FATAL ALCHEMY

JULIE MORGAN

Copyright © 2017 Julie Morgan
Julie Morgan, Author

All rights reserved. No part of this publication may be reproduced, stored in a retrieval system, or transmitted in any form or by means mechanical, electronic, photocopying, recording or otherwise without prior permission from the publisher.

This is a work of fiction. Names, characters, places and events are fictitious in every regard. Any similarities to actual events or persons, living or dead are purely coincidental. Any trademarks, service marks, product names or featured names are assumed to be the property of their respective owners and are used only for reference. There is no implied endorsement if any of these terms are used. Except for review purposes, the reproduction of this book in whole or in part, mechanically or electronically, constitutes a copyright violation.

Published in the United States of America in April 2017 by Julie Morgan. The right of the Authors Name to be identified as the Author of the Work has been asserted by them in accordance with The Copyright, Designs and Patent Act of 1988.

*For the imagination in all of us,
and to those who listen to the voices...*

PROLOGUE

*P*ANIC SET IN AS his eyes twitched behind closed lids. His breathing became erratic and voices sounded like mere echoes in his mind.

"I hear his heart, and he has a pulse!" came the voice of a woman.

Or were they actually talking to him? He was not sure, at least not yet. What he knew in this moment was this...he had died. The bite of death claimed him a year ago. Blood lust took over what he had left of a life...if one considered being an Undead living.

But now...air filled his lungs. He felt blood pumping through his veins. The panic built bigger. He had not felt anything outside of blood lust since his transition. And now? Now he felt everything.

The touch of a human, air pushing through his nostrils as he breathed, saliva pooled inside his mouth. Pain coursed through his body, from the headache threatening to split his head apart to the excruciating throbbing in his toes; pain so hot it were as if someone were extracting his toenails.

His chest vibrated with a sound so harsh, so loud, he wondered briefly if an animal was near him.

Bloody wolf-beasts, pieces of shit, he thought.

"I hear him," came the voice of the same woman.

Huh? he questioned then the voice returned. In this moment, he realized the voice came from him, from his chest.

His head shook left to the right. Soreness in his neck would be desired over what he currently felt.

"Wh-" he attempted as his lips moved. "Where…"

"You are in the hospital" came the woman's voice. "Your life has been saved, sir. You live!"

His eyes creased open as the light of the lanterns in the room shone. He squinted and his sight landed on a woman with brown hair pulled to the nape of her neck. She had dark skin and even darker eyes. She wore a white cap on her head, and immediately he knew she had to be a nurse.

"How?" he asked as his eyes closed once more. The pain became too much. Someone took his arm and bent it. He yelled as the ache shot through his body. "Bloody hell!"

"Oh, I am so sorry," exclaimed the woman. "Sir, please, do you have a name?"

"Of course, I have a name," he growled. His fingers twitched and he made a fist, and then relaxed his hand. Something sharp hit his elbow, and he looked to see a male had inserted a needle into his arm.

"We are giving you some pain-killers. Opium helps to relax those in pain," he told him. The man appeared to be quite a bit older than the woman. He had completely white hair and his skin aged him to be about sixty-five.

"Let me out of here. Why? How? Who…" his words trailed off as the opium took effect almost immediately. The pain lessened, replaced with drowsiness. "Who cares," he mumbled.

A soft hand held his and gave it a squeeze. "You were brought back to the living, sir. You are our first miracle cure!"

He barely opened his eyes to a smile so bright, so cheerful, it almost broke his heart. "Maxwell. James Maxwell..." his eyes closed and blackness settled over him.

~

THE NURSE SMILED upon the sleeping man. She glanced up at the doctor and nodded as he handed her paperwork.

"Make sure Mister James Maxwell recovers completely before he attempts to leave. We do not know, fully, the side effects of Miss Rimos's *cure*," he put emphasis on the word, as if he were bored, "will have on the cadaver."

"Yes, sir," she told him. Upon clearing her throat, she asked, "If I may, sir, she did indeed cure him, did she not?"

The man sighed and after a brief hesitation, he nodded. "Yes, so it seems."

"I would believe then, sir, the lasting side effect would be life."

He raised a brow to her and shifted the weight on his feet. "Are you volunteering to be his maid servant once he awakens fully?"

She shook her head no and lowered her gaze.

"Then do not speak to me in terms you do not understand. Are we clear?" He pulled at his tie and loosened it, then removed his lab jacket.

The woman nodded again and took a seat in the room. She began writing information on the form and as she heard the doctor leave, she rolled her eyes. "A real doctor would wait to see what he might do. A real doctor would be concerned for his patient. A real doctor would not brush off this miracle," she gazed upon James Maxwell's body with a soft smile, "and discover what Miss Rimos has uncovered."

A softness brushed against his lips. He thought it to be a kiss, until his eyes peeled open. The breath he felt was his own. James glanced to his right and focused his attention to the person next to his bed.

Her hair was dark, and her skin, it was like chocolate. She had a radiance about her, a beauty that only a fine painter could capture.

Pain suddenly erupted in his throat and he tried to gasp. Was he choking? Did something block his breathing passage? He coughed and the sound stirred the woman.

"Oh, James! Hold still! You will give yourself an awful fright!" She poured something into a cup and made to push her hand behind his head. She heaved him to a sitting position and placed the cup to his lips. "Drink, sir! You need fluids!" She had panic in her voice and James knew she was quite serious.

He coughed again and his eyes landed on hers. She pleaded with him again to drink and when the solution touched his lips, it almost burned. His skin was extremely dry and moisture hit like running lava.

Reluctantly, he opened his mouth and allowed the mixture entrance. It had no taste and as it slipped down his throat, the burning subsided almost immediately. She emptied the contents too quickly and he grabbed her wrist. Sitting up on his own now, he pulled her closer.

She gasped and her eyes widened. He recognized this instantly: fear. He looked to the pitcher then back to her. She nodded knowingly. "Sir, release me and I shall pour you more water."

"Water?" he croaked and released her wrist. "The sustenance I require is not water, madam."

She poured the clear contents into the cup again then returned it to his lips. "You do need water, sir. It will hydrate you and–"

He cut her off with a growl. "Madam, I require blood, not water. I am not a filthy human!" He coughed hard and lay back on his bed. Once the fit subsided, she assisted him to sit up again. She placed the cup under his lips and he took another drink.

"Do you not remember why you are here, sir?" she asked with patience in her voice. She smiled to him and tilted her head.

He swallowed again and shook his head. "Should I know why I am here? I woke up and found you and the older man looking upon my body."

She nodded and smiled a little wider. "Sir, that is true. You were the first successful case in receiving the cure from Miss Amelia Rimos! You were found dead and when brought into the lab–"

"What?!" he roared and slapped her hand away, sending the cup bouncing on the tile floor. It landed against the wall and the contents left in it sprayed across the room.

"Y-you were f-found, sir," she said in a nervous voice. "You were brought in as a cadaver. A successful experiment proved the cure, X-280, indeed works."

He shook his head. "No, no, no." He sat up, his legs moved to the side and his feet grazed the floor. "I am," he closed his eyes and took in a deep breath, then slowly released it, "I was an Undead so how could I possibly be a cadaver to toy with?"

The nurse lowered her gaze and her dark curled hair moved with her. She stepped back a few steps as James Maxwell stood from his bed. "I...I do not know, sir. I simply had been assigned to your case."

He nodded and ascended toward her, then leaned on a table near his bed for support. "And the person who did this...cure? This Miss Rimos? Where may I find this woman?"

The wall hit her back and she could no longer move further from him. James moved in and blocked her. Her heart picked up rhythm and her chest rose with erratic breathing. "I do not know, sir."

"Not good enough," he groaned as he bent against the wall. "Do you realize what you have done by making me...human?" He grit his teeth and shifted his body weight to the woman. "If I were still a vampire, your blood would be in my body and your head on the floor."

She panicked, then screamed. Then...silence.

1

John Hawthorne's lips pressed gently to his wife's, Amelia's, temple. He listened closely, hearing the sounds of her breathing deepen as she fell further into unconsciousness. He stood from the bed and gazed upon his wife, her belly protruding from the oncoming offspring. He smiled, the tenderness he displayed often reserved only for her, his thoughts carried away briefly.

It is my fortune alone this woman allows me to call her my wife. It is a sheer miracle she is still alive as she carries our unborn child. Is she carrying a human child, or shifter like me?

John sighed as he gently brushed a loose strand of hair from her face. Her brows moved slightly and her lips twitched with the hint of a smile.

Humans were not meant to carry our kind, he thought. *I need to speak with her midwife again, find out what else we need for this delivery. First and foremost*, he stood from the bed and straightened the dark gray night clothes he had on, *her life will be kept. If it comes down to choosing between her and our child, the choice will always be her. She may not like it, but that is my decision.*

John crept softly across the floor, the occasional floorboard squeaking with his weight. He picked up the candelabra from the dresser and pulled the door closed behind him. Waiting for a moment beside the door, his thoughts briefly turned to his enemy - Michel.

Time had passed since he defeated this enemy. The times have been without ease. The occasional attempt on a wolf from a vampire happened. Seldom would John allow Amelia out of his sight, now more than ever as she carried his child. He had scouts around his property and spies in town. Everyone had a job post and everyone reported on the shortcomings of their town.

Some days were easy. Nothing to report other than the occasional fight in town, a dispute over a bar tab, sometimes a dispute between a bar whore and the 'John'. Other days were more involved. Vampires moved at night, setting up residence in town and they began to spy on the wolves. Having his own spies in town, John had good working knowledge when something would change.

If a new residence came in overnight, it was likely a vampire had moved in. If a person moved in during daylight and were not to be seen again, again, good chance they set up residence for a vampire. John knew the town chairman who ran the books. The chairman knew everyone who came in and out of Savannah. John having the chairman in his pocket has also helped; having immediate, working knowledge of who is who and who is where, well, he could not not pay for this service.

Staring down the flight of stairs in front of him, John took the steps down until he reached the main floor. Adam, his Beta, sat at the dining room table and shoved a piece of sandwich into his mouth. His red hair gave the appearance he just climbed out of bed. Disheveled, he looked a mess. John glanced to the side of the room and found Sophie, Adam's mate, as she prepared coffee.

John raised a brow and looked back to Adam. "Late night?"

Adam glanced up and swallowed his food, then nodded. "Yeah. Patrol last night with the others." He watched as Adam glanced over to Sophie. "Coffee ready?"

She nodded, her white hair bouncing around her face. She glanced up and her violet eyes met John's. "How is the missus this morning? Is she getting more sleep?"

John nodded and lowered his gaze. Amelia had been struggling with sleep since discovering she was pregnant. Between the dreams she claimed to have and the rapid growth of the child inside her, it was astonishing to him she actually could sleep. "She is doing better."

"That is good," she told him as she made her way to Adam. She sat a glass down and poured in the black contents of coffee.

Adam picked it up and gently blew the top, then took a sip. He sat the cup back down and glanced over to John. "How much longer are we going to keep up the antics of patrol? When I agreed to be your Beta and agreed to your mating of your wife, I did not think it meant resorting to this type of punishment."

John growled low in his throat. In a flash, he was on Adam and had him pulled from his chair. Gripping the collar of his shirt, he pulled him close. "Want to try that again?"

Adam pulled his head back and his eyes widened. "Let me go," he demanded in an almost whiny tone, then in a lower octave, "please."

"Do not patronize me, Adam. I am still your Alpha. And she is my wife, mother to my unborn child, and the mother to our pack. Do *not* forget that." John explained to the pack after he married Amelia that she would become something of a den mother to the wolves when they needed her. Amelia openly agreed to the idea almost immediately.

Adam flinched to his words and as John sat him back onto the floor, he nodded. "My apologies, but honestly, John, she is not one of us."

"She is so long as she is married to me." He glanced over to

Sophie who, in turn, raised both hands in the air as if offering surrender. "Good." John glanced back to Adam and watched him for a moment longer. "As soon as our child is born, and everyone is healthy, we will be able to back off the patrols. Till then…"

Adam interrupted him. "You really think patrols will back off once your son or daughter is born? Really, John, if anything, patrols will be doubled. Why would you not want your child protected?"

He raised a brow and knew Adam had a point. He leaned in and smirked. "Fine, then you will be appointed as guardian to my unborn child until I find a more suitable replacement."

"What?!" Adam exclaimed.

"Since it seems you are determined to be an asshole in this day in our lives, why not allow you to be an asshole a little while longer?" He glanced over to Sophie who had her lips pressed together. "Oh, you are very much a part of this, too. I imagine you will enjoy helping Amelia with…well, let us just say clean up duty."

Sophie grinned and nodded. "I love children. Why not?"

"How can you love children, woman?" Adam asked her. "You have never had children. How do you know you would love them?"

"Just because I do not have something does not mean I do not want, or wish to care for it." She shrugged and looked to John with a triumphant grin. "I will be happy to assist Amelia with anything she needs."

Adam shook his head and turned back around in his chair, then took another sip of coffee. John winked at Sophie and she grinned.

"I have something I need to take care of. Please keep your ears open for my wife, in case she calls out."

Sophie nodded and took a seat next to Adam. Leaving the dining room, he heard the couple begin to argue over what was just discussed. John shook his head and stopped in front of the basement doorway. He glanced sideways at the door handle. He knew what waited for him on the other side of the door. His prisoner had been here since the day of his capture.

Since that day, John had only been down a few times to check on the man...well, monster. Amelia made notes in her notebook regarding the appearance of her 'test subject.'

"It seems as the days pass, so does his aging. In a matter of days, he has aged at least twenty years. Considering how old he really is, I have to ponder when his human body will actually wither and die." Her words returned to John as he continued to stare at the door handle.

He reached for it and held the knob for a moment, then turned it. The chamber clicked as it pulled into the door. He pulled it gently and it creaked once it left the frame of the door. Light from his candelabra glowed bright orange around his hand and forearm, offering a soft glow onto his face.

John took a few steps down into the basement. Once inside the room, a lamp sat on a wooden table. He sat the candelabra down and pulled matches from his side pocket. He struck one of the heads and it lit. An orange glow lit up around his hand and on instinct, he glanced to his left and right, then behind him.

Nothing came from the shadows, nothing made a sound. John lit the lamp and once the wick caught aflame, he turned the knob, causing the fire to burn brighter. The room filled with the orange glow and shadows began to appear on the floor from the wooden table, the empty chairs, and from his prisoner.

Taking a few steps forward, John knelt down in front of his former nemesis. Michel Gauthier's body sat strapped to the chair. His mouth agape, eyes open, and he was completely dead faced. At some point during the transition of vampire to human after receiving Amelia's cure, his body began to deteriorate.

"I do not think Amelia realized exactly how rapidly this would occur or I would have brought her down for this." John grinned. He tilted his head as if the deceased Michel spoke something. "What was that? I am sorry, you were saying?" He lifted a brow and smirked, then blew a tuft of air as if blowing out a candle. The body once owned by Michel Gauthier began to fall apart as ashes billowed and fell to the floor, surrounding the chair his body once occupied.

Feeling satisfied, John stood and brushed off any of the dust that may have landed on his clothes. He snuffed out the lamp on the table and picked up the candelabra again. Ascending the stairs, he closed the door behind him and heaved a heavy sigh of relief.

"Sophie?" he called toward the dining room.

"Yes, John?" she called back and moments later, stood to his attention near the basement door.

"Tonight, we celebrate," he grinned a little wider. "The vampire turned human in our basement is now nothing but a pile of ash."

She grinned and her violet eyes lit up. "This is the best news I have heard all day!"

John raised a brow. "Considering it is still morning, that's not really good news then."

She laughed and shook her head. "Well, the best news I have heard in a good month then." She reached up and patted John on his bicep. "Congratulations, sir."

He smiled and looked toward the stairs that led to the bedroom he shared with Amelia. "Plan a party for tonight. We have much to celebrate."

She nodded and made her way toward the dining room, a bounce in her step as she called for a few of her pack friends. As John reached the stairs, he felt a hand on his shoulder. Turning, he found Adam behind him. Turning to face him, he raised his brows as if suggesting, 'go ahead and speak.'

Adam cleared his throat. "I would have to assume with his final death, word would go out to the Undead."

John nodded and lowered his gaze for a moment. He considered Adam's words then felt almost confused, as if it were maybe an accusation. "I would assume they knew him to already be deceased. Why would it be any different today?"

"To our understanding, and correct me if I am wrong, but the ones they created themselves have some sort of link to one another. I recall something about emotional bonds through blood? One would assume if he finally died, his bonds would be completely severed."

John tilted his head slightly and lifted a brow. "One would have considered said bonds to have been severed once he was administered the cure."

Adam nodded and took a step back. He said no more, but his features spoke otherwise.

"Out with it," John ordered. "What plagues you?"

Adam glanced to his Alpha. "If I may be so bold?" John nodded his approval. Adam sighed and continued. "I think it is foolish to celebrate the death of the vampire king, as he self-proclaimed himself to be. With his final death, I would imagine his coven would be on our doorstep any moment, wanting to wage a war they have no chance in winning."

John grinned and nodded a few times. "You are right."

"I am?" Adam asked.

John nodded. "They have no chance in winning. Stop worrying over something that will not come to pass. Celebrate with your mate…"

"She is not my mate," Adam interrupted.

John raised a brow. "Does Sophie know that?"

Lowering his gaze, Adam shuffled his feet side to side, then shrugged slightly. "We have never formally discussed it."

John leaned in and placed a firm hand on Adam's shoulder. "Maybe you should. Never know what could happen if this war you are predicting would come to pass. I would hate for something as small as not declaring her your mate not be respected in the pack." John stood back and grinned. "As I said before, I do not pretend to understand what you two have, but if appearances speak anything, it looks as if you do love her."

Adam turned on his heel and left the room abruptly. John took the steps two at a time as he raced up the stairs to wake his sleeping wife. Wanting to share the news was one thing, celebrating the news, well, this was something else entirely.

∼

AMELIA BLINKED AT the news. Her heart raced and for a moment, she thought this afternoon's lunch would revisit her. She swallowed and closed her eyes, waiting for the reflux to subdue itself. Having control over her stomach once again, she opened her eyes and stared into the brown eyes of her husband. "He is…gone? Ash?"

John nodded and adjusted himself on the edge of her bedside. "I went into the basement to check on his status. Honestly though," he paused and shook his head a few times, "I did not expect to find only his ashes. I was not surprised by this fact, considering each time we saw him, he aged more and more." Taking Amelia's hand in his, he ran his thumb over her palm. "When you did the testing in your lab, how far did the subjects make it after they contracted the cure?"

Amelia sat up in her bed, relaxing her back against the headboard. She yawned and releasing John's hand, stretched, holding her arms above her head. When she relaxed, she raised a brow at the way John stared at her body. She glanced down, then back up to him. "What are you staring at?"

He grinned and met her gaze. "Your breasts are absolutely delectable. They have swollen in size and if I may say, damn." John reached for them and palmed both breasts gingerly. Amelia had complained of the tenderness she experienced at the beginning of her pregnancy. Although the pain had passed, she slapped his hands away on any account.

"We are having a serious conversation and you wish to place your hands upon my breasts?" She pulled the sheet up to her arms and rested them on top of it, covering her swollen bosom.

"I am a man and you are my wife. I love your breasts. Allow me to suckle them." He growled and leaned into her, growling softly into the nape of her neck.

Amelia grinned and made every attempt to not giggle, but failed miserably. The sound escaped her and when it did, she released the hold on the sheet. John grasped it and pulled the material away, then lowered his head to her swollen breasts. He gently kissed her soft, creamy flesh and he lightly pinched her nipples.

Gasping, Amelia closed her eyes and smiled. "It seems so long since you've touched me, John." Her voice had a rasp to it.

John glanced up to her and grinned as she clearly enjoyed herself. He pulled the sheets down further, exposing her swollen belly and bare legs. Pushing her nightgown up her body, he slid his hand in between her thighs. Not giving him a fight about it, Amelia pulled her legs apart, bending her knees.

Grinning to himself as he discovered his wife wore no panties, he gently stroked her sex. Her body flinched slightly as she gasped softly. He did it again and this time, he felt her become wet for him.

"Mmm, seems you have missed me, my wife. What shall I do about that?" He growled between her breasts as his finger teased the hood covering her clit. Pressing his fingers through it, he gently rubbed the swollen bundle of nerves.

Amelia gasped and her back arched slightly. "I cannot possibly lie on my back while we make love."

"Who said anything about making love?" John grinned as he sucked the hardened flesh of her nipple into his mouth, his tongue whipping against it.

She gasped again as his finger massaged her clit in a back and forth motion, while his tongue assaulted her nipple. "John, oh my..." She gasped again as her words trailed off.

John grinned to himself and slipped a finger inside her. His thumb pressed against her clit as his finger turned up, massaging the hardened mound inside her pussy.

"Oh god, John," she whispered. "You will make me reach orgasm before I have had a chance to even touch you."

He growled against her flesh and his finger teased her that much harder. She gasped and a moan filled the silence of the room. "I need to taste you, woman. I need you on my face." John removed his fingers from her pussy and he brought them to his mouth. He sucked his fingers clean.

Amelia watched him and her eyes dilated with need. She pushed her legs further apart while John settled himself between them. He leaned down toward her pussy then gently ran his hands underneath her thighs. He gripped her and pulled her down just enough to open her pussy for him a little more.

"Perfect," he said in a heated tone. He looked up to her and found her biting her lip. John grinned at her anticipation, loving the expression she wore, this longing to be claimed again.

He leaned in and his shadowed cheek rubbed against her thigh. He had not shaved yet this morning. Amelia told him when he allowed himself a day in between shaving, she found it sexy, although it hurt like hell on her lips.

Although on these lips, he thought to himself, *she will enjoy the roughness immensely.*

He rubbed his cheek against the place where he marked her as his mate. The scent of the pheromones filled the room and it caught Amelia's senses. She moaned softly and rested her head on the headboard.

"John, baby, please, no more teasing."

He grinned and leaning in, he rubbed his mouth against the inside of her thigh that sat next to her pussy. He did the same on the other side. Amelia began to move her hips in rhythm with him as he continued to rub his face against her thighs.

His fingers gently pressed against the hood that covered her sex. He pushed them apart and exposed her clit. Her pussy glistened with her honey as she seeped with anticipation.

Lightly, he flicked her clit with his tongue. He watched as the small bulb quivered and swelled just slightly more. Amelia lifted her hips up in an attempt for him to do it again. She groaned and her legs shook slightly.

"Are you all right?" he asked her and glanced up to catch her gaze.

She looked down and nodded. "Yes, just please, John, stop teasing and bring me to climax."

He grinned and lowered his head back down. Opening his mouth, he shoved his tongue inside her pussy. She gasped and her fingers pulled at his hair. John swirled his tongue inside her then ran it up the length to her clit. He sucked on it and assaulted it with whips from his tongue.

She moaned louder and began to grind her pussy against his face. John's grip on her thighs tightened as he pulled himself closer against her. He licked her from pussy to the top of her sex again, focusing his assault on her clit.

Amelia moaned louder and her honey dripped from her pussy onto his chin. John pushed a finger inside her and turned it up, massaging the hardened area inside her. Her hips bucked and he sucked hard on her clit. His finger pumped inside her harder and harder. Her back arched and she pulled his hair, pulling him harder against her.

"Shit! John!"

He pushed another finger inside her and his tongue continued to assault her clit. Her pussy clamped down on his fingers and he knew she was going to orgasm very soon. His teeth gently nibbled on her throbbing nub and he growled. The vibrations enhanced the sensation against her clit and a second later, Amelia's back arched and her orgasm hit.

John pulled his fingers from her and reached for her swollen clit, pinching it as she came. She groaned louder and her hips bucked, then she pressed herself hard against his hand. "John! John, fuck! Yes!" Her body shook as the waves of her orgasm began to subside.

Releasing her, John rose up from between her legs. Amelia's eyes were still closed as her chest heaved with rushed breaths. As she opened her eyes and gazed upon him, John swiped his arm across his face, removing any evidence of her orgasm.

"Get on your knees and turn around. I need to be inside you." His voice came out in a growl and Amelia's body shuddered.

She nodded and slowly began to reposition herself. John grasped her hips and pulled her bottom up toward him. He reached forward and palmed one of her swollen breasts and the nipple pressed into his hand.

"I love you," he told her in a lower, deeper tone.

"I love you, my beast."

He growled and pressed her shoulders toward the bed. As she lowered herself down, resting her cheek on the mattress, John lined his hardened cock up to her entrance and pushed. He slid inside her and he grasped her hips.

Amelia gasped and closed her eyes. "My god, you feel good inside me."

"Yes, baby, damn, you are so wet." He pulled back and gently pushed back inside her. "Let me know when it is too much."

She nodded and her lips parted. A gasp left her lips as he pushed harder against her. "You are not hurting me. If anything," she glanced up from the bed to him, "you are teasing me."

He grinned and his fingers tightened into her flesh. John

pulled back and thrust hard against her. A loud moan left her as he did it again. His balls twitched, needing their own release.

Amelia moaned again. "Harder," she whispered.

"What did you say?" he asked and pulled back, teasing her with small movements inside her. Amelia pressed back against him and he growled out loud. "Do not move, and I asked you a question. What did you say?"

She looked up to him and grinned. "I said, harder." Her voice had a firmness to it and John grinned.

"That is what I thought you said." He gripped her hips and thrust hard and fast against her. His balls slapped against her clit. Her voice rose higher and higher as John came closer to his own orgasm.

He closed his eyes and his head titled back. His teeth grit hard inside his mouth and as his balls clenched tight, a deep, low growl began to emit from his chest and billowed out through his mouth. His growl grew progressively louder and Amelia screamed in unison. Her pussy tightened around his dick and John came hard as she reached another orgasm.

John's body thrust twice as his hips pressed firmly against Amelia's backside. His grip loosened and he released her. Pulling out, he helped her lie back onto the bed on her side and he collapsed next to her. He panted for a moment and when he opened his eyes, he smiled to the sight before him.

Amelia's face was red and flushed from being pushed into the bed. She returned the smile and leaned in to kiss him. "I love you, my beast."

"I love you, my wife." A moment later, John closed his eyes as sleep overtook his heavy lids.

2

*A*MELIA STOOD IN her claw-foot tub as John took her hand to assist her as she stepped out. He wrapped a towel around her body, then kissed her softly. His fingers gently pulled through her long, dark locks as he smiled.

"Care to venture to the market today?"

She nodded and leaned into him, her rounded stomach prodding against him. "That would be nice. It is a beautiful day and walking would do me good." She gasped and pressed a hand against her abdomen. "John! He is moving!" She quickly took his hand and pressed it against her swollen belly.

He chuckled. "He, huh? Are you sure he is a boy?" John grinned as he watched her belly, then he quickly looked to her. "I felt him."

She smiled. "See? He is a boy." Amelia kissed him and wrapped the towel tighter around her shoulders.

He tilted his head slightly and raised a brow. "I wonder..." he squatted and placed his hands on either side of her stomach, then leaned in. He kissed her belly gently. "Son, I cannot wait to meet you. Your mother is an amazing woman. You will have a family full of love and support. They are all waiting anxiously to meet you, too."

Amelia grinned and watched her husband. "I am sure he can hear you."

"I hope he can," John told her as he continued to look upon her belly. He leaned in again and his eyes flashed gold, then he growled.

Giggling, Amelia touched his head. "What are you doing?"

"Hoping to communicate," he said as he looked up to her. "Find it funny, do you?" John stood and touched her chin, tilting her head up. He kissed her on the lips then rubbed his nose softly against hers.

"Communication by growling, should I try that sometime?"

He grinned. "Only in bed."

She laughed and patted his cheek, then walked into their bedroom. Amelia sat clothes out on the four-poster bed prior to her bath. Dropping her towel, she reached for her undergarments. Warm hands positioned themselves on her hips and she smiled as she glanced over her shoulder. "Plan on helping me?"

"Out of them, yes. In them? Where is the fun in that?" He kissed her bare shoulder.

"Please?" she pleaded.

He sighed and held his hand out. Amelia placed the garment in his hand and turned to face him. As John bent over, she held onto his shoulder and lifted one leg, slipping it through, followed by the other. He pulled the under clothing up her legs until within her reach.

Amelia grabbed the material and pulled them up; the ruffled bottoms billowed out from her thighs, the latest trend by the aristocracy from France. She took her undershirt and slipped it on, covering her breasts and torso.

John sighed and stood as he watched his wife dress. Mating outside the pack was not exactly his plan when he sought a mate. Then again, he did not plan on meeting Amelia, or falling in love with her.

We have no idea what she will birth, he thought. *Human with wolf genes or pure human?* He sighed and turned to the sound of a knock on their bedroom door.

"That must be Sarah," Amelia told him. Sarah was another Alchemist who worked alongside his pack, and as of late, had become friends with his wife. "She is right on time."

John made his way to the door. He unlocked it and opened it enough to peer out.

"Hello, John," Sarah smiled. Her blond hair was set in curls and pulled to the side of her head and a small hat sat opposite.

He pulled the door open and stepped to the side. "Morning, Sarah. She is all yours." He smiled at his wife then offered her a wink.

Amelia smiled at him, then opened her arms for her friend. She hugged her tightly. "Good morning, sweet Sarah."

"Good morning, Missus Hawthorne."

Amelia giggled. "You are right on time. Please help me into these clothes. John is taking me to the market today."

"Oh, very nice," she commented, and as Amelia turned her back to her friend, Sarah opened a white blouse with thin brown pin stripes. She placed it at Amelia's hands and shifted the material up her arms. Sarah repositioned Amelia to face her, then took the dark brown hoop skirt and bent over. Once Amelia stood inside the gathered material, she shimmied it up her body. "What do you plan to look for today?"

"Oh, I do not know. I have had a craving for carrots and honey. Together! Can you imagine?"

Sarah laughed and tightened the skirt enough to not fall off Amelia's body. Fluffing the bustle in place, she buttoned the blouse about halfway and bit her lip. "I am afraid your breasts have swollen to the point the tops will not close."

"Oh, well, what do you suggest?" Amelia turned around again and Sarah helped her remove the top.

"You will need something that does not require buttoning or fastening. Do you have a shawl handy?"

Amelia nodded and made her way to her dresser. Opening the top drawer, she pushed the contents around for a bit, then smiled. She pulled out a dark brown shawl, laced with fabric that appeared to be contemporary. She made her way back to Sarah. "How is this?"

Sarah grinned. "Perfect." Taking the garment from Amelia, she helped pull it over her head and set it over the skirt. It blended well, but did nothing to conceal her swollen belly. "Soon, we will have you in a corset again."

Amelia nodded. "Well, I have quite enjoyed myself not wearing them, to be honest. I like to breathe, thank you."

Sarah clicked her tongue in disappointment. "You tell yourself that now, but soon, you will be loving to see your waist."

Setting Amelia's hair, Sarah placed a few pins that held amber colored stones. They complemented the dress well. Amelia touched rouge to her cheeks and lips, then turned to her friend.

"Presentable?"

"Beautiful," Sarah told her. "Now, do your outing with your husband. I will be here to help you change when you return."

Amelia grinned. "What is that supposed to mean?"

Sarah rolled her eyes. "If your husband has any say about it, he will be happy to undress you."

"That I would," John said as he entered the room. "You are a vision, my wife." He nodded to Sarah. "Thank you for your assistance, as always."

"You are quite welcome. I will see you later then."

Amelia grinned. "Maybe."

*T*he carriage came to a stop in town. The sounds of the market filled the silence between the affection John provided his wife by way of kissing. He touched her neck gently and tilted her head as he deepened the kiss. His tongue slipped across her lips and she gasped against his mouth.

The door snapped opened, invading their moment of privacy. The sun shone inside, the warmth offering her comfort as a chill set in the air. Winter was coming and it would not be forgiving.

Savannah grew extremely hot in the summers, and John would often frequent the watering hole with Amelia. Swimming nude was his preferred option, unless the pack was around. Swimming naked had never been an issue, until he married. He did not like the thought of anyone seeing his wife's naked body but him.

*O*nly one other had witnessed her naked flesh, and that man was now dead. Michel, the old vampire king, and the pack's worst enemy. The thought made John growl.

"What is the matter?" Amelia asked him. "Do you not wish to be here today?"

He looked upon his wife. Her gentleness, the patience, the love she gave to him freely...he loved her more than himself. Now that she carried his child, she deserved his devotion and life...if occasion called for such.

John shook his head. "No, I am all right. Let us go to the market."

She smiled and slipped her hand into the driver's. He assisted her down and when she looked up, she gasped. "Adam? I did not realize you would be joining us. It is a pleasure–"

"I was ordered. Shall we?" he said in a monotone voice.

Amelia gazed upon his red hair and fair complexion. She

raised a brow and stepped closer to him. "I do not understand your quarrel with me, but I have always given you the respect you deserve, especially as his Beta. A little respect in return–"

"No," he cut her off again. "I take orders from him and him only. Not his pregnant wife," he spat. Immediately, John growled and grabbed Adam by his throat, thrusting him against the carriage.

"What is your problem with my wife, Adam? You swore allegiance to me!"

Adam's eyes widened. He looked between his Alpha and Amelia. Settling on John, he grabbed at John's fingers. "I swore fealty to you, not her!"

"She is your den mother," John barked to him. "She is my wife and my equal. You will treat her with respect!"

"She is not one of us! She will never be one of us!"

Amelia gasped and took a few steps back. John growled and shoved Adam away from him. "You will be punished for this when we return home. You will not retort in such a manner, as I am your Alpha. You will absolutely not disrespect my wife, either."

Adam shook his head. "I did not like the selection of your mate, but as you are the Alpha, I was not left with a choice in the matter."

John raised a brow and took a few steps toward him. "You had every right to denounce her, and it would have been so."

"You would have sent me away?" Amelia asked with almost a squeak to her voice. She shook her head and took another step away.

"Pack laws," John told her as he continued to stare at Adam. "I would not have sent you away. We would still be involved, I would not be able to claim you as my mate, though." He turned to her and raised a brow. "You would still be mine, regardless of what the laws state. I love you, woman."

She smiled a small smile and lowered her gaze. She turned

toward the carriage and leaned against it, giving her back to John and Adam.

Amelia glanced at them once more, then back to the scenery in front of her. *I had no idea he could have sent me away,* she thought. *I knew Adam was not happy with our pairing, mating, whatever he wishes to call it, but he seems to be the only one against it. Sophie has never given issue. Why does he disapprove?*

Coming from her thoughts, she looked up when a hand touched her shoulder. She turned and faced her husband, resting her hands on his thick chest. She could feel him as he breathed. "Is all well, now?"

He shook his head. "No, but it will be. You need not to worry over it."

She nodded and lowered her gaze. "Shall we?" she asked as she looked up again. He nodded in return and took her hand in his. They made their way across the dirt road to the farmer's market. Fresh fruits and vegetables awaited for tasting and purchase. The vast variety of flowers added a floral scent to the air. John sneezed and Amelia looked up to him with a grin.

"Too sweet for you, love?"

He chuckled. "Something like that."

She released his hand and stepped toward a cart filled with green and red vegetables. Picking a few, she brought them to her nose and inhaled the fragrance. She smiled and handed them to the vendor, then offered a few dollars. He handed back a bag after placing her purchase inside.

Amelia turned to locate John, but instead found herself staring into the eyes of a stranger.

But was he a stranger? She knew him from somewhere as he seemed familiar...felt familiar.

She took a few steps toward the man who stood in the shadows of the building. He wore a dark gray suit with a tie, a black bowler hat, and held a cane; a silver snake's head held the perch. His brow lifted in a manner suggesting he knew her as well.

"Hello," Amelia smiled. "Pardon me for asking, but do we know one another?"

He shook his head and returned her smile. "I am not sure, madam. I would remember a beauty such as yourself." He removed his hat and the man took a casual bow. "If we may make the acquaintance once again, may I offer my hand in assistance today?" He rose once more and as he pushed his hand to her, Amelia gasped at a set of hands gripping her shoulders.

She turned and found John behind her. "Who is your friend?" he asked with a hint of a growl in his voice.

Jealous fool, she thought. She smiled and turned back to the stranger. "I am not positive, yet, as he was going to introduce himself. Sir, if you would be so kind? My name is Amelia Hawthorne. If we had made an acquaintance prior, I do apologize for not recalling your name. However," she paused and tilted her head, "maybe we met when I went by Amelia Rimos."

The man's eyes lit up. "Yes! That is it. I knew you were Miss Rimos, the Alchemist!" He chuckled and held his hand out. "I am an admirer of your work, Miss Rimos." He glanced to John and smirked. "My apologies, Missus Hawthorne."

She smiled and glanced to John. "I am fine here, but stay close?"

"You can count on it," John whispered for just her to hear. He glared at the man then took a few steps back, leaving them to a private conversation.

Amelia smiled and turned back to her new friend. "Please, sir, what is your name?"

He motioned for her to step closer, in which she did, but only slightly. "James Maxwell, madam. Word has it you rescued me, once upon a time."

She stared into his eyes, unsure what he meant by saving his life. Amelia studied him and James lifted his head slightly, a smirk playing to his features.

She mentally flipped through her memory bank of people she worked with at the lab, the patients she helped treat at the hospital and anyone her departed sister, Rachel, may have known or courted.

No one came to mind. As she opened her mouth to let him know she was not aware of who he was, a different recollection teased her. She closed her lips and her brows furrowed, then it hit her.

"OH MY GOD!" she exclaimed. "You…you are the cadaver I…the man who…you received my…" She could not complete a sentence as her thoughts raced to manic mode. She shook her head and her hand clamped over her mouth to keep from either screaming or laughing…maybe both.

"James Maxwell is my name, madam, as I told you. And when I was a vampire, someone took me to your lab, insisting I was dying…apparently."

She nodded and smiled so wide it hurt her mouth. "I cannot believe I am actually talking to you!" She shook her head and reached to touch him, then thought better of it. "How…please, tell me how you are coming about with the, well, with the change?"

James grinned and lowered his gaze. He looked up past her and raised a brow, then met her gaze. James grasped her arm and jerked her close. Amelia gasped as her lips opened to say something, but he cut her off. "You listen to me, Amelia Rimos." His voice dropped an octave and took on a menacing tone.

"Ow," she pulled at him in an effort to break free. "You are hurting me, Mister Maxwell. Release me, now!"

James shook his head. "Not until you hear me out, woman." He gritted his teeth as he looked upon her. "I did not wish to be changed to human again. You took that freedom from me. You took it without hesitation and without asking or cause. Why?"

He shook his head and closed his eyes. "Do not answer that. I no longer care *why* you did it." He opened his eyes and peered into hers as he leaned closer. "You will hear me now, Amelia Rimos. I will find a way to turn back into an Undead and when I do," he glanced down to her swollen belly, smirked, then into her eyes, "I will come for you."

Releasing her arm, James stepped into the shadows. Amelia watched him for a moment, not positive on what to say, or what to do with this threat. Her heart began to slow from the attack, but it did nothing for the uncomfortable nature she felt in her lower belly. The baby moved and kicked with a fierceness. She wondered briefly if he heard what transpired.

It would not make any sense if he did, she told herself. She absently rubbed her hand underneath her belly, as if to offer comfort to her unborn child. *He will come for me? He did not wish to be changed back? Why would he want to be an Undead again?*

Her thoughts kept her mind busy and she did not realize John came up from behind. His hands touched her shoulders and Amelia yelped in a startle.

"John!" she screamed as she turned to face him, eyes widened. "Do not sneak up on me like that!"

He stepped back with raised brows. "I did not realize I was sneaking, Amelia. My apologies. What happened to your friend?" He looked past her, then back to her eyes.

She shook her head and waved it off. "Nothing, it is nothing we cannot discuss back home," *which we should,* she thought. "I am ready to leave. Did you find everything you needed?"

John nodded and stepped closer to her. "Are you sure you are all right?" His hands gently massaged her arms and he leaned in, then kissed on her on the forehead.

"Yes, of course." She smiled and lowered her head slightly, feeling a weight on her shoulders: the anger and hate of her former cadaver patient.

He took her hand and tucked it into the crook of his elbow. "Then we shall be off. The driver is waiting."

3

*J*OHN LAID OUT the meat brought in from the latest hunt, then cut it into quarters. He seasoned it then set it aside. "Amelia," he turned to his wife, "fetch me a knife for the vegetables?"

*A*melia made her way across the kitchen. The walls white with brown cabinetry, tin and glass cups adorned the shelves. Amelia insisted on having nice dinnerware for guests to entertain at some point. John argued, but soon gave in.

She opened a drawer and pulled out a knife. Having recently been sharpened, she took it to John, then leaned against the counter. She crossed her arms over her chest as they sat on top of her swollen belly. She watched him rhythmically cut the carrots from today's purchase in the market.

She thought of what happened with her cadaver…no, former cadaver patient, and felt John needed to know. She sighed and looked up to him. "Can we talk about something that occurred at the market?"

"Does this have to do with that man upsetting you?" he asked as he glanced sideways to her, then to the vegetables.

She nodded and lowered her gaze. "Yes." *How do I tell my husband and Alpha of a pack of werewolves a man threatened my life?* She sighed and almost felt she were facing a firing squad.

She may have well been.

"The man in the market...I recognized him because he," she turned away from him for a moment. Pressing her palms onto the counter, she called on courage buried deep inside her.

I fought off Michel. I married a werewolf. I am carrying his baby and I am scared to tell him what happened?

"He used to court you?"

Amelia looked up and blinked. "What?"

"The man, did he used to court you?" John finished chopping the vegetables and wiped his hands on his pants.

"Oh, no, I wish it were that easy."

"Then tell me. Out with it."

Uneasiness settled over her and she looked away from John again. Rubbing her temples, she bit the inside of her cheek.

"Amelia, come on, tell me. What is it?" John placed his strong hands on her waist and leaned in, kissing the side of her neck.

She closed her eyes. "John, that man," she twisted out of his arms and faced him. "He was the cadaver I tested my first batch of X-280 on." She let out a breath she had been holding and waited.

He raised his brows. "Is that all? Well, that is better than a former beau. I thought I would need to fight for your honor for a moment." He chuckled and headed back toward the cutting area.

"John, there is more and I wish you would not make light of this."

He looked to her over his shoulder. "Then what happened, woman?" He pivoted toward her and bowed against the counter.

She shook her head and swiped at a tear that raced down her cheek. "Oh, John…I made a mistake. I never should have created that, that… concoction! I have made a horrible mess of things!" She sobbed into her hands and when she felt his warm presence wrapping around her body, she rested into his chest and hid her face.

"What did he tell you? And I believe it is safe to say he was not as old as the former Michel."

Amelia looked up to a smirk on John's lips. "To say he is upset about the situation would be taking it lightly."

He raised his brows and stepped back slightly. "Did he threaten you?" His voice took on a growl and lowered an octave. She could hear the wolf in his voice and her body began to shake.

"John, please, calm yourself."

"Amelia! Tell me! What did he say?"

The back door to the estate, near the kitchen, opened and slammed against the wall. Adam and Sophie came in and his eyes glowed for a moment. "What happened? I could feel something…something not right."

"I think we all felt it." Sophie glanced between John and Amelia, then back to her Alpha.

"Apparently the cadaver Amelia brought back to life found her today," John explained, "and it seems he is none too happy with her about it."

"Is that so?" Sophie asked as she crossed the room, standing next to Amelia. "Well, if he feels the need to threaten my pack mother again, then he can answer to me."

Amelia softened, grateful for Sophie. She smiled to her friend.

Adam roared, "I told you this would not be a good idea!"

"Adam!" John yelled back.

"Both of you, stop it!" Sophie spoke up. When both men

glared at her, she shook her head, then turned to Amelia. "What did he say to you?"

Amelia looked to John and fear crept up her spine. Not fear of her husband, but fear of how he would react. She glanced to Adam. Nothing but pure hatred emitted from this man. *I have no idea what I ever did to him,* she thought. *Probably just the fact I am here.*

She glanced to Sophie and stepped closer to her. Maybe putting her in between the men would serve as a cushion if any blows were to come about, not that John would ever hit her.

"He helped me remember who he was exactly. I did not recognize him at first, you see." She lowered her gaze and as quickly as she smiled, it left her face. "He was not happy with me on administering the cure to him." She glanced up to Sophie, then looked to John. "He plans on seeking someone out to change him back into an Undead."

John raised a brow. "He would rather be a filthy blood eater?"

She nodded and lowered her gaze again. "Apparently so."

"Is there anything else we need to know, Amelia?" Sophie asked as she placed a gentle hand upon her shoulder.

Amelia nodded. She held her breath, knowing this next part would absolutely, without a doubt, upset her husband to a new degree she had not yet witnessed. "Yes, he said once he is changed back, he plans on coming for me."

"What?!" John roared. "Coming for you? COMING FOR YOU?" He slammed his fist onto the counter and Amelia jumped back. "He made a verbal threat to you WHEN I was in the market with you? Why did you not say anything then?"

"Because you would have reacted just like this!" Amelia yelled back. "This is why I had to wait! You would have drawn too much attention!"

"And you should be so good to judge this?" Adam spoke.

"You, the one who created this mess in the first place?" His words were like venom.

Amelia watched her husband glare at Adam, then he put the same glare toward her. "Is there anything else?" he growled through gritted teeth.

She quickly shook her head.

"She is under our protection, sir," Sophie spoke up. "I will guard her–"

"I do not think that is necessary," Adam said.

"What?" Sophie asked.

"She is married to our Alpha. He can guard her just as easily." Adam glared at Amelia once more.

"You will remember your place, Adam, and remember Amelia is my wife," John growled.

Adam stared at his Alpha for a moment, then nodded. "I meant no disrespect." He then turned on his heel and left the kitchen.

"That was unexpected," Sophie mumbled. "I will go after him."

John nodded, then looked to Amelia. "So, avoiding this confrontation to save yourself from public embarrassment?"

She gasped, not expecting this from her husband. "No! I did not tell you so you would not react this way in public and possibly KILL someone!" Amelia held her tongue for fear of regretting her next words; although he deserved them.

She slowly exhaled, then continued. "I was not avoiding public embarrassment, John. I cannot believe you would say that. He threatened me. A threat to me is a threat to our child. I would have thought that meant something to you."

A chuckle laced with darkness, rather than humor, sounded in the kitchen. John closed the distance to her and turned Amelia to face him. "Of course it means something to me. You are my world now, Amelia. You and our child. Do you not understand that? I would give my life for you in a second. Never doubt that. You have my heart, my protection, and my family, if it is ever needed."

She nodded and lowered her gaze. "I am so sorry I did not say anything earlier. John, truly I am. And Adam, oh God, he hates me so much and I have no idea why!"

"Adam is an asshole. Do not worry about him. Him, I can take care of quickly. You? I would not be able to move on in life if you were not in it."

Amelia leaned into her husband and sobbed into his chest. His thick, strong arms wrapped around her frame and held her close. His hand smoothed down her head, then to her back.

"I love you, Amelia. Never would I allow anything to happen to you."

She nodded and glanced up. "Never would I allow anything to happen to you, so long as I can help it anyway. I mean," she lowered her head and wiped at her eyes, "you are so much bigger than I am. It may not be much of a fight."

John grinned and a rumble vibrated against her body. "That I am."

"I love you, too, John." She paused for a moment. "Before you go, let us make plans to walk the forest trail. I love the evening strolls."

Tilting her chin up, John kissed her softly. "Sounds like a plan. Let me take care of Adam. I will be back in a while. The oven is readied with the fire wood. Cook up the vegetables when you are ready." He kissed the top of her head and smiled to her once more, then left the kitchen.

~

THE CHILL IN the air whipped around John's body as he stepped outside. He glanced to his left and right, but did not see or hear Adam and Sophie. "Where did they go?" He sighed and mentally went over the events of today in his mind.

A man threatened my wife. Yes, he will most definitely die, Undead or not.

Adam needs to be set back in line. He was out of order earlier.

I need to talk with Sophie. She made a great point in guarding Amelia. If I am not around for her, there is no one more I trust to guard her than Sophie.

He made his way farther into the yard. A yelp caught his attention and John quickly turned in the direction of the sound. He took a few steps toward the area and felt adrenaline rush through his body.

"Adam?" John called and waited, but no answer returned. "Adam! Sophie! Answer me!" When nothing returned but the sound of the wind, John gritted his teeth. *Where the hell did they go?*

He took a step forward and an old twig broke underneath his footing. He continued walking as he made his way toward the side of the house. In the distance, the forest behind his estate came into view. The trees were changing with the season providing a lush volume of reds, golds, and purples.

Glancing down the estate line, no one was present. He knew some in the pack were hunting today, where others were with family. Tom and Katherine were off duty and most likely at home. He thought of his friend and knew when he filled Tom in on the occurrence of today, Tom would be ready to fight when called upon.

Adam swore fealty to him, but he was not positive he could count on Adam to guard and support Amelia unless forced. Katherine did whatever Tom asked of her. The woman knew how to handle herself and shot with a straight eye. *She could teach Amelia a thing or two on self-defense.*

As the uneasiness subsided, a pain erupted in his head and John fell to his knees. As warmth seeped from his temple. He looked up to the man in the market today, and a metal pipe coming down on him again.

4

*C*LEANING UP FROM dinner, Amelia waited by the dining room table as the sun set. The candles had burned down and the golden hue they provided began to subside. She sighed and leaned back in her chair as the baby moved in her belly. She placed her hands over her bump and smiled.

"Soon, my son, soon."

"So you think you are having a boy?"

Amelia turned to the voice of Adam. She nodded and stood from her chair. "Yes, I do." She lowered her voice, chagrined. "I will leave you since my presence seems to disgust you."

"Amelia," Adam sighed and stepped into the room. "It is not that." He paused and Amelia lifted a brow as she watched him. "It is you are not wolf. You are not part of what we are and you will never understand what that means."

She stared at him for a moment then with a boldness she rarely mustered, she crossed the room and pointed a finger in his face. "How dare you presume to know anything about me when you can only assume I am some weak human woman? How dare you!"

"You will remove your finger, madam. Now, if you are done, I will explain further."

She shook her head. "I have heard enough. You can explain to John when he returns." *Where the hell is my husband*, she thought. "Leave me be."

"Amelia, please listen to reason," he continued.

She sighed and knew she would regret this later, "What reason would that be?"

"John was to mate within our pack, or at least another were pack. Since he did not, there is no guarantee he will pass on his linage to his child."

Amelia stared at him. On one hand, she understood what Adam said. Hell, John even discussed this with her, but in a way that did not come across so abrupt and rude. On the other hand, Adam seemed to enjoy rubbing this in any time he had the opportunity. She shook her head.

"Regardless of what our child will be when born, he is still *our* child. Leave it be, Adam. Why do you not tell Sophie how you feel rather than discuss something you obviously know nothing about with me?"

Adam growled. "Are you challenging me as Beta in the group, Amelia?"

She laughed. Amelia knew Adam had never cared for her relationship or marriage to John, although this was a bit too far. As Beta, from what she understood from John and the pack, he would protect her as if she were the Alpha, not treat her this way.

"Is that what you think?" She shook her head. "I am not challenging you, Adam." She laughed again and raised a brow. "What I am saying is tell her how you feel rather than tell me about children."

He growled then left the room.

Amelia walked to the dining table and leaned onto it, then blew out the first candle. John was not coming home tonight.

Something obviously came up that needed his attention. She blew out the next one, leaving one final candle on the table. Picking it up, she walked across the floor to the lantern in the room, then lit it. As the glow grew around her, she blew out the final candle and made her way to her bedroom.

~

MORNING CAME AND Amelia stretched in bed as the sun shone through her bedroom window. The warmth felt comfortable on her exposed skin. As she reached out, she felt across the bed, feeling an emptiness where John should have been.

Her eyes opened and she glanced to his empty pillow. A sadness built in her stomach, at least until her body alerted her to do something with the pressure on her bladder. Quickly, Amelia rose from bed and made her way to bathroom.

"Amelia? Are you in here?"

Amelia smiled to the familiar voice of Sarah, her friend and fellow Alchemist. "I am here, in the bathroom."

"Are you ill?" Sarah called from the bedroom.

She smiled. "No, I am all right. Is John downstairs?" Amelia finished then came to greet Sarah. "I woke this morning and he appears to have not come to bed."

Sarah shook her head, her blond hair moving with her. "No, I am afraid he is not. I will be happy to ask where he is."

"Thank you. Allow me to freshen up with a good brushing and I will be downstairs."

Sarah smiled and left the bedroom. Stepping into the bathroom, she brushed her teeth then ran a hairbrush through her locks. Pulling her hair to the top of her head and securing it with an elastic, she set the hair in drop curls. Satisfied with the result, she pulled a robe around her body and tied it above her belly.

Opening the bedroom door, she took a few steps downstairs and paused when she heard the conversation between Adam, Tom, and Sarah.

"No, she informed me John did not join her in bed last night," Sarah told whomever.

"I will check the parameters," Tom said. Amelia kept quiet and her gaze followed Tom as he left the house.

"I will check in with the patrol from last night to see if they saw anything unusual," Adam's voice whispered. "Do not alert Amelia to anything yet. It may be nothing, but the Alpha would never leave without notice, or at least letting his Beta know."

Amelia could actually picture Adam's chest swelling, right along with his head. She rolled her eyes and completed her descent of the stairs. As the step creaked from her arrival, Adam made eye contact with her first, followed by Sarah.

He raised a brow, then left. Amelia took a place next to Sarah and leaned close. "Please, tell me what is happening."

Sarah stared into her eyes for a long moment, then sighed. "How much did you hear?"

Amelia shrugged slightly. "When you told them he did not join me in bed last night."

Sarah's mouth made an O shape and she lowered her gaze.

"Understand something, Sarah. He is my husband, and their pack master. I appreciate their need to know, but do you not think he would have informed me as well if something were going on?"

Sarah nodded. "Of course."

"Then I cannot imagine something is actually happening, otherwise we would all know—"

Sophie ran into the room. Her white hair mussed and skin flushed from running, completely out of character for her. "Good, you are here!" she panted.

Sarah and Amelia hurried across the room toward her and

Sarah placed a gentle hand on Sophie's shoulder. "What happened?"

Catching her breath, Sophie looked into Amelia's eyes. "Something has happened to John."

The blow of the news did not hit Amelia at first. Instead, her thoughts began to make sense of why Sophie seemed out of breath. *The woman is in great physical shape. There is no reason for her to pant after a run. Although with this news, she may not be out of breath from running, but from panic.*

Panic.

John is missing.

Sarah suddenly had Amelia in her arms and Sophie leaned in and assisted. "Amelia!" Sarah yelled. "Amelia, let us get you to the couch."

The women, each taking an arm, escorted her to the sofa and sat her down. Sarah placed a hand on Amelia's forehead.

"No fever," she mumbled.

"Why on earth would I have a fever?" Amelia asked.

"The news of John?" Sarah remarked. "Fainting usually comes with a fever or a shock..." She stopped, realizing her own words. "Oh, Amelia, I am so foolish." She pulled her into her arms and hugged her. "Forgive me."

Amelia sighed as she leaned against Sarah. "It is fine." Looking to Sophie, she asked, "What did you find?"

Sophie shifted on the couch and cleared her throat. "There was blood..."

Amelia sat up from Sarah's embrace and her eyes widened. "John's, I pray not."

Sophie lowered her gaze and nodded. "It was his. Adam confirmed it a moment ago."

Adrenaline quickly shot through her, warming her body. She wrung her hands and stared at Sophie. "Find out what happened. If Adam had anything to do with this–"

"Are you suggesting he did?" Sophie asked with a curious glance. "Because if you are, that is treason against the pack."

"Well," Amelia pushed herself to her feet. She looked down to a sitting Sophie. "According to Adam, he made it quite clear last night, I am not pack nor ever will be pack, so who would I commit treason against?"

Sophie stood and the fierceness she normally carried faded to sadness. "Me," she said in a lowered tone.

Amelia's heart sank as Sophie left the room. "Sophie!" she called after her.

"Let her go," Sarah told her and took her hand. Standing next to her friend, she placed her other hand on Amelia's arm. "Let us go outside and see what news we can find?"

Amelia sighed. "My husband may be missing and I completely upset one of the few pack members to ever have my back. I am off to a wonderful start this morning."

Sarah rubbed gently on Amelia's back. "John is a strong man, more power behind him than the rest of his pack. Did you know he takes on the knowledge of prior pack leaders? He also has the ability to call upon the strength of them if so needed."

Amelia nodded. "Yes, I was aware, or so he told me once upon a time. Now let us stop wasting time and start searching for him."

"Actually, let us get you something to eat first," Sarah insisted, "get your nourishment up. Then we can venture outdoors and begin our search."

Amelia sighed. "All right, let us go."

"How can anyone get onto our territory without us knowing?" Tom asked. He crossed his thick arms over his chest and stared at Adam. "Were you not on patrol last night?"

Adam nodded. "I was, but not the only one. Trust me when I say I heard nothing and smelled nothing different."

"Who said it needed to be different?" Tom accused. "Do you not think a human would venture onto our land? Do you only smell for the Undead scum?"

"If you are suggesting I had something to do with this," Adam began and stepped closer to Tom, "you better be ready for a fucking fight. You are my friend and I do not wish to go there, but if this accusation continues, we will." His eyes flashed gold and he snarled.

"Is that a threat?" Tom asked.

"You tell me."

"Would you two stop?" Katherine yelled, then put herself between the two men. "Just stop! We know you had nothing to do with this, Adam," she said to him, then looked to her husband. "And you! You know better than to challenge him on such things! What has gotten into you?"

Tom continued to stare at Adam then slowly, the resolve began to fade. "I...I do not know." He lowered his gaze to his wife's and held it for a moment. "John was attacked and taken, yet no one saw, heard, or smelled anything different. How can that be?"

"What?" Everyone whipped their attention to Amelia.

"Hell, when did she come out here?" Katherine whispered. "How long have you been listening, Amelia?"

Amelia blinked and she looked from pack member to pack member. "Did you say...he...no, no! NO!" Amelia screamed and she fell to her knees, taking Sarah with her. "NO!"

"Oh shit," Katherine yelled as she quickly made her way across the lawn. "Amelia! No, do not worry yourself. Trust me, John can handle anything that comes his way. He is a tough man!"

"Whose blood was found on the ground?" Amelia yelled. "Who did this? Who?" She stared at Adam, then Tom and back to Adam. "For fuck's sake, someone please tell me something! I have a right as his wife and your pack mother to know!"

"You are not–" Adam began and Tom cut him off.

"We are working on it, Amelia. Trust me. Whatever happened, we will find an end to it." He glared at Adam, then made his way to his wife. "Do you wish to stay with Amelia?"

Katherine looked to Amelia and raised her brows. "I will stay with her," she said.

"Then it is settled," Tom began. "We shift and hunt."

A growl emitted from Adam and his face turned a dark shade of red. Anger did not begin to cover what seemed to claim him. "No! I give the orders! I am Alpha when the Alpha is detained or indisposed!"

Tom raised a brow. "How convenient... What shall we do, new leader?" He glanced across the field to a few of the other pack members:

Wyatt appeared to be in his early twenties. Amelia met him a few years ago and he had always been cordial with her, but never went out of his way to talk. He seemed shy.

Tyler, maybe in his early thirties, came into the pack just before Amelia met John. Being one of the newer members, he did not say much, nor had a say in much. However, today, he seemed upset at the turn of events. "Seems a little trigger happy, if you ask me."

Adam snarled, and Tyler returned it.

"Leave 'em be," Wyatt drew out. "He does not mean nuthin by it," the man spit on the ground and Amelia's stomach churned.

"What I want to know is," Sophie asked as she stepped up, "where the hell IS John?"

Amelia glanced to her and watched as Sophie made her way to Adam and stood by his side. She lowered her head and made a play of fealty to him.

Adam smirked and glanced at those around him. "I will be

your Alpha in his absence. You will follow my order and my rule. Understood?"

No one said or did anything, except Sophie. She glanced to Amelia and rose a single brow, then cast a chagrined look to the rest of the pack.

"Understood?" he yelled. The others flinched slightly, then one after the other, the pack nodded.

Everyone is submitting to this man, Amelia thought. *He had something to do with this, I know it!*

She stood strong next to Sarah and leaned into her embrace. "Be ready to depart at any given notice," she whispered.

Sarah nodded. "I will be with you wherever you go," she whispered back.

"Thank you," Amelia mumbled.

5

*P*AIN THROBBED IN John's head, and a sigh emitted from his lips. Crust pulled at his lids as he tried to open his eyes. A damp darkness surrounded him as well as a pungent smell. His stomach immediately churned and he vomited. The smell of death invaded his senses and he knew exactly where he was.

The Undead captured him. But upon seeing the man, for a brief second, who attacked him, John knew he was definitely not an Undead.

John growled and a low, guttural sound rumbled in his chest. "James Maxwell! Show yourself!" The pain throbbed harder in the back of his head and the chains around his body that strapped him to a wooden chair were so taut, he could barely move. He bit back a snarl when the metal touched his exposed skin.

Silver. They were prepared for this.

"James Maxwell, show yourself, now!"

A chuckle rose in the silence of what seemed to be a cave echoing his words. Hands pressed on John's thighs and a lantern followed, placed next to his legs. As John's eyes came into focus, the familiar face of James Maxwell stood before him. "So the beast is tamed, I see." He grinned. "Nothing more than a puppy," he spat.

John closed his eyes and considered an attempt to shift, but thought it better to wait and conserve his energy for the right moment. "What do you want?"

"Oh, was your pregnant wife not clear? Or did she not tell you?"

John growled. "What do you want from Amelia?"

"I WANT MY LIFE BACK!" He had become mad, his arms flailed about. "She took everything from me!"

"She saved your worthless life! You are a disgrace to humanity!" John yelled back.

"Maybe we should change you into one of us?" came a female voice. She had an accent, and sounded faintly familiar. "Then again, it would be so criminal of us to do that sort of... injustice to a wolf-beast."

"Come out of the shadows, you demon whore!" John yelled. "Face me!" he snarled and moved against the chains, snarl growing louder as the pain ignited.

"Nothing but a pup," James remarked.

"I shall take it from here." A new voice, a male with a Spanish accent spoke up. "Allow me to introduce myself." The man paused for a moment, then fingers snapped. Lanterns popped ablaze throughout the cave. Dark limestone glinted from the glow of the lanterns and a faint drip-drip echoed softly. Stalactite ice cycles formed from the dripping ceiling onto stalagmite columns. The air felt and smelled of mildew.

One by one, the Undead appeared, and as they did, the fear of being outnumbered, out of his element, and knowing there was no way to escape alive began to sink deep within him.

When the final lantern lit, the man of the voice came into view. He stood tall, tanned skin, dark hair that could be black hung to his shoulders. He was slender in build and wore a suit with a top hat. Upon it were blades, gears, and a few other gadgets within easy reach for self-defense.

He picked up one of the lanterns and held it closer to his face. When he grinned, fangs displayed, most likely for John's benefit. He took a few steps forward and bowed slightly, bringing his free arm across his chest.

"I am Tomas Hector Santiago Mendez. Please, address me as Tomas. Since the demise of our king, I have taken over as leader." He smirked and took a few steps forward. "As I have learned, it is you who is responsible for his death."

John swallowed the bile gathered in this throat. "I would do it again in a second."

Tomas smirked. "As such, it is only fitting we now attack your land...while we have you in custody. Seems we are at a fair advantage now, no?"

His accent rolled off his tongue to make him appear suave. He carried himself and talked as if he did not have a care in the world. Tomas smiled as he approached one of the females in his coven. He lightly touched her cheek and the woman appeared to have melted. John feared he would vomit again.

"We shall attack tonight," he continued to touch the female and his finger slipped over her bosom, to her corset. "That is, of course, unless you hand over the Alchemist, Amelia."

"NEVER!" John yelled.

Suddenly, a wind rushed over John as Tomas appeared in his face. "Then you have chosen death, *mi amigo*." He grinned and his fangs gleamed against the firelight in the room.

John attempted to not breathe in the decay that seeped from Tomas. "Death would be a better alternative than your lot."

Tomas grinned, grabbed John by his hair and as he yanked his head to the side, his fangs sank deep into his neck.

The sound that escaped John thundered throughout the cave. A few chuckles and yells from the Undead echoed. Tomas released him and as he stood, he raised a brow. "Not bad, honestly. Salty...maybe if blood could be salty."

The pain in John's throat throbbed, giving a momentary reprieve from that in his head. Warmth seeped down his chest as his vein pulsed his blood. He would heal soon enough.

"It is the mutt in him. What you did is completely disgusting," came the familiar female voice again.

Glancing up, John found a dark figure resting against the wall in the corner. Listening in the entire time, she finally pushed away from the wall and made herself known to him.

As she came into view, her dark hair, light skin... "No," he mumbled, "you are alive?" Last time he saw her, she was underneath him as he fought to rescue Amelia. Michel's lover, and right-hand man, René was here and did not meet her demise, as she once predicted.

She smiled and squatted in front of him. She now wore a patch over one eye. "Do you think me so fragile, mutt? And to think you knew me so well." She stood with a smirk and walked away. "When your dogs went after Michel, I fought my way through the house and escaped unscathed. Well, almost.

"Michel eventually caught up to me and followed through with most of his promise. He took my eye as punishment, then made Tomas promise to slowly and deliberately remove the other, along with the rest of my body parts."

She paused, then turned to John. "Consider what you did for me a favor. Said favor offers one in return." She glanced at Tomas and raised her brows. He bowed forward as if to grant her freedom for whatever she wished to mutter next. She bowed slightly in return. "For said favor, we shall not kill you...tonight. We shall, indeed, attack your land and we will do it with you in tow."

"What of me, mistress?" James asked. John almost forgot he was present.

Amelia, he thought, *they have to protect her. They have to protect one another, not that they could not. Adam will lead them. Tom will be there, as well as the others.* René was allowing him to live, but to watch as they attacked his pack. He had no way to warn the others.

"Oh, yes," Tomas smiled as he approached the now human male. He lifted one of his arms, opened his mouth and bit into his arm. He offered it to James as he bled onto the floor.

John shook his head, willing the man to not drink the blood. James immediately brought the arm to his mouth and latched on like a leech to a willing victim.

John closed his eyes and lowered his head. James, once vampire turned human, had a second chance at life. Then in that second, he threw it away.

A sound shot through the room like a howl from an injured man. Tomas stepped back and held his arm to his chest. The howl shifted to a scream and when John looked up, James dropped to his knees and fell onto his back. His body thrashed. John noticed the other vampires backing away.

"What is happening?" asked René.

Tomas simply shrugged. "Who knows? He was administered that whore's *cure* and now James is changing."

"Changing into what, exactly?" she asked.

John pressed against the chains, ignoring the pain as his skin burned. He needed to escape to warn the others, to leave and save his own life. He had no idea what this would do to James, if he would still be the same man...or vampire he once was...or if this could have an alternate effect on him.

If Amelia were here, she would know. He inhaled deeply and held his breath as he also held onto an image of his wife on their wedding day.

She wore a white, lacy gown the other Alchemists she knew made for her. Sarah brought it to her the day she could finally try it on for a fitting. He recalled walking into the den as she stood on a table while women placed pins on the inside of the dress.

He chuckled and Amelia turned to the sound. She screamed for him to get out, then yelled as a pin poked her. He laughed even more and quickly left the room.

"WHAT IS HAPPENING?" James's voice was shrill, ripping John from his thoughts. He watched the man writhe on the floor. Blood seeped from his mouth, most likely Tomas's, unless he bit his tongue off. The thought made John smirk.

"Hold him down," Tomas ordered. A few of the Undead approached the body as it jerked this way and that. They made an attempt to restrict him.

His arms and legs kicked and pulled. He snarled and bit at the ones restraining him. "Release me!" he yelled. His voice had changed, taking on a deeper tone.

He flailed again and when one of his arms punched upwards, a vampire flew backward and crashed into the cave wall. Tomas shuffled backward and watched with a smile, as did René.

"What have you done to him?" John asked. "This cannot be better than death! Look at him!"

"Yes, look," René followed, "look at our beautiful...monster." She grinned and met John's gaze. "And our new weapon."

John shook his head and James...or the man formerly known as James, kicked. Another vampire hit the wall and the crunch of his skull left a sickening feeling in John's gut. The injured vampire moved on the floor slowly, then got to his feet. John knew they healed in a similar way, but he would definitely be slower.

The monster's body stilled. The others holding him reluctantly released him and moved away. Sounds escaped from him that resembled wheezing, maybe seething.

"Rise," Tomas ordered. "Rise and join us!"

The monster growled and made his way to his feet. The white flesh of James Maxwell had been replaced by dark, tarlike skin. The light from the lanterns shone against his face and John found his eyes completely black.

The monster snarled. Elongated fangs came from his mouth and saliva dripped from the point.

Tomas stepped closer and reached for the creature, touching his arm. It flinched, then roared at the self-proclaimed leader. "You are absolute perfection."

The creature rumbled once more and snapped at Tomas, then lunged forward. Knocking the leader onto his back, the creature snarled and drooled on him. He leaned in as if to bite; guards quickly yanked the creature away, then pulled Tomas to his feet.

"Enough!"

John looked up to another woman who suddenly made her presence known. She stepped toward the light and as it cast shadows over her body, her lips pressed into a smirk. She lifted her hand, palm forward, and mumbled.

What happened next shocked not only John, but the other vampires in the cave; at least John thought by the wide-mouthed stares.

She had the creature calmed and under her control. He stalked forward and stood in front of this woman, an occasional snarl emitting.

"Irina," René began. "Glad you decided to join us."

The woman named Irina glanced at her and raised a brow. "Are you?" She grinned. "I do not believe you." Irina held up her other hand, and suddenly, René's body jerked and moved across the floor.

What the hell? John asked himself. *Is she controlling them?* He pulled at his chains. The sound scraped across the chair, causing the creature to shift his attention to John.

A snarl erupted. John held his gasp and closed his eyes as a thick, heavy breath invaded his face. Then a howl with an ear-piercing scream drilled into his aching head.

"Hold yourself, my love," Irina told him and the creature backed away from John.

He opened his eyes and found the body of a man who looked to be James Maxwell, but no longer held his soul, humanity, or any of the sort. Now stood the shell of a man who had become an abomination.

John looked to the woman named Irina and found her staring at him. "Oh, we shall have fun with Mister Hawthorne. Oh yes, we will."

6

AMELIA HELD HER breath as her belly pained her. Their son, for lack of a better term, kicked her in the ribs.

"Son, please, be careful with your mother." She sighed and sat on her bed, then stared at the empty wall before her. The pain subsided and she relaxed, some. *John is gone but who took him?* She had thought over the last few hours, and the only conclusion would be the Undead.

"But what quarrel do they have with us? I mean, other than the obvious? Is revenge for Michel worth the price for taking John?" She sighed and shook her head. "Maybe? Possibly?"

Then she considered something. She met her cadaver patient yesterday in the market, James Maxwell. "There is no possible outcome other than death to a human taking on a werewolf, especially if said wolf is the Alpha."

"Amelia?" Sophie's voice interrupted her thoughts and as she looked to the entrance of the room, the woman stood in her doorway. "I was hoping we could talk."

Amelia nodded and patted the side of the bed where she sat. "Please, have a seat." As Sophie made her way into the room, Amelia admired the way her hair had been tied with a few hair pins. A dark red stone sat in the middle of the pin and provided a contrast to the white of her hair.

Violet eyes looked into her own and she smiled softly. "I was hoping to talk about what transpired earlier today."

Offering a nod, "Which part, exactly?" Amelia began. "The part where John's blood was found on the grounds while Adam was on duty? Or when Adam declared himself Alpha after discovering John's disappearance?"

Sophie blinked at her words, then her brows furrowed. "I do not have a quarrel with you, Amelia. I do not wish to start one, either. Accusations against Adam are treacherous in pack laws–"

Amelia lifted a hand, waving it in front of her face. "No, to me it is not, being I am not part of your pack. Adam made sure to clear that up for me the other day, thank you."

Lifting a brow, Sophie turned her cheek to Amelia. "So I heard, but please rest assured, Adam had nothing to do with this."

"How can you be so positive, Sophie? Honestly, the man was on patrol the night John was attacked. He has no idea of his location and no idea what may have transpired without a scent. How can any of this not seem suspicious to you?"

Sophie's jaw tightened as she glared at Amelia. Her eyes flashed from violet to golden, then returned to their normal color. Amelia sat back a little as Sophie cleared her throat. "No, it does not seem suspicious to me, Amelia. I know Adam, more so than you may think. He is a good man and has always had John's back, no matter what. Hell, he approved of your marriage! Does that not count for something?"

Amelia shook her head and stood. She clinched her teeth and closed her eyes as she breathed through the pain she felt pulse through her body. *My God, another one of those will bring me to my knees.*

As it began to pass, she breathed through it and turned to

face Sophie. She noticed the woman studied her. "You do realize John would have married me with or without Adam's approval?"

"Yes," Sophie's gaze moved away from Amelia, focusing on the wall. "I believe John would have said or done anything to make you his." The foul tone in her voice was evident.

"Wow," Amelia whispered. "I have looked to you as something of a sister in this pack, but honestly, right now? You need to leave my room…and my presence. I cannot be around you while I am close to birth."

She turned her back to the woman and felt her eyes burn with tears. As upset as she felt, she did not wish to provide Sophie with the satisfaction of hurtful emotions. However, in the same breath, she wanted to put this wall behind them and move forward.

With Adam as the wall, that option was not doable.

"All right," Sophie whispered and as Amelia listened, she turned slightly toward the direction of the door. The last thing she saw was the white hair of Sophie as she rounded the corner.

Amelia sat on the bed and softly sobbed. *Where is John? How can Sophie feel this way about Adam? I think the best thing, right now, is to leave with Sarah.*

"Amelia! Where are you, Amelia?!" Suddenly, the yelling voice of Sarah filled the empty void of Amelia's bedroom. She stood and made her way toward the entrance of the bedroom.

"Sarah, what—"

"Get inside. NOW!" Sarah ran toward the bedroom.

"What is happening?" Alarmed, Amelia stepped back and watched as Sarah locked the bedroom door. "Sarah, talk to me, what has happened?" *What has her so riled up?* she thought. *Did something transpire with Adam? Even if that were the case, I do not imagine he would actually pose any physical danger.*

"We are under attack." As Sarah turned to her, she gasped at the dirt and residue on her friend's face.

"Sarah?" she asked in a whisper, already knowing the answer. The vampires.

"The Undead have arrived. And Amelia, they have John."

Her brain momentarily stopped; she stared into Sarah's eyes. Her lips became numb, her mouth went dry. Her fingers felt cold...hard. Her body...weak.

"Oh no," Sarah lunged quickly and caught her as Amelia began to fall toward the hardwood floor. "I have you, love, I have you." Helping her toward the bed, Sarah sat Amelia down and held her cheek in her hand. "Amelia, can you hear me?"

Amelia blinked as she stared at her friend. Her blond hair had been rattled, maybe from running. Her face and neck had dirt smeared across them, and possibly bruises. "Sarah, how... what happened to you?"

"Did you not hear me? They have John! They are outside now and closing in. I was attacked and I fought, got away to find you."

Amelia's gaze dropped to the floor and her body felt empty, save for her child. Her heart beat loudly in her ears, and her chest felt about to seize. She slumped and clinched the material over her heart. The words were finally registering, a tear slipped quickly down her cheek.

"They...John...he is..."

"Yes," Sarah whispered. "And he is alive."

Amelia's head snapped toward Sarah and the emptiness was quickly replaced with anger, rage, determination. Her fingers pulled in and her hands became fists. She could only see red. "Where?"

Sarah took her arm and clutched the elbow. "Amelia, you are to remain in my custody until the fight–"

"WHERE?!" she screamed and jumped to her feet. "Tell me now or I will go throw you down and find John myself! He is my husband and father to our unborn child! Where the FUCK is he?!"

Her chest heaved as she spat her last words from her lips. No longer the proper lady, Amelia was the beast her husband may need to survive. Pregnant or not, she had no plans on losing him again, or burying the love of her life.

"Outside, in the back. He has been tied to a cross with what looks to be silver chains. He is badly injured, from what I could see, but it is nothing we could not–" Sarah startled as she ran for the door. "NO! Amelia, come back! Do not go outside! It is too dangerous!"

⁓

THE PLATFORM CARRYING John's body bounced hard in the crevices of the earth. His head jolted this way and that. A groan emitted from his chest as the silver chains cut into his wrists, waist, and ankles.

John attempted to open his swollen eyes, when the monster, formerly that of James Maxwell, snarled as he snapped at John's face. His eyes squeezed shut as searing pain crupted on his chest. His jaw clenched as the warmth of blood oozed and mixed with what had previously dried.

The monster's constant mutilation of his body, bites and slashes from dagger-like nails continued to grind, dig, and tear at his flesh.

"STOP!" came the voice of a woman. The monster ceased and pulled away, a slight whimper in his voice.

What the hell? John thought. *This monster has been thinking on his own, acting on his own, then someone orders him to stop and he sits aside as if nothing had occurred. No one has power over this beast, yet something, or someone, does.*

"John Hawthorne," came the same voice, yet this time, close to his ear. "Can you hear me, John?"

The platform bounced again and he groaned, the pain

becoming almost too much. He slowly lifted his head and opened heavy lids.

He found a woman in front of him in a black dress, the neckline bound to her upper neck and sleeves covering her arms to her wrists. The dress came down in a hoop skirt, similar to what Amelia wore, except again, all black. He glanced at her eyes and found her to be amused.

"Fuck you," he mumbled and lowered his head.

"Oh, I think not, mutt. However, if you do not find it in yourself to change your mind, I am sure my friendly...thing here... could be quite persuasive." A growl began to build halfway through her sentence, unrelenting to grow as she spoke.

John glimpsed the woman again, and as the platform jerked once more, his body flew forward and he seized as the chains pulled against his skin. He howled in pain, and as his body fell back into position, he found the woman smirking.

"What do you want with me?"

"Oh," she stepped closer, "nothing really. Just maybe your wife."

His head snapped to attention and a pain ripped through his body from the onslaught of muscle movement. Regardless of what or how he felt, this was Amelia's life. "What the hell do you want with my wife?"

The woman smirked again. "Let us make a trade, shall we?" She pressed a finger into an open wound on his chest. John gritted his teeth and she pushed harder.

She wanted him to submit, but he could not, *would not*. John held his head up and stared her in the eyes. "I am not trading my life for hers. Kill me now."

She grinned and pulled her finger free, then wiped it on what was left of his shirt. "Oh no, I am not killing you, nor will I give your life for hers." She folded her hands over her bustle and stepped toward the edge of the platform. "You will give me her or I will kill you both." She gazed at him over her shoulder.

"Unless you have another Alchemist in hiding, Mister Hawthorne, I need Amelia to return with me."

He growled and pulled against his restraints. It was no good; the silver clung tightly to this body and gouged into his skin, leaving it raw. "You will not take her without a fight!"

She smiled and twirled toward the front of the cart. "So be it."

7

Amelia made it as far as the stairs before she paused. She inhaled deeply, then took the first step before she was immediately grabbed. The grip on her arm did not let up and Sarah turned Amelia to face her.

"Let me go or I will force your hands free of my body! That is my husband out there, Sarah! You cannot stop me from helping him, if I can."

Sarah took a few steps closer until she came nose to nose with her. "And what do you plan to do, exactly, once you are outside? Run to John and free him? Help him walk? You are due to have your child, Amelia. You cannot possibly put that much strain on your body and what of your child?"

Amelia began to speak and Sarah held a hand up. "I will not begin to pretend to understand how you are feeling, for I am not married. But if I need to, I will stop you."

Amelia lifted a brow. "You may try, but you will find yourself at the bottom of the stairs. As for my child, I am not a fool. I will protect him at all costs. I will not be responsible if you die, but if you live, I expect you by my side while *we* help carry my husband inside."

Sarah lowered her gaze and took a step back. "It is obvious I have made quite the impact on you today as you refuse to listen to reason." She held her arm out, offering the way for Amelia to lead. "After you. I will help in his rescue, but when I say for you to stop, Amelia, with God as my witness, you will stop. Do you understand?"

Amelia quickly nodded and smiled. "One day, when the time is right, you will understand what I am doing today. Now, let us go!" Gradually, Amelia made her way toward the bottom of the staircase. She found Tom and Katherine running toward the back with rifles and handguns, followed up by Sophie.

Stopping in her tracks, Sophie did a double take to Amelia and Sarah, then back to Amelia. "And where do you think you are going?"

"Get out of her way, Sophie. She knows what she is doing. Or so I hope," Sarah told her.

Sophie nodded and took a step toward the women. "These rifles are loaded with your liquid sun. Use if needed. The rest of us, well…you will see." Sophie's eyes shifted gold and her fingers twitched. "Time to fight! My Alpha is outside and needs us!"

Amelia grinned at hearing her words and cocked the rifle. She glanced to Sarah and lifted her brows. Her friend did the same. They followed Sophie to the back door and stopped.

A battle scene unfolded in front of the women. Vampires moving so fast on the greenery, they appeared as moving streaks in the air.

Then the wolves…she smiled as she saw her pack. Fighting between the Undead and the wolf pack reminded her of what may have transpired when John came looking for her.

Back then, Michel held the forces of the Undead together. Now? She had no idea who held the ranks. She assumed René perished in the fight as she never saw her again

The wolves delivered death to the vampires tenfold. Snarls sounded and body parts flew. A loud whimper filled the air and when Amelia sought the cause, she paused as one of her wolves fell forward in a heap.

"No," she yelled. Aiming her gun, she fired a shot and hit the vampire in the back. His body fell into a seizure as chemical sun exploded in his body, burning him from the inside out. Then his corpse fell into ash.

"Who is the wolf?" Sarah asked.

Amelia shook her head and tore her gaze from the fallen wolf. She cocked her rifle and when she looked up, her eyes landed on a wooden platform. She gasped and grabbed Sarah's arm. "There!" she yelled and pointed. "He is there! I see him!"

"Wait, Amelia, who is that? The woman next to him wearing black?"

Amelia shook her head, not having an idea. "She is too far; I cannot tell, but Sarah," she looked to her friend, "there is something you need to know." Amelia quickly filled Sarah in on the cadaver she saved with the X-280, how he found her in the market the other day, the threat and his disappearance.

"I do not know what has happened to James Maxwell," Amelia continued, "but I have a feeling he may be here, fighting with the Undead."

"Would they have taken him back into their coven?"

"Why would they not?"

Sarah shrugged. "I am not positive, but it would seem unlikely to me. He is a vampire who became human again. I would assume, to the Undead, he would be…taboo?"

Suddenly, a shrill scream ripped through the clearing. Both women flinched and stepped back. They glanced from one side of the field to the other for the source.

"Oh my God," Sarah whispered. "What is that?" She pointed with a shaky hand and as Amelia followed the direction, she gasped. His skin was blackened and he had the appearance of a demon.

"No! Oh no, that is him! That is James Maxwell!" She shook

her head and watched the man...no, creature as he made his way across the field.

His arm swung swiftly, and with such power. Blood sprayed from the wolf he attacked and he snarled. He continued to thrash his hands into his victim, punching repeatedly. Blood spewed around him and the body no longer moved with life, but only with the torment that continued against him.

Amelia lifted her rifle and aimed it toward what had once been her cadaver. She looked through the crude sight, and slowly the creature turned his gaze to where she stood. She gasped and held her breath. He was across the field, yet he seemed to be directly in front of her.

"Amelia! Fire your gun!" screamed Sarah. "Shoot him!"

Her finger pressed against the trigger and as she was about to pull, the creature's body suddenly hit the ground, face first. She lowered her gun and glanced at Sarah, who had lowered her own rifle. They watched as a wolf snarled and bit onto the creature's body.

"We need to get John! Maxwell is under control right now. Sarah, now! We need to go!" Amelia checked the bullets she had left.

Sarah continued to watch the field, shock having stricken her. "What the hell happened to him?"

"I do not know but we have to get John! Right now, Sarah! Come on!" Amelia grabbed her arm and pulled her forward. The thrust of movement pulled Sarah out of the daze holding her. Both women stepped onto the field, and as much as Amelia tried to run, she made her way in a fast-paced walk.

Sarah grabbed a hold of Amelia's arm and remained by her side. Snarls from the Undead grew louder, as well as growls from the wolf pack. Amelia slipped on the ground and when she caught herself on Sarah's arm, bile rose in her throat from the blood on the ground.

"Are you all right?" Sarah asked her.

Amelia nodded. "Yes, just...oh my God, so much blood." She swallowed hard to keep her breakfast in her stomach. "Come on, we are almost there!"

As they reached the platform, Sarah climbed on first then took Amelia's hands, helping her up. Amelia rushed to John and took his face in her hands.

"John! Can you hear me? It is me, it is Amelia! John! Look at me, John!"

His eyes fluttered slightly and he groaned.

"He is alive!" Amelia shrieked. "Sarah!" She shook her head when she turned back to him. "Oh my god, what did they do to you?" His face battered and bruised, cuts fresh on his neck, cheeks, and forehead. Amelia fought tears as they stung her eyes.

"I am working on the restraints," Sarah called. "Keep talking to him."

"Am..." John mumbled, then his eyes widened. "NO!"

Amelia glanced to her right and the woman in black stood next to the platform. She grinned at Amelia and tilted her head. "Do you not recognize me, Alchemist?" The woman smiled a little wider, displaying her white teeth.

Amelia panted slightly as she clung to John's wounded body. "Should I?" she asked her.

"Oh, child, you should." The women stepped closer and placed her hands, palm down, on the platform. "We are cousins, of a sort."

"No, I have no family other than my husband and child. Who are you?" Reality struck from her own words as thoughts of her sister, Rachel, and her father came quickly to mind.

"Amelia," John groaned, "she is..." he groaned as his body shifted, one arm falling to his side. "I do not know what she is," he mumbled. "She controls them."

Amelia held onto John as Sarah continued with the

restraints and released his other arm. His body slumped forward as the chain on his waist gave slack.

"I do not understand," Sarah questioned. "They bound him as if to have him released."

"I am not questioning it," Amelia started. "Let us get him inside before she or anyone else stops us!" Amelia glanced to the woman again with a plea in her eyes. She shook her head, not about to believe the words to come from her lips. "If we are cousins, as you say, please help us with passage back to the house. This man–"

"Beast. He is nothing but a beast, Alchemist. He needs to be destroyed with the rest of the lot."

Amelia's mouth opened in shock and she stood, staring at the woman. "He is many things but he is not something to be destroyed. Why would you want to kill off their kind? Do you not realize one cannot live without the other?"

"Of course, I realize this, Alchemist. My kind created the beasts."

Amelia stared at the woman in black. She blinked, processing this information. She side glanced to Sarah who looked to Amelia.

"Is she a witch?" Sarah whispered.

"Oh, indeed I am," the woman said as her brow rose. "I am much more than a witch, child." She lifted her hand and the creature that once was James Maxwell stopped moving. He froze as if she controlled him like a puppet on a string.

Amelia watched in shock and she pulled her eyes away. She looked down to John, then to Sarah. She swallowed the lump in her throat, then glanced to the woman. "Are you a…necromancer?"

The woman smiled and lowered her arm, then pointed her hand toward them. "Yes, you may call me Irina, while your mutt is still alive."

Amelia's eyes sought the creature, finding him closer. He

made his way quickly toward them; his mouth drooled blood. She felt John's hands working to grip her body.

Taking ahold of their arms, John pulled himself up and before shoving the two women behind his back.

"John, no!" Amelia screamed as she pulled her rifle up to her shoulder. She aimed it at the creature and as he leapt into the air, he just as quickly fell to the ground. Sarah screamed, John flinched and reached for Amelia as she held her rifle trained on the lifeless body.

The scene unfolded in unfathomable chaos as Amelia tried to figure out who took down the creature. Copper fur matted with blood stood on end as the wolf snarled. Then Amelia gasped, realizing who it was. "Adam! Adam! NO!" Amelia screamed, but she was already too late.

A shot fired in the air, then everything stopped; the fighting, the killing, even Adam and the creature. Adam's wolf form shook on the ground as blood seeped from his side. Amelia looked around for the culprit. Who shot the firearm, but could not locate him.

Irina stepped closer toward his fallen body and pressed her foot against him. Adam groaned then coughed.

Amelia looked to a grinning Irina, who returned her stare. She lifted a brow and turned her back on them, making her way toward the forest. Amelia looked to Sarah then back to Adam. Vampires drew closer and encircled Adam's body. He twitched as they touched him.

"Why can I not move?" Sarah questioned.

She looked to Sarah, then John. She pulled at her leg, but she also could not move. Panic set in as the vampires lifted Adam's body into the air. "NO! Where are they taking him? What is happening?"

John attempted to move and barely shifted his foot. As soon as Irina disappeared into the greenery of the forest, the vampires quickly behind her, the hold suddenly released.

Amelia willed her sight beyond the horizon in an effort to see where they were taking Adam. She could not make out any figures that far, nor could she make it on foot if she tried.

"NO!" came a rough, familiar voice. When Amelia and Sarah both looked, Sophie's wolf form ran as fast as she could toward the vampires.

Tyler, one of the pack members, quickly grabbed Sophie by wrapping his thick arms around her body. He held her in place as she struggled to free herself. Her legs kicked in the air and she pushed away from him. "Let me go this instant, Tyler! Now! They have Adam," she screamed.

"I cannot do that, Sophie. I am sorry, but I cannot." Tyler continued to hold onto her and when he glanced toward John, he offered him a nod. Tyler returned it and continued his hold on Sophie.

She wailed as she sobbed and finally gave up the struggle. As Tyler slowly released her, her body collapsed in the bloody grass. "Adam! No, no, no, NO!"

Tears slipped from Amelia and she reached for Sarah. "Oh my God," she whispered. Palming her tears away, she looked back to the battleground and found fallen comrades and mounds of ash where a few Undead lost their own fight. She returned her attention to the scene unfolding in front of them.

Opting to shift into her human form, Sophie screamed from the pain as her bones broke. Her body shifted and contorted on the ground until her human form returned.

"Adam, no, baby, please, no!" Sophie cried again.

"Tyler, stay with her, please," John ordered and Tyler returned with a nod. Being cautious as he climbed down from the platform, John bent over Sophie's body. He gently touched her back. "Take your time," he told her and stood again. He began to make his way back to Amelia and Sarah. "Are you two all right?"

Sarah nodded and squeezed Amelia's hand, then left her side and went to Sophie's.

John touched Amelia's belly, then looked into her eyes. "You were completely foolish to come out here."

"You would have done the same," she told him. "Scold me later. We need to mend your wounds."

"My wounds will heal themselves in time, woman." John grinned softly as he pulled Amelia close. "Please, never be this foolish again."

"RELEASE ME!" An unknown source broke the silence in the air. Amelia and John turned and discovered one of the Undead did not make it out with his coven. John immediately pulled Amelia behind him.

"Oh, well, if one remained behind for us," John announced, "seems I have a kill on my hands, after all."

Amelia looked past her husband to the man in custody. Tom, one of John's most trusted pack members, held onto a vampire. *He was an Undead*, Amelia thought, *but why did he not leave with the others?* "John?" Amelia asked as she reached for his arm. "Who is this? Why is he your kill? What happened?"

He contemplated Amelia's question and placed his hands on her shoulders. "I wanted a chance to tell you later but since he is here, my wife, this is one of the blood leeches who imprisoned me. And now it is my turn to benefit the favor of torture." John grinned and side glanced to the prisoner.

"What?" she asked. "He did this...all this to you?"

"Not all of it, but yes, he assisted," John told her and faced the vampire. He stared at him for a moment. "You realize you... and the others, are simply pawns in her game."

"I shall end you!" he snarled.

John grinned and shook his head. He sighed. "I learned quite a bit during my imprisonment." He paused for a moment and lowered his gaze.

"Just tell me," she whispered and took his hands.

He raised his eyes to hers. "René, she is still alive. She has become one the leaders, if not the top leader."

She gasped and took a step back. "She is…René is alive?" Amelia shook her head in disbelief. "No, she cannot be. She was destroyed in that house! The pack told me as much! Katherine and Tom both…"

"We were not in the room when John found you, Amelia," Tom explained. "We assumed she died by Michel's own hand."

She looked from Tom back to John. "Was she behind today? Did she orchestrate this?"

"Yes, but not just her," John began. "Tomas fed his blood to James Maxwell." He lowered his stare and explained the change James went through in the cave. "It seems a vampire who had been turned human and made vampire again actually becomes a soulless monster."

"Any worse than what they are when they first turn?" Katherine asked and she chuckled. "Honestly, they are nothing but leeches!"

"We have no further need for this one," Tom announced.

John grinned. "Then let us get this over with." He took a step toward the vampire and the Undead man screamed in protest. As Tom held onto his body, John met his scrutiny. Tom nodded and John snarled, pulled his fist back and it landed not just against the vampire's chest, but through it. When he pulled back out, he held onto his spinal cord.

The Undead fell to his knees upon his release, turned to ash and floated away in the breeze.

"Adam…he was coming to save us," Amelia whispered. "I accused him of your attack, John." She looked to him and tears welled in her eyes. "I accused him of treason and turning you over to the Undead for his own benefit."

As John began to clean his hands, he opened his mouth to retort and Sophie spoke up instead. "I hope you now realize… and see…Adam had nothing to do with all this." She jumped to her feet and stomped toward Amelia. Her violet eyes lit gold, then returned to their natural color. "NOTHING!"

Amelia flinched and stepped back. "Sophie, I did not know... I am so sorry."

She shook her head and looked to John, "With your permission, I wish to hunt for him."

"Not now, not while you are in this state. You will get yourself killed."

"Oh, you prevent me from hunting for my love, yet it is all right for *her* to commit treason!" She pointed toward Amelia and if venom could come from the look she gave her, it would have killed her. "She all but pulled the trigger on him herself!" John began to speak, but Sophie spun on her heel and left the yard, returning to the house.

As John was about to call after Sophie, Amelia spoke up. "No, she is right, I did. I will spend a lifetime making this up to her." She lowered her head. "I am such a damned fool. I am so sorry," she whispered, "so sorry."

John touched her shoulders and shifted her to face him. "It is over now. We need to rest and recover. Next, we will strike and take them down and find this Irina. Where she is, we will find Adam."

"If she is here," Sarah joined Amelia and John, "this cannot be good. If there is one, there will be more. If her coven is about, there has to be a reason. If a necromancer is working with vampires, it is not to be friendly." She sighed and continued by raising her voice for all to hear.

"Necromancers control the dead. They have the ability to take away any will they may have and do their own bidding. We all saw it with the creature tonight, as well as the other vampires." Sarah looked to the others and made eye contact with almost everyone. "There is a reason they are here."

John nodded. "I, personally, do not feel the Undead have any kind of will to speak of, but nonetheless, let us go inside and start preparations on locating Adam and the others. There will be more to discuss from what I learned during my captivity with this Irina."

As the pack made their way inside, John filled them in on what he discovered about the vampires having the cure, ingesting vampire blood again, and the monster it created. "I am worried what testing and torture Adam will receive." He sighed and shook his head, then in a softer voice said, "He will be begging for death in the end."

8

*A*MELIA TOOK A seat in front of her vanity and gently brushed her curls. She stared at herself in the reflection then quickly glanced to the side as John entered the room. She smiled toward him and took in his outfit.

He wore a dark gray suit, white shirt, and vest. John ran his hands down the front of it and looked to her. "Am I all right in this? I do not feel appropriate wearing this suit while we bury our fallen."

He sighed and raised a brow. "Funerals should not have to be like this. Why is it required to wear fancy clothes?" Glancing to his wife, he shook his head. "No, I am not looking for an answer. It just does not feel decent, I suppose." He took a seat on the bed and watched as she continued to brush her hair.

"Well, I agree with you." She turned to face herself in the mirror while keeping John in her view. "John, I did not openly accuse Adam of having plotted against you, but may as well have. Who does that?"

She looked to him in the mirror. "Sophie will never forgive me." Her words trailed off and she quickly wiped at her eyes. "I just wish I had time to make it up to him, show him I was

74

wrong, so completely wrong. I feel horrible that our last interaction was me accusing him, turning on him." She hung her head slightly as she fidgeted with her dress. Her belly moved as her son rolled this way and that.

How could I be so stupid to blame him? she thought. *I am not worthy of being here.*

Amelia glanced up as a set of warm hands squeezed her shoulders lightly. She met John's gaze.

"You would not have known, Amelia. Do not blame yourself. Adam can be an asshole. He was stubborn and thickheaded. You saw it firsthand."

"It does not excuse the fact I accused him of treason, though."

John grinned at this. "I can see him now, in my mind. How did he take being accused I wonder?"

She raised a brow. "You would ask such things, John Hawthorne." As Amelia moved in her seat to stand, John reached for her hand and helped her to her feet. "Thank you, but I am quite capable."

"Yes, I recall you running across the field toward me during the fight. You and I will talk about that later." He pulled her hand into the crook of his arm.

She furrowed her brows. "Talk about what? That I ran to rescue you?"

He nodded. "Precisely. Now let us get ourselves—"

"No, you would have done the same for me," she interrupted. "Do not tell me you would have stayed inside and waited for someone else to get me off that platform."

"Now, woman, that is different and you know it."

"How?" she asked him.

"I am not the one who is carrying our son."

She harrumphed as they descended the stairs. As they reached the bottom, Amelia brought the subject back to Sophie, who stood before them with her back turned. She sniffed and her arms moved; Amelia suspected she was wiping her eyes or nose.

Amelia reached for her tentatively, then pulled her hand back. She looked to the ground and sighed. *How do I do this? She hates me now.*

"So I see you are ready to bury your enemy."

Amelia glanced up to the venom that spat from Sophie. Both brows raised in surprise, she quickly shook her head. "Sophie, no...please–"

"Please what, exactly? Please understand that you accused Adam of deceiving his Alpha?"

"Sophie, that is enough," John commanded. "I understand you are hurting, but she did not mean her words. You will come to accept that in time."

Sophie snapped her gaze from Amelia to John. "Is that an order?"

"It will be if you do not watch yourself."

She slowly shook her head and as she gnashed her teeth, Amelia watched as her jaw muscles clinched and released.

Five minutes alone with her, I do not think I would survive. No, I know I would not survive.

"Just keep your distance. I cannot...not right now." Sophie lowered her gaze for a moment and as she took a single step back, she lowered herself into a bowing position. "I am, and still, pledge fealty to you as my Alpha."

"I appreciate that, Sophie, but nothing has changed," John told her. "Even if Adam did step up as Alpha, I am back and all is where it should be."

She glanced up and her eyes glowed golden. "Not everything." Sophie turned away and headed outside.

Amelia sighed. "If she does come around, it will be a very long while. I do not imagine she will ever forgive me for turning on him."

"You were following your instincts. You think differently

from the pack. As human, you would. No one can fault you for that."

Amelia motioned with her head toward the direction Sophie left. "She does."

"She is hurting," John told her. "Give her time. Now," he set a pair of spectacles on the bridge of his nose; the glass color showed blue and he glanced down to his wife. "Let us go."

~

*J*OHN STOOD AT the head of the service and looked out over the field. His pack, and a few friends of the fallen, had gathered. John looked toward Amelia, who offered an encouraging smile. He lifted one corner of his lips, then glanced down.

"It is never easy to give a eulogy for the ones we loved. What do you say? Do we celebrate their life or do we mourn their death? Well, today I say we do a little of both." He paused for a moment, then decided now would be a good time to say a speech about Adam.

"I want to talk to you about Adam." He looked out over the pack and found a few nodding, others not moving, and Sophie with a look of disgust. "Adam came to me many years ago. He had come into his shifting as a wolf and his fur was the reddest I have ever seen."

John shook his head with a grin. "He had a mouth on him and had no idea how to control it. He wanted to be in a pack, and he also wanted to run free. 'You cannot do both,' I told him one afternoon.

"Soon, he began to grow as a man, and as a wolf. He drew respect from others around him, and in time, it was returned. What put him into the power of Beta," John grinned and looked out over the audience, then landed on Sophie. She held her hand over her forehead as she shielded her face. He sighed and continued.

"The role of Beta came to Adam as we took on pack wars. Another alpha wolf approached and wanted to take my territory. I remember when Adam shifted right then and snarled. The fight broke out and it only took a moment before Adam won. He tore into that man and Adam grew in strength. He took on what the other wolf-beast left behind.

"When his first battle came about with the Undead, he stood easily against three on his own. Then, he shifted." John nodded to the whispers in the crowd. "That is right, he took them on before he shifted. Absolutely dangerous, and he learned his lesson afterward from the ass kicking he received."

He heard a chuckle in the crowd and found Tom smiling.

"I sat Adam down that night and we talked about what he wanted out of this pack. He openly told me one day, he wanted to be on top. He was born to be an Alpha. I chuckled at this. He had a look of evil in his eyes when I did."

John grinned, then continued. "As the conversation continued between us, by the end of the evening, I formally announced him as my Beta. The strength and knowledge that comes with being in a position of power indeed came to him that night. His body grew, as did his mind and knowledge." John glanced to the ground and sighed. "He would make an amazing Alpha to this pack, or a pack of his own."

～

*A*MELIA TOOK A seat in the den of their home. The pack members crowded the room, as well as the front porch. Food had been consumed and liquor began to make the rounds. She watched as frowns began to shift to smiles and occasionally, she heard a chuckle.

"I hope they are telling stories about Adam," Amelia whispered to Sarah.

Sarah nodded and leaned toward her. "You know, we would have left that afternoon if the Undead filth had not shown up."

"I know." Amelia glanced across the room and found Sophie watching her. She wore all black today, respectively, in black fitted pants, corset and leather boots. Her white hair was such a bright contrast to the darkness she wore, and the darkness that seemed to surround her. Her eyes glowed golden, then slowly shifted back to their violet.

Clearing her throat, Amelia glanced toward the floor, then to Sarah. "Please stay by my side until she calms."

Sarah nodded. "Absolutely." Adjusting herself in her chair, she glanced to Amelia and tapped her chin for a moment. "What on earth would a necromancer be doing with the Undead?" She paused and crossed her legs toward Amelia, the white of the bone cage under her bustle peeking through. "I understand the concept of *why*, but…why?"

Amelia shrugged softly. "Honestly, I do not know." She raised a brow. "But I intend to find out. We are not far from being necromancers ourselves. I am sure–"

"Never compare me to them, Amelia," Sarah retorted quickly. "I would never resort to fighting alongside the Undead."

Amelia grinned and nodded. "My apologies, but she may think the same of us for joining sides with the were-beasts."

"Then she is in for a big surprise, is she not?"

Offering another nod of agreement, she said, "Yes, she is… well, they are. I am certain there is more than one, but what would they be after with the Undead?"

"I do not know, but the thing…the creature they created. What the hell was that?"

Amelia shook her head, then looked up to locate John. She waved to him and he nodded, offering her a finger to indicate he will be over in a moment. "I think it is time we find out what happened to my cadaver...well, to James Maxwell."

She took a drink of her water then sat it on the table. Her swollen belly contracted suddenly and Amelia held her breath. She reached for Sarah's hand and gave it a squeeze. As it passed, she glanced to the woman. "That was not pleasant by any means. It felt like my entire front side seized up and pressed against me."

Sarah's brows raised. "Are you possibly going into labor?"

"I do not know, having never had a child before." She glanced up as John crossed the room toward them. "Nothing about this, not yet," she motioned to her belly and Sarah nodded.

"Did you need me?" he asked his wife.

Amelia nodded. "Tell us what you know about this creature. You went into it a little in the field but now that we are all here and together, it may be good to get everyone informed."

He stared into her eyes for a moment and his nostrils flared. Anger did not touch his face, but Amelia could see something was...wrong.

"What is it?" she asked him.

"Something seems altered, smells have changed about you," he told her.

Sarah snorted and covered her lips.

"I took a bath today!" Amelia told him in a stern voice.

John grinned and shook his head. "My apologies, that is not what I meant by smell, my love. Something is different." He leaned in and sniffed and Amelia raised her brows. "I believe you are going to be in labor soon."

"You can *smell* that?" She sighed and placed a gentle hand on his shoulder. "You need to make your story known first, then we can discuss what you believe to be *labor smells*." She enunciated the last two words with humor in her voice.

John grinned and kissed her cheek. He cleared his throat and spoke. The Alpha tone, loud as it was, carried throughout the room. The vocal command his pack could not ignore even if they tried.

Amelia had watched on occasion as a few of them tested it.

"OUTSIDE!" he ordered. "THERE IS MUCH TO DISCUSS!"

As the others filtered out of the room, he motioned them toward the back of the house. He remained with Amelia and Sarah until the others had cleared the room. Sophie remained for a moment, then pushed off the wall to join the others.

John looked down to his wife and lightly touched her cheek. "I love you."

"I love you, too," she told him with a smile. He left the room and Amelia watched him, then waited. She listened to the silence envelop the room, then turned to Sarah. "I think my water just broke."

Sarah glanced down and her eyes widened. "I do believe you are correct in that assessment. Let us get you upstairs."

~

*J*OHN WAITED FOR everyone to join him outside to get the pack updated at the same time. He glanced around, and satisfied he had their attention, he turned to Sophie. He nodded to her and she returned it.

"We have casualties and others are still missing. I trust the missing will turn up soon, if not, we will hunt for them as we would. There is a lot to tell and a short amount of time to tell it. I will be needed upstairs soon," he motioned to the house, "My wife is going into labor."

Gasps sounded and congratulations ensued. A firm grip on his shoulder, John turned to Tom.

"Congratulations, my friend."

John smiled and nodded. He inhaled deeply then began to

account the turn of events in the cave. He explained about Amelia's cadaver she turned human, the vampire Tomas sharing his blood, then the creature it created.

"It seems once a vampire has ingested the cure Amelia created, then attempts to turn vampire again, it causes...well, unknown side effects is the best I can say for now," John explained.

"Why, exactly, did the man want to become vampire again?" Tyler asked.

John looked to his pack member and shook his head. "Honestly? He stated he never wanted to be human again, and Amelia took that right away from him."

"Sounds familiar," Sophie mumbled.

"Sophie?" John looked to her with a growl. She lowered her gaze and crossed her arms over her chest. He glanced back to Tyler. "The man's name was James. Once he ingested the vampire blood, he began to change."

"Is that what we saw out there today?" Tyler asked.

John nodded. "It is. He seems to have lost every bit of his humanity. There was nothing left of James, just this monster. He turned and attacked a vampire next to him and that is when I first noticed the woman."

This seemed to catch Sophie's attention. "What woman, John?"

"The woman here today who controlled him, as well as a few other vampires on the field." He looked to his pack members. "Did anyone else witness this today? Did anyone else feel the pull she had on us?"

Tom held up a hand. "I did, at one point I could not move. I saw her do something with her hand, like a twitch to it or something similar. The vampires suddenly changed direction, as well as that creature. He headed straight toward you, Amelia, and Sarah. That was when Adam jumped in front of it."

The pack grew quiet. A few heads turned toward Sophie. She

nodded, then stepped forward. She raised her head and looked to John. He gave her the floor to begin.

She sighed and stepped farther out, then turned to face the pack. "Adam put himself in harm's way to save our Alpha, his unborn son, and our Alchemist."

"Is Amelia okay?" Tyler asked.

Sophie spoke up first. "I was talking about Sarah." A firm hand grasped her shoulder and pulled her back. Looking up to her Alpha, she sighed and lowered her gaze.

"That is enough, Sophie." He looked to Tyler. "She was fine. She and Sarah worked to get the binding undone and that is when all three of us realized something was wrong. The restraints were too easy, aside from the silver.

"As soon as I had been freed, the creature came running. The necromancer had been waiting for it, I think, to happen so she could unleash him on us. Amelia and Sarah thought the same. Amelia knew who the woman was and Sarah had a good idea. It was not until later I learned of who and what this woman is."

"So the necro...person can actually control the dead?" Tyler asked.

"Yes, they can," John answered.

"So, if this...witch was to go into a cemetery, she could control a corpse?"

"Yes, I believe so. They control the dead and a corpse is absolutely dead." John looked to his pack. "I need you all to understand what this means. James felt his free will had been snatched from him. Imagine the battle today where only this witch, for a lack of a better term, influenced a handful of vampires. Going against that, I have no idea how we would fair, other than destroying them."

"And that is different how?" Sophie asked. The others looked to her with surprised expressions. She shook her head. "Oh, do not look at me like that. Every one of you were thinking the same thing. You are just too weak to ask it. So," she looked back to John, "how is this any different?"

He raised a brow. *Adam is gone and she is hurting, lashing out. She will calm in a few days' time.* "It is different because they are forced to fight, rather than wanting to fight. I would not want someone to control me like a puppet, would you?"

She shook her head. "But I am not an Undead filthy vermin of Earth, either."

"True," he said, "but imagine, if for just a moment, these witches were able to control you. How would you deal with that? It is not like you could fight back or fight the compulsion."

Sophie shook her head. "I do not have an answer for that, other than kill them before they do it to us."

"Kill them?" he asked her and she nodded.

"Yes, kill them. Do you not see they have the upper hand here?"

"Yes, I do, however, you need to realize they have the upper hand on the Undead, not on us."

"Not yet," she said as she turned away from John, then made her way through the crowd. "I will fight for you, John, but I will not subject myself to compulsion."

John watched her as she left, then let out a long sigh. "We need to get a few men on the inside of this. We need to, somehow, find a way to talk to a vampire on how this works, how the necromancers are able to control them…and if their ability does go any further than this."

"Can they work spells to force actions upon others?" Tyler asked.

John shrugged. "I have no idea, but we will find out." A scream sounded from inside the house and John smiled. *My son is coming*, he thought and smiled wider. "That is my signal to return to my wife. We will continue this later."

9

Sarah helped Amelia up the stairs and closed the door to the bedroom. Helping to remove Amelia's clothes, she handed over a long nightgown. Amelia put it on, groaned and sat on the bed. The pain was stronger now, almost like pressure had been applied to her abdomen in a way to squeeze her child.

Sarah dropped to the floor in front of her. She smiled and touched Amelia's knees. "Let me check you, we will see about getting started, all right?"

Amelia designated Sarah to be her midwife during her third month of pregnancy. She knew the woman to be capable of many things and trusted her completely.

Amelia nodded, then groaned, closing her eyes. "Sarah, fuck, this is…oh, God!"

Sarah pressed her fingers to Amelia's knees and pulled them apart. "You need to try to relax and lie back on your elbows. Here," she placed the heel of Amelia's feet on the end of the bed. "This will help."

As Amelia lay back, she stared at the ceiling, then suddenly jumped. As her legs fell further apart, Sarah inserted a few fingers inside her. She closed her eyes as another contraction began.

"It will not be long now," she told her and stood. Hearing footsteps on the wooden floor, Sarah opened the door to Katherine on the other side.

"I am here to assist with whatever you may need," she told Sarah. "Amelia, you will get through this."

She nodded and looked to Sarah. "I need water."

Katherine nodded and quickly left the room. Sarah called after her, "Bring me whatever clean towels are available."

Amelia breathed through another contraction, her breaths almost panting. *Should it hurt this much?* she wondered. "Oh… Sarah, dammit!" She gritted her teeth and rather than breathe, held her breath. *Fuck, fuck, fuck!*

"Amelia, listen to me, listen!" Getting her attention, she smiled softly. "I need you to breathe and try to calm down. It appears the contractions are coming faster."

Amelia nodded. "I hope John finishes his story soon." She sat up as the contraction passed. "I need to walk around a bit."

Sarah nodded and stood next to her. She rubbed her back and her shoulders, then as Katherine came back into the room, she handed over a pitcher of water.

"I am on my way for towels now."

Sarah smiled and took the pitcher. "Thank you, Katherine. Amelia," she poured water into a glass, "here, drink this." She handed it over and crossed her arms over her chest. Tilting her head slightly, she smiled. "Can you tell me what it is like?"

Amelia drank the water then handed the glass back. "Tell you what?"

"What it is like to be pregnant. I do not have a lover, nor am I married. I do not know if that is in my future or not, so I am hoping to maybe have an understanding."

Nodding, Amelia continued to pace the room, hands on her lower back. "Well, I suppose you could say it is like putting a small child inside your belly who continues to move about, no matter what you do. If you eat something they do not like, you may vomit.

"Then there are the cravings. I wanted salty things and sweet, sometimes at the same time." Sarah grinned at this. "The first time I felt him move, I thought for a moment it was gas," Amelia grinned and Sarah giggled, "then realized it was actually him changing position."

Her hands absently rubbed against her belly. "You get so used to him moving about that when he sleeps, you want to shake him awake just to know he is all right.

"Then there are times he will kick me right in the ribs. Oh, Sarah, that is the worst. It hurts so much." She shook her head, bent over and pressed her palms on her thighs. Another contraction began to rise and she breathed in deeply, then slowly exhaled.

"Fuck me, this hurts." She glanced up to her friend. "Imagine something inside you, eating with you, drinking with you, sharing blood with you. Now this something is going to push himself out of an opening absolutely too small to even consider…OW!" She inhaled a sharp breath and her nails dug into her knees.

"I have you," Sarah told her as she quickly came to her side. "Here, let us get you on your knees. Bend over to your hands and relieve some of the pressure on your back."

Amelia nodded and lowered to the floor. Sarah had made a makeshift pad at some point. It was nice to have the support of the cushion for this. Her hands now pressing to the floor, her back felt at ease for a few minutes, until another contraction hit.

"Sarah, oh God!" She groaned through the pain and gritted her teeth. "Get. John." She told her between breaths.

Sarah glanced up to a waiting Katherine. "You heard her, go get him."

Katherine quickly ran from the room, leaving the echo of her boots in her wake.

"I need to check if the head is surfacing. This may be uncomfortable, but it will allow me to see how much time we have until your son is born into the world."

Amelia nodded to her. "So you feel I am having a son as well?"

"I am assuming as much since you two have insisted you are having a boy." Sarah smiled to her.

Katherine returned with more towels and washcloths, and John. "Allow me to dampen a few and we can keep any fevers down that may spike."

"Good, thank you, Katherine," Sarah stated. She glanced up to John. "Come down here. Your wife needs you."

John stepped inside into the room. "Amelia, I am here."

She glanced up to him and tears ran from her eyes. "Never, ever ask me to give you another child, John Hawthorne! I hate you for this! Do you hear me? HATE YOU!"

He raised a brow and glanced to Sarah. "It will pass soon."

"The baby?" he asked with a questionable look.

She smiled. "No, the hatred."

"SHUT UP!" Amelia screamed. "Oh God! Sarah, get me on my back; he is coming!"

Sarah immediately helped her lie down. She motioned for John to come closer. He took her head and placed it in his lap.

"I am not sure what to do," he confessed.

"Whatever she needs," Sarah whispered. "For now, just hold her, tell her you are here, stroke her hair and hold her hand. Oh," she handed him a washcloth. "Make sure she does not gain a fever. Keep this on her forehead and help keep the sweat from her eyes."

He nodded and pressed the cold cloth to his wife's forehead.

Amelia closed her eyes and whimpered at the pain.

"All right, Amelia, I see his head beginning to crown. When I tell you to push, you push. Do you understand?"

Amelia nodded then let out a sob. "What if I cannot do this?"

"You can, and you will. You have to," Sarah instructed her. "Now push, Amelia, I need you to push!"

She pushed as much as her body would be willing. "OH MY GOD IT HURTS!" Her voice came out as a scream and John held her squeezing hand.

"You can do this. You will be all right. I love you so much," he told her. "Just think, the more you push, the faster he will be out and we can begin to grow as a family."

"Stop talking!" Amelia yelled at her husband. "I will never forgive you for this amount of pain you have inflicted upon me, John Hawthorne!" She inhaled and yelled out at the same time. "Oh my God! Get him out!"

"Amelia, you need to push harder! Push now! John, help her sit up!"

He lifted her shoulders, then moved close behind her. "Push, baby, you can do this. I have you. I have you."

Amelia closed her eyes and held her breath; she focused on the sound of John's breathing. She heard him in that instant, as if hearing his heart beating next to her ear. Maybe it was her own heart, but regardless, she focused on the sound. Then she pushed.

"PUSH!" Sarah yelled to her. "He is coming!" Amelia screamed this time as she did. John held onto her body as she pushed.

Then she fell slack. A cry sounded in the air. A laugh of joy from John followed shortly behind.

Amelia opened her eyes and slowly blinked. John continued to hold onto her and as Sarah glanced up to them, she smiled.

"Congratulations, you have a boy."

10

*I*RINA CLOSED THE door behind her and kept her fingers pressed against the wooden grain. She stared at it for a moment, then grinned. *My plan is working perfectly*, she thought.

"I did not realize Amelia had become so...pregnant."

Irina glanced over her shoulder toward the woman who spoke. Her dark brown hair cut short, the woman held an elegance about her that exuded excellence. Vampirism seemed to restore youth in some, where others were not so fortunate.

"Well, what do you believe happens to a woman when she becomes pregnant, Elena?" Irina left the door and stepped toward the woman. She raised a brow and smirked. "Pray tell, you did not already forget when a woman conceives–"

Elena cut her off and as her lip pulled in a snarl, she growled. "I will have you know I *do* know how a woman gets pregnant. What I meant was I did not realize she had grown in her pregnancy at the rate she did." She rolled her eyes and shook her head. "Honestly, Irina, you think so little of me?" She turned away from the necromancer and approached another door. It had a deadbolt attached, keeping the prison secure. Scratches scarred the wood from interrogations they had from time to time.

An interrogation had been planned the evening before for one of the wolves captured in the fighting. Irina cut the woman off as she reached for the lock. She looked Elena in the eyes then smiled softly. "I have been waiting patiently to attend to... well, attend to my prisoner. Now, if you do not mind, I need my quiet space to think."

Elena raised her brow this time, then crossed her slender arms over her chest. She frowned with chagrin and made a huff of irritation. Irina noticed how thin Elena's frame appeared and also saw scars on her skin.

"Help me understand," Irina began, "how it is you came by these scars? I thought vampires healed from wounds inflicted?"

Elena's frown dissolved softly and in its place she appeared more herself. "I had these before I was turned." She held her arms out facing up, then turned them to bare her inner forearms. "It was not a pleasant experience, from what I recall." She shrugged and her arms rested by her sides. "Nonetheless, why will you not allow me entrance?" She carried a slight whine in her voice.

Usually Irina found this cute, almost sexy. She enjoyed the body of a woman as much as a man's. Elena's body definitely had sex appeal and she knew how to get Irina's attention. However, this time, this was business and not a place to make sexy talk, or have sex in general.

"Listen, Elena..." Irina sighed and stepped closer to the female. She lightly touched her cheek and smiled. "I need to do this alone. I cannot afford any distractions."

"But I promise to not distract you." She leaned into Irina and lightly pressed her lips to her neck. Her tongue teased Irina's earlobe. "Let me watch. I will let you watch later."

Irina closed her eyes and she swallowed hard. Elena skimmed her fingers across the top of Irina's breasts as they pushed over the material of her corset. In a blink, Irina snatched her hand and jerked it away, then put distance between them. Elena gasped and her eyes widened. "I told you I need to be alone for this. You will do as I command; do you understand?"

Elena snarled at her lover and dared a step forward. "What will you do to me if I do not? Will you hurt me? Punish me? Throw me away like a used doll?"

"If that is what it takes, then yes. I have no issue using my power over you if needed, Elena. Now," she leaned in and smiled softly, "be the good girl I know you are and go into the den. I am sure the rest of your flock would love to see you."

Elena gritted her teeth and she quickly turned on her heel. "I am not happy," she mumbled as she stomped out of the room.

Irina shook her head and turned back to the door. She unlocked it and pulled it open slightly. Darkness held the other side. She lit a candelabra, clutched it at the entryway to the stairs. The room lit a golden hue and as she pulled the door open wider, she heard a set of footsteps come up behind her.

"We finally have a healthy live one, do we not?" Masculine hands rested on Irina's waist and he leaned in close. His breath eased over her neck.

"We do," she whispered. "Are you ready to try this experiment again?" She turned to face Marcus, one of Tomas's guards, and smiled. Marcus's skin appeared tanned, which was impossible considering he was a vampire.

At one point, Irina wondered if this man was Brazilian. His hazel eyes stared into hers. Irina wanted to reach up and run her fingers through his dark hair. It was a little long on top, but did not hang past his ears.

His body, damn, he had a body. Sexy as he was, he was a vampire. She made a false attempt to straighten her skirts to cover the blush touching her cheeks.

"I am ready," he told her. Marcus sidestepped and took the

candelabra. His fingers barely grazed hers and their eyes met again.

Any thoughts Irina had regarding sex with Elena were gone. As he headed farther into the room, the light faded after him. Irina reached for the door, noticed Marcus had placed two guards outside, and she grinned. She offered a nod of recognition, in which they returned. She reached for the door and slowly pulled it closed, then locked it from the inside.

Irina began her descent toward the stairs Marcus already took down. She had something to experiment on and the thought made her grin. It was not often they were able to capture a live beast, but when they could, the possibilities were endless.

As much as she wanted to work alone without distractions, and as much as a distraction Marcus could be, she knew he wanted this as much as she did.

The experiment would likely force the beast into something like James Maxwell became, or it would kill him. Either way, Irina knew the beast captured would soon be dead.

"It is unfortunate, really," Marcus began, "will he live?" He narrowed his eyes as he watched the beast on the other side of the silver lined bars. "Or will he die?"

"Stop playing, Marcus. We have work to do." Irina removed the jacket she had on and stood in a corset and bustle skirt. Her shoulders were bare and a slight chill in the air caused gooseflesh on her exposed skin.

Marcus raised a brow and grinned. "Is that for me?"

"Later, maybe," she teased.

"Good enough." He unbuttoned and hung his jacket then rolled up his white sleeves and opened the first few buttons of his shirt.

Irina grinned. "So, is that for me?"

"Could be," he teased her. "Now, love, if you may?"

She nodded, opened one of the drawers and pulled out a

metal syringe, glass beaker, and her goggles. Irina pulled on the goggles and stared through the glass lenses.

"James, be sure not to damage these lenses, will you, darling? The spell that makes them show the chemical compounds is a bitch to create." She glanced at him. "I'd hate to recast it using all your vampiric blood required." No reaction from Marcus.

Since Amelia created her cure then destroyed the evidence, the only link to it resided inside the body of James Maxwell. This beast of a vampire and human with the components of the potion Amelia created was the only indication, only source Irina had in possibly recreating it.

She put the instruments together to draw blood from the beast, then paused with a thought. *Since we took their Beta, the entire pack will mourn.* The thought made Irina grin. *There is a good chance I could send someone in, someone to play spy. I could have them bring some mutt along for the ride of their life, and in the process, convince them to give up the one person who brought on the pack's mourning: Amelia.*

She grinned, liking this idea, but for now, decided to keep it to herself. She did not want anyone knowing her plans, at least not yet. She had a coven of her own to return to soon. They would want news of the vampires and werewolves. They would want information regarding this cure and to know if it were possible to gain more.

They would seek to destroy everything if...

"Irina?" Marcus brought her from her thoughts. He raised a brow to her. "Yes?"

"Oh, nothing, love," she answered with a sly grin. "Just... plans for later is all."

He grinned and shook his head. "Is the instrument ready?"

She nodded and approached the cage. The beast inside snarled and snapped towards them. Upon his capture, Irina had injected him with a concoction she created that forced the man to remain in his beast form. His copper fur matted from blood.

"If you can hold him still long enough to shove this inside his arm...leg? Whatever that is," she pointed to the front leg of the beast, "I can get what I need."

Marcus nodded and unlocked the cell. In a flash, he had the beast pinned to the ground and held his front leg out. The wolf fought him but exhaustion seemed to be working against him, and in their advantage. Having not rested in his human state since the fight had drained him of his power as a two-natured beast. The full moon gave them the power, so she understood, and remaining in wolf form for too long could have the alternate effect.

Almost as if living with a welcomed curse.

She shoved the metal syringe into his arm and the beast howled in pain. Blood began to fill the glass cylinder and soon, she would have enough for what she required. As soon as it filled, she yanked the metal out of the beast's leg.

He bled onto the floor and panted. Marcus stood and watched over him for a moment. "Not so beastly now, are you?" He grinned and followed Irina out the door. He locked it into place once again.

Irina placed the glass beaker on the counter then picked up a thin tube. One end came to a point and she inserted this end into the beaker. The other end had a device Irina pulled. Blood sucked into the tube and she pulled it out and put some in a small petri dish. Setting the tube back into the glass beaker, she pulled the dish closer and waited.

Slowly, the components of the beast's blood began to identify themselves to her. The make up to what he was as a two-natured put itself on display to her like particles of dust in the air. Some moved this way while others moved that. She raised a brow and tilted her head.

"Well? What do you see?" Marcus asked.

"Nothing of consequence yet. Just his makeup. Hand me the blood taken from that monster...James."

A moment later, Marcus came to her side and handed over a small glass tube. The contents inside were darker than what she removed from the beast. Irina took it and smiled, but did not look away from the dish. Slowly, she let two drops of blood hit the dish and she handed the tube back to Marcus.

Then it began to happen. The blood she dropped in attacked the blood from the beast. She watched as the darkened blood assaulted in small amounts, the beast's. "Remarkable," she mumbled.

"What is happening?" Marcus questioned.

"Hold on...a moment. Wow," she leaned in closer. "Hand me the tube again." She held her hand out and the tube slipped over her palm. She grasped it and slowly dripped a few more drops of the darkened blood. Irina inclined in even closer and smiled. "This is absolutely amazing."

"Irina, I will not ask again. What is happening?" Frustration in his voice, Marcus leaned against the counter.

"Give me a few more minutes to confirm my suspicions?" When she did not hear a remark from him, she took it as acceptable...maybe hurry the hell up.

Regardless, she tipped the contents of the darkened blood into the dish until almost all of it had been covered. She watched and as the darkness covered the light, almost as if the darkened blood ingested it, consuming it.

"Remarkable!" Irina stood and removed her goggles. She smiled and gave her attention to Marcus.

"Finally!" He rubbed his hands together and grinned. "Tell me what you have learned."

"Since James had become vampire...well, beast...whatever he became, it is likely his blood will continue to act as if he were vampire."

"And?" Marcus raised a brow.

"And there is more. His blood actually began to eat the blood of the mutt over there. Through my lenses, I watched as it took place, as it was happening! Oh, Marcus, this is bigger than any of us could have anticipated!" She looked back to the petri dish again and grinned. "She had no idea what she came across when she created this cure, Marcus."

"What makes you believe it is her cure doing this to the dog's blood?" he asked.

"I believe this because if a vampire attempted to bite or drink the blood of a vampire, and help me if I misspeak, Marcus, but if a vampire attempted to drink the blood, it would have no effect on you, correct?"

He nodded. "From what I hear, it is an acquired taste."

"Exactly. Well, here," she pointed to the dish, "I am seeing the blood of James overtake the blood of the mutt in the cage."

"And?" Marcus asked her. "Please get to the point."

She frowned in frustration. "I am telling you his blood will kill any wolf-beast it comes into contact with. Do you see now?"

He raised his brows and Irina smiled. "You mean that if I were to inject the blood of our own beast into the dog in the cell, it might... kill him?"

She nodded. "Yes, it *will* kill him. If I were to inject this in a vein, he would die in a matter of minutes."

He stepped closer to her and touched her chin, lifting her face up to him. "Have I told you how remarkable you are?"

Irina grinned. "Not enough, it seems." She removed his hand and turned away as his lips kissed her cheek.

"Why do you tease me so," he mumbled and took the keys off the counter. "Shall we test your theory?" Marcus made his way back inside and toward another cage that held a different were beast.

She nodded. "I would love to. If this works as I am assuming it will, I want you to take it with you to the wolves. I want you to lure someone. Convince them they need to bring Amelia back with her. I need her, Marcus. Will you do this for me?"

He leaned down to the beast and pressed a knee to his head and his hands held down his legs. "Then leave the beta we took as bate. We could use him to lure her out. This one here, he is of no use to us. Besides, it is not like you are leaving me much of a choice. I do it..."

"Or I will make you," she finished for him. Irina emptied the syringe of the wolf's blood, then put the tip of it in the tube Marcus brought her. She stepped inside the cage and as she bent down, she casually ran her bare hand over the fur of the animal at her feet. "Shame, such a waste." She plunged the syringe into the neck of the wolf and he howled.

He writhed with the energy he had left, Marcus held him down. The thrashing began to soften and soon, he ceased. His chest stopped moving and a last sigh left his mouth.

Irina stood over the dead carcass and raised a brow while holding the syringe. "Yes, definitely take some with you, or just take the beast along as your pet. I do not care how you do it, so long as you do it. Feel free to release him on the pack."

She turned on her heel and left the cage, then tossed the empty syringe onto the counter. It shattered and the blood left in the tube spilled. As she made her way with the candelabra, Irina turned to gaze at a surprised Marcus.

"I told you he would die. Now do as I ask or I shall force it upon you."

Marcus stood and slowly made his way from the cage. He looked upon the counter at the remaining contents, then up to a retreating Irina.

"Fucking bitch," he muttered under his breath.

∾

IRINA MADE IT to her designated room while she stayed with the coven. After locking the door to keep her actions private, she pulled a silver bowl from a nearby shelf. She picked up a pitcher of water and emptied the contents inside it. She made her way toward the window and set it on the sill.

After pulling a chair out, Irina took a seat and stared into the dish. She waved a hand over the top.

"See me," she spoke while looking into the basin. Her own reflection stared back, then it began to shift. A murky appearance developed over the liquid, then it rippled as if something dripped into the center.

The contents settled, then the murkiness dissipated. Her garden on her island came in to view. Gray columns stood with ivy clinging to it as it grew. The sky materialized as bright a blue as she remembered.

"Is someone with me?" Irina asked. "I need an elder, please. Amara, are you there?"

"Child," came a woman's voice. Then a woman who appeared no older than thirty smiled as she took a seat. "Irina, have you found it?" She wore a mask, of sorts, at all times to hide her age and who she really was. Amara appeared around seventy years of age, but rumor had it she was closer to three hundred.

Irina nodded. "In a way, Amara, yes. I found they—"

"That is not what I asked you, child. Did you find this cure created or not?"

Irina gritted her teeth for a moment, then tried again. "Yes and no."

Amara sat back in her seat slightly. "Tell me how you allowed this to happen. There is much riding on the failure you are about to deliver."

Irina wanted more than anything to reach through the water, grasp the old woman's neck, and squeeze as hard as she could. Most days she hated Amara, then on others, she was treated as if she were the old woman's child. She hated the hot and cold…more often the latter than anything else.

"I did not fail you, Amara. Allow me to explain what I have found."

The woman sighed and beckoned with her hand to continue.

Irina cleared her throat then explained Maxwell's transformation and how his blood killed the wolf-beast.

"So you see, all is not lost. I have charged Marcus with—"

"Stop," Amara ordered. "You mean to tell me you have found a blood type to kill werewolves?"

Irina nodded with a smile. "Yes, that is correct."

"Well, that changes things." She sighed and brushed a few of her locks away from her face. "Who is this Marcus?"

"Marcus is one of the guards to the vampire coven. I tasked him to lure Amelia back to me so I can bring her home, where she belongs. There is only one complication."

"Aside from your obvious failures today? Please, tell me." Amara breathed heavily in melodramatic boredom.

Irina lifted her upper lip in a snarl. "I would appreciate some level of respect for the mission I am on."

"When you actually do what is asked of you, I will be happy to show said respect. Now, finish. I have things to attend to."

Irina heaved a sigh and nodded. "The complication is Amelia has had a child with the Alpha of the pack."

This seemed to have caught Amara's attention as the old woman snapped her gaze to hers. "She did what? How? That is not possible!"

Irina grinned and sat taller. "It is possible because it has happened."

Amara turned away to speak with whomever was near her. "It seems we have a baby born of Alchemy and the wolf-beast." She paused for a moment and shook her head. "No, I am hoping to get more soon." She turned back to Irina. "Continue, and make it quick."

"Yes, madam." She cleared her throat. "The wolf I administered the blood to died within moments of injecting it. I sent

Marcus to the wolves to get Amelia by any means necessary. He took James…well, the creature, with him."

"Good. Now get Amelia and get back here immediately. We have a lot of preparation. The next moon is coming."

As Irina opened her mouth to respond, the communication cut off. She groaned and sat back in her chair. "I would give anything to kill that bitch off," she whispered to herself.

11

Irina put the bowl away after emptying the contents of the water. She unlocked her door and opened it, finding Elena on the other side. The woman looked up and a softness claimed her face.

Her dark brown hair famed her features in a way that made her appear youthful, beautiful. Irina smiled and opened her door wider, then moved to the side. Elena took one step and stood in front of the necromancer. She lightly touched Irina's cheek, allowing her finger to trace the outline of her jaw to her chin, then to her lips.

"You kept me waiting," Elena told her. "I do not like to wait."

Irina smiled and leaned in. "Waiting makes the heart grow fonder."

"If I had a heart that beat, maybe that would count for something." Elena sidestepped her and walked into her room. She glanced around, then turned toward the woman. "I had hoped to have you before you left. Please grant me this favor."

"Of course," Irina smiled and closed the door, locking it. "I have a few more days here, then I shall be on my way." She closed the distance to the young vampire and smiled. "You are absolutely beautiful," she cupped her face and leaned in, lightly kissed her chilled lips. "Do you realize that?"

"So you tell me," she answered and kissed the necromancer back.

When the vampire touched her lips, a coolness lightly brushed over her. Irina grinned and looked into her eyes. "No more talking." She captured the woman's lips again. Her skin chilled to the touch, Elena's tongue pressed for entrance. She gave it and pulled the vampire closer.

As they kissed, Irina felt the sharpness of fangs in the woman's mouth. *She will want to bite me*, she told herself. "My thigh," she whispered. Understanding without asking what she meant, Elena growled against her lips.

Elena gripped her body, pulling her closer. Her hands moved up Irina's back until she reached her shoulders. Grasping her hair, Irina felt the pang when she pulled, forcing her head back. A gasp left her lips as Elena kissed along her neck.

Fingers tugged on the corset strings and as it loosened, Irina quickly worked the busk enclosures. Freeing herself from the confines of the corset, it dropped to the floor. Irina's breasts hung loosely against her flesh and immediately, Elena grasped them, then lowered her mouth to a waiting nipple.

She licked it, nibbled the tautness of it. Irina gasped and she worked the tie of her skirts. Pushing them down her legs, she managed to kick them away as Elena continued to suck and tease her breasts.

Cold hands made their way across Irina's backside, down the garter on her hips. "I want to taste you," Elena whispered against her flesh. "Then I shall feed from you."

Irina nodded and she gently touched the woman's cheeks, releasing her lips from her breast. Immediately, the vampire kissed the necromancer and a heat of gasps and whimpers filled the air. Irina pulled on the strings of Elena's corset and in a moment, had it off her body.

Elena pushed against the necromancer's body and as she fell back onto the bed, the vampire shimmied out of her skirts, leaving herself in her garter and nothing else.

Irina grinned with approval, then casually spread her legs. Elena licked her lips and lowered herself to her knees. Grasping Irina's legs, she yanked her in a quickness toward the edge of the bed. She pushed the lips apart that covered the clit, then looked up to capture Irina's gaze. She licked her lips again, then in a speed only a vampire could move, she buried her face in her pussy.

The necromancer moaned and lay on her back, her fingers tangling in the vampire's hair. "Oh my God," she whispered. "Yes, Elena, yes."

The vampire slipped two fingers inside her and began to pump. Irina moved her hips against her face. Elena flattened her tongue and licked from her pussy to her clit. Sucking the hard bulb inside her lips, she struck her tongue against it.

Irina groaned louder, almost in a scream. She pulled the vampire closer as she ground harder against her face. "Fuck, Elena, just…do not…my God, woman! Yes!" Pulling her fingers from her pussy, she pressed them against Irina's clit and teased her.

Lifting her head, Irina gazed to her vampire, then grinned. "Do it."

"With pleasure," she told her in return.

Irina lay her head back and closed her eyes. Fingers continued to furiously work hard against her clit and she knew in a matter of minutes, if not seconds, she would come to orgasm. As soon as Elena decided to bite into her flesh, the orgasm would double, if not triple, the pleasure, but also add pain.

Pain that, in this moment, was completely doable.

She heard the vampire snarl, then it happened. Teeth sank into her inner thigh and her lips sucked against the skin, as if latching on. Irina bit her lips and her back arched upward. She then opened her mouth and a moan mixed with a scream filled the air as she came to orgasm.

Elena continued to torment her clit as she sucked on her thigh. Warmth enveloped her cool hand and when the vampire glanced upward, she released her leg with a snarl. Her lips were ruby with blood, as were her teeth and fangs.

She sank her fangs once again into her leg and Irina cringed. The pain began to set in as her orgasm passed. She held her breath for a moment as the vampire snarled against her flesh.

"Elena, love, that is enough." The vampire continued the torment against her flesh. "Elena, I said that is enough!" She snapped her hand upward and the vampire's head pulled back in a quick crack, then she fell slack to the floor.

Irina had broken her neck and as she gazed upon her lover's body, blood pooled onto the floor from her mouth. Those with power over the vampires had the upper hand in moments like this, but for vampires, blood of a necromancer came at a cost.

The blood was more potent than that of normal human blood. Some are born with their talents naturally where others study a lifetime to achieve their potential. Even Alchemist blood was sweeter than human, but nothing like necromancer. She could not blame Elena for not wanting to stop, but if she did not, she could have killed her.

Sadly, she stood from the bed as blood ran down her leg. She placed her hand over it and made her way to the bathroom. Filling the tub in the room with warm water, she used a washcloth and cleaned the wound. Lowering herself into the basin, the brass of it chilled her backside. She relaxed and allowed herself to submerge fully.

She glanced to the ceiling, the water distorting her view as it moved about. Irina released a bubble of air watching it ripple on the surface.

I need Amelia.

Marcus has the blood and the creature as he heads toward the wolves' plantation.

The coven finds me ridiculous.

She came up for air and inhaled, then took in a breath as a hand pushed her down.

"HOW DARE YOU SNAP MY NECK!" Elena's injury healed faster than she accounted for. The vampire pulled her up for air and as she gasped, and attempted to say something else, she was pushed back under again.

"I allow you into my bed, feed on you, tell you secrets and for what? For you to fuck me, kill me, then leave me?"

Elena pulled her up again, and this time, Irina was ready. She held her hand out, palm up.

"You will release me now, Elena."

Not a second passed before Elena freed her hair and took a step backward. "Let me go now, necromancer bitch!"

"Do you hear yourself? You were going to kill me if I did not stop you! Now, leave my room and do NOT come back here!" Irina moved her hand toward the bathing room door and Elena's body moved in an unnatural way.

Elena fought the compulsion but was losing. Her body jerked left and right, her head snapped one way then the other, her legs bent as she tried to keep herself from walking. The event reminded Irina of a marionette doll. Unfortunately for Elena, the blood on her lips added to the effect.

"Now leave me, Elena. You are NOT welcome back!"

"Why? Irina, I am sorry. I am so sorry! Please, release me! I will be good for you, please! I am sorry!"

"No! Now go!" With the force of her words behind it, she left Elena no choice. She heard the vampire scream as she was removed from the room. Her screams filled the emptiness of the hall as well as the beating she put on the walls. The vampire could no longer come inside unless welcomed back.

Hearing a few male voices, Elena quickly quieted. Irina was

not sure if it was because they forcefully eradicated her, or if they also snapped her neck.

Irina tried to relax once again, but it was pointless. She sighed, removed herself from the tub, and wrapped a towel around her body. She looked at herself in the mirror. Her skin flushed from the anger and fear she just experienced. She rolled her eyes and groaned.

"I should have fled with Marcus." She shook her head and took a seat at the vanity to brush her wet hair.

12

Marcus led the way toward Amelia's home, the wheezing creature by his side. He glanced at him and raised a brow, curious of what he was, if there was any of him left inside the shell of a broken man.

"Can you hear me?" Marcus asked him, then came to a halt. When the creature did not answer, he crossed his arms over his chest. "You will address me when I speak to you. I may not have the power to compel you, but do know I have the power to end you just the same."

This must have caught the attention of the creature as he turned and glared at Marcus. His lips pulled into a snarl and his eyes furrowed in what looked to be anger. He still held the appearance of a human but with his tar-black skin, he did not appear…natural.

"Can you speak?" Marcus asked.

The creature formally known as James snarled and took a few steps toward the vampire. "If I did," his voice came as a deep growl, "would you stop talking?"

Marcus grinned and the timid fear he had slowly melted. "Most likely not."

The creature responded by turning away, then pulled his shoulders back, as if stretching. He growled and the sound rumbled through his body.

Marcus took a step closer. "Are you compelled right now? Are you following orders?" He placed a gentle hand on the creature's shoulder, which caused the monster to flinch. Marcus quickly removed his hand and absently wiped it with the jacket he wore.

"No," the creature growled.

"Then why do you not attack me?"

The creature turned his black eyes to Marcus. "My quarrel is not with you."

"Ahh," Marcus replied and before he continued, he considered his next words. The creature glanced at him, then back toward their path. He took a few steps forward and Marcus continued. "So, if I were to say, attack the first were-beast you see, you would?"

The creature growled and Marcus took this as a yes.

"If I asked you to not attack, to maybe just…hurt one, would you?"

Again, the creature growled but this time, he turned to look at Marcus. "Why?"

"Why what?" Marcus asked.

"Why not kill?" He turned his gaze back toward their walking direction. "Look what that whore did to me."

Marcus grinned and shook his head. "If it is all the same to you, allow me to put my perspective on the situation."

"Do I have a choice?" the creature asked.

"Not likely," he told him. "First, before I ask anything else, why lead the others to believe you are mute? Why not speak out for yourself?"

This question may have stumped the creature as he stopped. He turned and looked upon Marcus. "No one bothered to ask."

"Ahh, well, there is that," Marcus told him. "So, as I was

saying, you say this...whore did this to you. I assume you mean Amelia, the Alchemist?" The creature nodded and began to walk again. "Right. And was it Miss Rimos, oh wait, Missus Hawthorne, that brought you in, against your will, the night she administered the serum to you?"

The creature turned and glared at Marcus. "Watch your words, or you will be my next kill."

Marcus grinned. "It is an honest question. How *did* you find yourself in her care?"

The creature stopped walking again and visibly sighed. "If I tell you, will you stop talking to me?"

He grinned and shook his head no. "But I will keep it minimal, as I see fit."

Shaking his head, the creature started walking. "I had just fed for the night. I was messy, clumsy. I left my kill in the open. I had been taught to make it look like an animal attack."

The creature shrugged. "I did the best I could. I ripped his throat out and almost decapitated him, followed by slashing through his gut and spilling his bowels onto the alley floor. I felt satisfied with what I did, at least until I blacked out. Something, or someone, broke my neck and when I woke, I found myself in her lab.

"I was nothing more than a rat in a cage that she would experiment on. She injected me time after time with serums she created. She watched and took tissue samples and blood samples. She would threaten to throw me into the sun if I did not cooperate. She told me she made some kind of...liquid of the sun."

The creature sighed and continued explaining as he walked. "When she finally made the cure she was hoping for, she administered it to me.

"I still remember the smugness she had on her pretty little face. She told me, *'Now you will be human again. Is that not a fantastic reality?'* She did not give me an opportunity to answer her for I died that night, figuratively speaking." He lowered his head and lifted his arms as if to question himself in his own words. "How the hell can any of this be a fantastic reality?"

Marcus watched him for a bit and remained silent through his story. Once Maxwell finished, he pondered a moment longer. The creature looked to him and raised his brows.

"What, no questions?"

Marcus again waited, then thought on what and how he would ask. "From what I understand, you were the victim in this scenario, correct?" The creature nodded. "You felt violated in a way." Again, the creature nodded. "And when she poked you enough with these needles of hers, you never thought to break free? You allowed her to continue her testing until she found the right cure in order to make you human again?"

The creature turned on Marcus and snarled. He shook his head and quickly put himself in front of him. Marcus felt his pungent breath hover over his lips. "As if I had a choice? Silver cage? Sunlight? Liquid sun?" Giving Marcus a shove, he caused the vampire to stumble on his feet. "Are you making an attempt to call me a yellowback?"

Marcus grinned and smoothed the material of his clothes as if to straighten himself, to put himself back together. "Oh no, not at all. I am only suggesting that you are...no, were a powerful vampire and she was merely human." He held his hands up in the air in mock surrender. "I am only stating the obvious, James."

"Do *not* call me that name! I am no longer James! She took that from me!"

"No, James," Marcus snidely remarked. "You took that from yourself when you drank from Tomas. No one had any idea of the ramifications on what would happen if one were 'cured,' then fed vampire blood. You, my friend, did that on your own."

The creature snarled again and leapt toward Marcus. "How

dare you!" he screamed. The monster shoved him to the ground and when his hands surrounded its throat, it snapped at his face.

Marcus squeezed the flesh around the creature's neck and held him off. Drool pooled from his lips and began to trickle onto Marcus. "You filthy beast, get *off* me!" With a hard shove, the creature rolled to his side. Wiping his neck with the sleeve of his shirt, he raised a brow. "You wish to fight me? I will tell you now, *James*, you will lose."

The creature steadied himself on his feet and once again snarled. "Why do you torment me? Why do you bring these points up? What do you have to gain?"

Marcus grinned. "Strength. Knowledge. Most of all, your anger. You need to be strong, James." He circled the creature and continued. "You need to take out these wolves and allow me to capture the Alchemist. You need to be swift and silent...well, not silent. I do not believe you have the ability. You grunt and groan so often..."

"Do not pretend to know anything about me, Marcus. Do not pretend to have my best interests here. If you have an ulterior motive, Irina and René, as well as Tomas, will hear about it!"

Turning his back on the creature, Marcus continued talking to himself as he made to formulate a plan of action. "Not if you are dead," he glanced back to him, daring him to speak any different. "Dead men tell no lies, James. Dead men do not talk."

The creature snarled and lowered his head.

Satisfied, for now at any rate, Marcus continued walking, putting his hands into his pants pockets.

I need to investigate the home. The layout I know, but how to distract the others to capture the woman? I might need to befriend someone. He laughed at his inward thoughts. No wolf would hesitate to end him as soon as they saw him.

As they approached the plantation, he reached for the creature and lowered himself into a crouch. "Look, they are about, scouting the area. I am counting...three here in the back." Marcus paused for a moment and looked to the left side of the home, then the right. "I believe there are two on each side." He turned to the creature. "Can you take out the back, leaving me the sides?"

The creature nodded and his hands dug into the dirt, preparing to race toward the home. Marcus laid a hand on his shoulder and when the creature looked to him, he shook his head no.

"You will wait for my signal. If you run in too soon, they will end you, James."

"My life is already over. She did this to me. She will pay with her life." The creature lifted and as he had been about to sprint, Marcus caught his leg and pulled him to the ground. His body hit hard and the creature quickly turned toward him.

"I should kill you for that, Marcus."

"Ahh, but you will not," Marcus told him. "You run in now, I am telling you, you will give our cover away and get yourself killed. Where will that end for you? In the ground as ash, that is where. Is that what you truly wish?"

"Yes," the creature growled. "Now, allow me to run or I will hurt you. And by hurt I mean to rip your appendages off and toss them in many directions. I will then tear your heart out and eat it, followed by your eyes. After that, I will..."

Suddenly, a distraction caught the creature's attention and he turned. A blond woman left the back of the house and took a seat in one of the chairs. They both watched her and Marcus spoke up first.

"She is human, I can smell her from here."

"She will be first to die then. No human should live if they have anything to do with the wolves."

Marcus did not allow him to continue. He quickly grabbed his head and in a snap, broke his neck. He sighed as he laid the creature on the ground. "Well, my friend, that will not happen tonight, or any other night." He stood and observed as the blond woman relaxed, the wind gently moved her hair to and fro, followed by a few strands across her face.

Marcus watched her with delight. It had been a few centuries since he had any love affairs with women. They would usually end up turned, or worse, dead. If this woman held herself with the wolves, she could be the key to gaining access to Amelia.

Marcus grinned to himself and shifted his gaze to the creature at his feet. He did not kill him, but temporarily put him into a slumber. "He will become an issue at best," he told himself. Squatting, Marcus pushed the hair from the creatures face and studied him.

"I am sorry, so sorry, my friend, that the unforeseen circumstances have happened to you. I, however, am not sorry for ending your third attempt at having a life. You should have remained human and became somewhat of a spy for our cause."

With that, Marcus brought out his dagger and held it in the air, then in a swift move, he plunged it into the chest of the creature.

Dark blood oozed from his torso and Marcus quickly pulled a vial and held it to the wound. As the contents seeped inside, he yanked the dagger free and wiped the blade on the grass. Marcus then watched the man formerly named James die, a third time. His skin began to dry and shrivel; his eyes billowed inward as well as his stomach. In a moment, James was no more, and when the breeze reached them, he simply became dust, returning to the earth.

13

*A*MELIA HELD HER son close as he nursed. She gently slid her fingers over his scalp and smiled. John stood in the entryway of the door and watched.

"Louis Jonathan Hawthorne," he said with a smile. "If my father were alive, he would be very proud of the name. It is strong, an Alpha."

Amelia glanced at her husband. "An Alpha? Who is to say he will be two-natured?"

"Who is to say he will not?" he answered as he stepped farther into the room and sat on the edge of the bed. He leaned over her legs, resting an arm on the other side of her. John leaned in and softly kissed his son's head. "Regardless of who he turns out to be, he is my son first."

She smiled. "I am happy to hear you say that, John." She watched her son as he nursed. "I never knew what it would be like to experience this kind of love."

"How do you mean?" he asked his wife.

She sniffed softly to herself then wiped at her eye. "I feel as if my heart is on the outside of my body, and it beats for him. Everything I am, everything I have, it is now for him."

John nodded. "I agree." He sighed and leaned his head onto his wife's thigh. "How are you feeling since the birth?"

"Honestly? Pretty good. I want to go outside later with him, allow the sun to warm our bodies and maybe read to him on the swing."

"Then I will make sure we have enough guards outside so you may do so."

She lowered her gaze to her son as he stopped feeding. Pulling him to her shoulder, she lightly rubbed his back. "Have you spoken with Sophie?"

John shook his head. "I have not seen much of her."

Amelia nodded then as her son burped, she smiled and pulled him down. "Maybe it is time to talk to her about what happened. She may continue to blame me for Adam's abduction, but she will eventually need to learn it was not me who took him, and to accept what happened. Then maybe one day, she will no longer blame anyone and move..."

"Blame anyone?"

Amelia quickly glanced toward the door and found Sophie there. She looked more pale than usual and her unkempt hair had not been washed for a few days. "Blame anyone?" Hate spat with her words and Amelia knew it was toward her.

"Sophie, please, I did not intend this fate for Adam."

"How dare you call his name!"

Amelia flinched and clutched her son to her chest. At the same time, John flew off the bed and grabbed Sophie by her shoulders. He shook her then pushed her against the wall.

"How dare you talk to your pack mother that way!" John's voice came loud with a growl. The Alpha tone had been evident to everyone, even Louis.

Her son began to cry and Amelia bounced her arms softly as she cooed to him. "It is all right, baby, it is all right. Daddy is upset, it is all right."

"She is not my pack mother!" Sophie yelled back.

"She is my wife! She is every part of this pack as you are!"

"She was going to LEAVE us, John! She was going to take that other Alchemist and leave! She retaliated against us when you were gone and Adam stepped up! She blamed him for your taking!"

"I know exactly what she did and why she did it. She does not hide anything from me. Now, I suggest you either apologize now or leave the room, so help me, I will punish you if you disturb my son one more time!"

He shoved her out the door and Amelia flinched again. She knew he would not leave her a choice to apologize, as the words would not come. At least not now, maybe for a long while. She hoped one day they would but until then, she would make do by being ignored, snarled at, maybe ridiculed.

John closed the door to the bedroom and leaned against it. "I am sorry," he offered in a lowered voice. "I did not mean–"

"No," Amelia interrupted, "you did what you had to. I know she is hurting but what she did was not right."

Nodding, John moved from the door and opened it. Finding it clear, he turned to Amelia. "I will return shortly. Can I bring you anything?"

"Yes, I do need something to eat, and some water."

"Consider it done." He smiled and left the room.

~

SARAH JUMPED AT the sound of John's voice upstairs. She had been enjoying the peaceful evening alone with her own thoughts. If Amelia had called for her, she would be by her side in a moment's notice, but the call did not come. Instead, a sobbing whisked past her with a head of white hair.

"Sophie?" Sarah called. The woman stopped just outside the door and her shoulders shook as she continued to cry. "Sophie, what happened?"

She shook her head and sobbed more. "Adam being taken, that is what happened." She turned and glared at her, eyes moving from hers to her feet, then back to her eyes again. "You are every bit to blame as she is."

Sarah blinked and raised her brows. "Blame? For what exactly?" She stood from her chair to face Sophie.

"Adam's taking."

"I had nothing to do with this, Sophie. Neither did Amelia."

A second later, Sophie stood directly in her face. "She had every bit to do with it, just as you did." Sophie snarled, her lips pulled over her teeth like a wolf would when readying itself to attack. "If you knew better, you would gain better company. You were with her when the two of you freed John. You were both there when Adam sacrificed himself to save you. He put himself in harm's way to save your worthless lives."

A slap sounded in the air. Sarah gasped and took a step back. Her hand stung from the force she put behind it in slapping Sophie's face. "I am sorry, I did not mean…"

Sophie snarled, then disappeared from the scene. Sarah released the breath she had been holding and bent over. She pressed her hands to her knees and closed her eyes. Taking in a deep breath, she focused on trying to not hyperventilate.

"I almost lost my life to a woman I used to call friend." She shook her head and when the fear finally passed, she stood and gathered herself. She glanced around but did not see Sophie anywhere. She felt a pang in her chest, but also relief from not seeing her again so soon after.

As she stood outside, the evening breeze billowed around her body. She thought of the fight and her freeing John; the images of the battle played in her head.

The necromancer controlling the beast running toward them.

Adam jumping in front of him to stop the attack.

The necromancer stopping the vampires after that, taking Adam's still body, then retreating.

It did not seem to make any sense to her.

She closed her eyes as the breeze enveloped her and strands of hair tickled her face. When she opened her eyes, in the distance something caught her attention. She strained for a closer look and as quickly as she saw it, it was gone, nothing but darkness.

Ignoring it, she said, "My mind is playing with me since the attack," she told herself. She quickly made her way inside.

Sarah gave up living in her own home when Amelia needed her. She stayed here with her friend to help as much as she was needed. Her Alchemist friend having married an Alpha, then giving birth to his child, Sarah was not sure of the ramifications, if any, Amelia may have brought upon herself.

Giving birth to a child born from an Alchemist, well, that was one thing. Mix in a two-natured Alpha male? Well, Sarah was not sure who the child would turn out to become.

It would be most likely he would not become an Alchemist. Typically, females took on this trait, with Amelia's father being the rare exception. Then again, it was not often two-natured mated outside their pack. She thought of the child and smiled.

"Regardless, he will be loved." She made her way toward Amelia's room and knocked lightly on the door.

"Come in," came her friend's voice. Sarah pushed the door open and found Amelia standing over the crib.

"Is he asleep?"

Amelia nodded. "Yes, in a deep sleep. He is full so he will be down for a while." She laid a light sheet over her son then turned to Sarah. "Come here, I need you." She held her arms open and Sarah crossed the room, embracing her friend.

"I heard and saw Sophie. She was not too pleasant with me, either, but I think she will be gone for a while."

Amelia wiped the tears from her face.

"Why are you crying?" Sarah asked her.

"I feel as if I lost Sophie as a friend. She was my first ally when John took me from Michel." She shook her head. "I am being silly."

"No, you are being human. It is all right." She hugged her friend again. "I am going into town for a few things." She took a step back. "Do you need anything?"

Amelia quickly scribbled a list on a piece of paper with the ink quill in the room. "Here, and thank you." She offered a few coins to her, in which Sarah turned down.

"No, please, it is fine. I will see you soon." She smiled and made her way toward the door.

"Thank you," Amelia told her.

Sarah nodded. "I will leave first thing in the morning. I will come to you as soon as I return." She left the room and headed toward her own room for the night.

Closing the door, Sarah leaned against the cool wall and closed her eyes. Her heart ached. She longed for someone to love her, someone she would give her heart to in return. She yearned to find the one she could call her own, could share a life with. So long as she lived under this roof with Amelia, she knew it would likely not happen; and she was all right with that.

On the other hand, she felt skittish, maybe scared, to put herself out there for anyone. She witnessed what Michel did to Amelia firsthand and the torment she went through, followed by the pain Sophie felt in losing her mate. She knew what happened with Michel is likely to not happen again, although she would not put it past a vampire to try as much.

"Maybe finding someone is not in the cards for me. I do not know how I would go on if I found someone, then lost them after a few years' time." She sighed and began untying her corset. As she pulled it apart, relief filled her body, then unhitched the busk. She sat it on her bed and removed the rest of her clothing.

She thought of her first love, Anthony. Meeting him in her school days, Anthony signed on with the military and was sent to war. They wrote a few times but in time, the letters stopped coming. She never heard if Anthony made it home, but she never took it upon herself to find out. If Anthony wanted to be with her, he would have made an effort as well.

She took herself to the bathroom and dampened a cloth, washed her face, then patted it dry. She took down her hair and brushed it out. She stared at her own reflection and turned her head to the left, then the right, examining her face. She touched her neck and lifted what she thought to be sagging skin, when in fact it was just as tight as the skin on her arms.

Sarah kept a slim figure and she did not stand too tall for her size. Somewhere around five foot and a few inches, Sarah knew she could use the help of a tall man around the house. She lifted a brow and humored herself. "When I have a house and a man of my own to keep, maybe."

Sleepiness teased her body as she yawned. Moments later, she turned down the comforter and laid her head on her pillow. She willed herself to have dreams of meeting someone she would eventually call hers, someone who would sweep her off her feet.

14

THE NEXT MORNING, Sarah dressed in a white button down top, light pink corset and light pink bustle skirt. She pulled on tan colored mid-calf boots and picked up her satchel. She headed toward the stable for a horse. The air became warm mid-morning in Savannah. She knew she would be sweating but did not want to be drawn in a carriage either.

Of course, no one had an automobile so a horse it was.

As she approached, the stable hand smiled and removed his hat. He was young and fairly new to the pack. Sarah could not recall his name so instead, smiled.

"Miss Sarah, how may I be of assistance today?"

She adjusted her hand clutch and smiled a little more. "I am in need of a horse this morning. I have plans to go to the market, maybe do some shopping."

"Shall I put the carriage together for you? I will be happy to escort you into town."

She shook her head. "No, thank you. What I need to pick up, I will manage bringing back. Just a horse, please. Preferably something…calm."

He chuckled. "Yes, ma'am."

Sarah stood off to the side of the stable, enjoying the cool of the shade. The horses neighed and the smell of the hay delighted her. The stable boy seemed to do well in keeping the grounds clean.

A moment later, he approached with a horse that stood tall next to her. His coloring was tan with a black mane and tail. His eyes were as black as his mane and he threw his head a few times.

"Oh, he is a beautiful creature," she whispered and touched his face. She patted his neck and the horse stepped side to side, as if enjoying her touch.

"His name is Buck. He is a buckskin breed. He is one of our most gentle horses here, Miss Sarah. He will do really good by you."

She smiled and looked to the boy. "Mind helping me up?"

"Not in the least." He quickly came to her side and as he put his hands together, she stepped in them and he lifted her. She sat sidesaddle and he helped her put her feet into the stirrups. "Miss Sarah, in town there are people who would be happy to help you. Just be sure they are gentlemen and not someone hoping to...well..." he shrugged, a blush touching his face.

Sarah grinned. "I thank you for your help today. I can look out for myself. I appreciate it." She set her satchel in the saddlebag then taking the reins, she pressed her heels into Buck's sides. He began a walk out of the stable and into the sunlight. "I should be back at least by nightfall. I plan on visiting the lakeside today with my new friend here." She bent over and patted his neck. "Please let Amelia know, would you?"

He nodded with a smile. "I will do that right now, Miss Sarah." He wiped his brow and waved to her as she made her way toward the dirt road. "Have a nice trip!"

"Oh, I plan on it," she told herself. She smiled at the quietness that surrounded her. Just her and the forest, the birds, the animals, the small critters that would scurry about. She knew she had taken a chance not telling anyone she would be out past dark, with the vampire attack that just happened, but no one had ever been after her.

In this war Amelia had become involved in, it was her they wanted, not Sarah. It was John they were after, not Sarah. She smiled to herself again at the oncoming liberation of freeing herself, even if it were just for the afternoon and evening.

She loved her friends, loved Amelia like a sister, and in a way, Sarah had become a temporary placement for her friend. When she lost Rachel, that was a loss she was not sure Amelia could possibly overcome. But she did as she settled down with John.

"In time, all wounds begin to heal," Amelia told her one afternoon.

"Maybe so," Sarah returned, "just know I am here, no matter what."

John's plantation disappeared in the distance and the quietness surrounding her gave her a tranquility she had not experienced in quite some time. She made her way toward town and as soon as her belongings had been picked up, she planned to spend the afternoon and early part of the evening at the lake. She might even take a dip in the water.

～

CLOSING BOTH SADDLEBAGS as they came close to overflowing, the shop keeper stood next to Sarah as she buckled the final strap. She wiped her brow and turned to him with a smile.

"I appreciate your assistance today. If I may ask one more favor?"

"You may," he said to her with a smile. The store owner had kind eyes and salt and pepper hair he kept cut short. He was tall, maybe six foot. His body was strong as he moved hay bales in his spare time, according to what he told her in their past conversations.

When Sarah came to his store, he fashioned helping her over anyone else. She knew he may have wished to court her, but Sarah never allowed it to go any further than shopping at his store. The owner may have been around her age but as it were, Sarah had not been interested in being courted.

"Would you be so kind as to offer me a hand up on my horse?"

He bent down to one knee and patted it. "Please, allow me to assist you," he offered with a smile.

Sarah nodded and as she lifted up her skirts, the shop owner blushed slightly. She smiled and tried not to allow herself to giggle. She stepped on his leg and as she rose, her foot slipped and she fell into his waiting arms.

"Oh!" she exclaimed and when she looked up, they were eye to eye.

The shop owner, stunned at first, held onto her, then slowly smiled. "Miss Sarah, how about I fetch a foot stool?"

Sarah cleared her throat and quickly untangled herself from him. She nodded. "Yes, please do."

When he left her side, she sighed and held her face in her hands. She laughed to herself and shook her head. Upon his return, he held a wooden step stool and set it next to her horse.

"If I were a few inches taller, I feel this would not be an issue."

"I do not mind in the least, Miss Sarah. And there is nothing you should ever change about yourself."

Sarah felt her face blush crimson and she quickly turned away and stepped on the stool. "I, umm, thank you for your help today, Mister…oh gosh," she covered her lips. *It would happen to me, his name has slipped my mind!*

"Jeremy Quincy, Miss Sarah. The name is Jeremy Quincy, and I am always at your service when needed."

She nodded. "I do apologize; it seems the heat has altered my mind in some way for me to misplace your name."

He chuckled. "Think nothing of it." He patted the side of the horse's neck, then looked up to her. "May I call on you sometime, Miss Sarah?"

She blinked and her lips parted. She was not sure she wanted to be courted, at least not yet. She stared at him for a long moment and when she did not say anything, Jeremy nodded.

"Well, if there is not anything else you need?"

"Jeremy…" she hesitated for a moment and when he met her gaze, her mouth became dry. She shook her head no and looked the other way.

He nodded and lowered his gaze. "Then I will see you next time, Miss Sarah." He patted the horse once more, then Sarah pressed her heels into his sides and the horse began to trot. She took him to a canter to quickly escape the embarrassment she brought upon herself.

"Well, that did not go as I had hoped for," she told Buck, maybe more to herself than the horse. "Maybe next time I could say, 'Yes, Jeremy, I would love for you to court me. Maybe we should marry and I will be your shop girl.'" Sarah rolled her eyes and slowed Buck down to a trot. "All right, boy, let us go to the lake."

∽

The afternoon sun had begun to settle in. Sarah removed her clothing and took to the water. Finding herself alone, she had no reservations on removing her clothing. She did, at least, leave on her undergarments just in case someone did approach.

She floated on her back as the sun warmed her body. Thoughts of vampires briefly touched her mind as she thought of their pale skin.

I could never imagine not enjoying the energizing rays of the sun, tanning my skin, enjoying the warmth of the summer afternoons horseback.

She smiled to herself as the breeze flitted over her body, causing her nipples to become erect as they chilled. Opening her eyes, she noticed the sun had begun to set. "Just a few more minutes," she told herself. Sarah plunged under the water once more to swim, then came up and smoothed her hair back.

Glancing to the bank, Buck continued to eat on the grass near the tree she had tied him to. She smiled and swam toward shore. The sun had completely set and as her feet touched the bottom of the lake, she stood. Her body wet with her clothes, nipples standing through her white material, she gasped and quickly lowered back into the water.

A man appeared on the bank and he smiled, tilting his head to the left, then the right. He looked toward her clothes, the horse, then back to her.

"Out for an afternoon swim?" he asked.

She swallowed hard and nodded. Her weapons, liquid sun, and pistol were in her saddlebags. Which were on the horse, who had been tied to the tree, on the bank, behind the man.

"Then I shall take my place away from here to offer you the privacy you deserve." The man bowed and draped an arm over his waist, then as quickly as he appeared, he was gone.

Sarah held her breath and waited. She had not come face to face with an Undead in quite some time, outside of fighting, that is. She continued to stare into the direction the man fled and satisfied he actually left, Sarah quickly made her way through the water and toward Buck.

She opened the saddlebag and withdrew a towel. She wrapped it around her body as gooseflesh rose on her skin and her nipples became taut.

Quickly drying as much as she could with wet clothes on, she pulled on her top and skirts. She grabbed her corset and fashioned the busk. As she reached for the strings, she felt a wind blow gently around her, and she froze.

"Allow me," whispered in her ear.

Sarah bit her cheek as cold fingers slipped over her hands, removing them from the strings and setting them to her sides. He pulled her corset into place and tugged all the while she held her breath.

"It would be in your best interest, madam, if you breathed."

She sighed and let the breath out, then turned her head slightly to catch a glimpse of her visitor. "What is your name?"

"My lady," he told her in a lowered voice and leaned in, "you may call me Marcus." His breath spoke softly over her ear and Sarah closed her eyes, partially in fear, partially from the invasion of her senses.

She had gooseflesh again, but not from the chill of wet clothing.

As he finished tying her corset, he set his hands on her waist and gently turned her to face him. As their eyes met, Marcus offered a smile. It was soft, endearing, and somewhat gentle. "And what shall I call you, the beautiful lady of this evening who has made my night more brilliant than I have experienced in a few lifetimes?"

"Oh," she gasped to the flattery of his words. She lowered her gaze to his chest, then looked back to his eyes again. "Sarah. You may call me Sarah."

15

*I*RINA STOOD BY the window, staring at the landscape that surrounded her. Trees were full and beautiful. Birds sang their songs to one another. She watched as a deer approached behind an oak tree. His antlers were absolutely enormous. Men paid good money to have antlers this size hung on their den walls.

She watched as the deer lowered his head, nibbling on the fodder.

"To lure one to your will, you must focus your mind and force their will to your hand." The words of her elder and mentor, Amara, came to her. Curious, she focused her mind and energy to the animal, willing it to bring his head upward and make eye contact. As she began to release her energy, a ruckus brought her from her meditation. Frustrated, she turned and glared over her shoulder, her gaze landing on a vampire in the shadows; Elena.

"What do you want?" she asked and turned her attention to the landscape. She did not have time for games, less for this vampire who seemed to believe she had a claim on her. Irina rolled her eyes to her own thoughts, then crossed her arms over her chest.

"To apologize, my lady. I am upset with myself over my own behavior." The woman paused, most likely in hopes of an acceptance.

Irina closed her eyes and infuriation built inside her. *I could care less what you want. Right now, I want to know where the hell Marcus is.* "Leave me be."

"Please, mistress, if you allow me to explain…"

Irina quickly turned and held her hand in the air in a claw-like shape. Elena's eyes widened and she coughed. Her hands rose to her throat and she gripped at an invisible force.

In a flash, she had Elena pinned to the wall as she strangled her. "There is nothing to explain except you are an incompetent fool."

She stalked closer and squeezed harder on the mental strangulation around the vampire's neck. "I allowed you a taste and in turn, you attack and attempt to drown me. Tell me how I should look past this? You have defied me and your coven. Honestly, Elena, I am surprised no one has ended your pathetic life."

"Mistress," Elena struggled, "please, Mistress! Allow me to help."

She tilted her head and a brow rose. "Help me? How can you honestly help me?" Irina grinned but no humor touched her features. "Pray tell, please."

"Release me and I will tell you."

Irina leaned closer, and her nose almost grazed the vampire's. "I should snap your neck over and over until your head is ripped from your body. I would then find a way to reattach it, to do it all over again."

Elena's eyes widened and she shook her head. "Mistress, please! No! Allow me to fetch René. She knew of the Alchemist Amelia. She was the lover of our fallen leader, Michel!"

"Do you play me for a fool?" Before giving her a chance to respond, Irina snapped the vampire's neck. The woman dropped to the floor in a heap. She took a few steps back and disappointment settled on her. She crossed her arms again and made her way toward the window.

A reflection in the glass caught her attention; she smirked. "Speak of the devil." She turned to the vampire who favored Michel at one point in time. "What do you need?"

René lifted a brow as she took in Elena on the floor. "I see you enjoy playing with your food before dinner."

Irina shook her head. "No, that is what you do, not me. I eat food, not blood."

"Would you care to change that?"

Irina lifted her brow. "Tell me what you came to say, then leave my presence."

René's eyes widened in rage for a brief moment and Irina mentally dared her to attack. She had no feelings for this vampire and felt she had become a liability.

After Michel attempted to kill René before his own capture, then losing him, she allowed herself to go on a blood lust rampage. She flew through the town of Savannah and killed innocents, and created a few new vampires to add to her self-proclaimed army. René seemed to believe the world now owed her something since the loss of her mate, Michel.

Irina saw it differently. When the timing was perfect, she planned to use René to her advantage. Unless she met her own demise beforehand, which at this moment, Irina had no problem instigating.

"I came to discuss the creature and Marcus. Why send them in without my knowing?"

Irina grinned. "I did not realize you had to be notified." She leaned against the sidewall and her gaze trailed down the vampire, then back up. "Seems to me you are not fit to be the one who…runs things here. You know, being as you allowed Amelia to escape and allowed Michel to perish."

"HOW DARE YOU!" In an instant, René charged the Necromancer with her fangs ready for a feast.

Irina grinned again and held her hand up, blocking the vampire from moving. "Stop," she commanded and René had no choice but to obey. "You honestly think you have any control over what I do? Or that you have the ability to attack me?" She circled the vampire and as she approached her backside, Irina leaned in to whisper in her ear. "How badly do you wish to destroy me? As much as you wanted to destroy Amelia?"

When René growled, Irina continued with a smirk. "How about the courting Michel took her on? I bet he could have slept with her if he pushed harder. He could have had her and replaced you like that." She snapped her fingers for effect. "You would be out and Amelia, well, she would be in."

She continued to circle her and as she made her way to the front, she touched her chin, lifting René's face upward. "Tell me, vampire, you attempt to attack me, you will not receive the glory of destroying the one who destroyed you. Is that what you wish?"

"RELEASE ME!" René demanded. "NOW!"

Irina smiled and shook her head. "No, I do not think so. I shall wait for Tomas to return, and Marcus. I will see what they picture fitting for you. Trust me," she leaned in, "they are on my side, not yours."

"They would not take your side over mine!" René yelled.

"Oh, would they not?" She smirked and leaned in again. She sniffed, then wrinkled her nose in disgust. "You smell of death. Have you been feeding on rats, René?" She grinned and stepped back. "It would suit you as much if you were."

René screamed and tried to struggle in the hold Irina had on her. "Release me, Irina, now." She groaned and made an effort to not struggle.

Irina grinned once more and tilted her head. "You wish to not fight me? You may be many years, if not a good century, older than I am, but I will not be played a fool. What is it you want with me?"

The woman attempted to calm herself, or so Irina thought. As she began to let the hold on her soften, René visibly sighed. She squared her shoulders and made to adjust her corset and skirts.

"The day of the fight, the Beta of the pack was taken."

"Yes, I know this," Irina told her. "Tell me something useful."

René snarled under her breath and took a step back. With enough distance between them, René took to the other side of the room and picked up a tumbler filled with a brown liquid. She poured it into a goblet, then turned to Irina. She lifted it toward her and smiled. "Whiskey?"

Irina heaved a sigh and accepted the glass, then set it down. "On with it."

"He had a mate. If she feels any semblance to the loss I did over Michel, well, you may be able to use that to your advantage."

The Necromancer quietly stared at her for a long moment. She turned away and looked out the window once more. "Anything else?"

René growled under her breath and footsteps sounded as she walked toward the entrance of the room. "I thought fitting to tell you this news for your advantage."

Irina glanced over her shoulder as René left the room. "I plan to fully use that to my advantage," she whispered under her breath, "after I destroy you for becoming a problem." She turned back to the window and smiled to herself. "Guard!"

Immediately, heavy footsteps thumped against the floor, followed by a voice that carried the deepest bass of a man. "My lady?"

She turned to face him. He was almost as thick as he was tall.

Dark skinned and hair in dreadlocks, he wore a monocle over one eye. She asked him once why he wore it. *"It provides a more human appearance, my lady."* Of course, she found humor in this. A fellow man who practiced the art of Alchemy, she brought him with her as a bodyguard of sorts.

"I need you to do me this favor. Please capture the vampire René and have her in a holding cell. I shall see to her later tonight. Do this for me and tell no one."

"As you wish, my lady." The man left the room and the sound of his steps quietly resolved the farther he went.

Irina turned back to the window. As the sun began to set, she knew the vampires would be out soon to feed. Lurking in the shadows to avoid daylight was one thing; sundown was something else entirely. She wanted to know how Marcus and James's expedition went last night with the wolves.

A movement caught her attention on the grounds. "Tomas," she told herself. She grinned and made her way out of her room toward the grounds.

Opening the doors, she ventured outside and the warm air of the evening tousled her skirts. "Tomas, may I have a word?"

The vampire approached with a smile. "But of course, my lady. How may I be of service to you tonight?"

She sighed and lowered her gaze, mock grievance on her features. "It is René. She has once again overstepped her boundaries." Irina looked up to Tomas and inched closer. She lightly touched his chest. "I had her captured and put into a holding cell."

"You did what?" he asked, almost alarmed.

She nodded. "I had her put into a cell. She threatened me and attempted to take my life earlier. Tomas, if I may be so bold," she paused and he nodded.

"You may, as you have already taken it upon yourself to put her in chains."

She lowered her gaze. "Yes, and for that I do apologize,

however, when she attacked me, I felt the need to protect myself." Irina slowly lifted her gaze to his.

Tomas looked into her eyes and if she were not in her current position in this plan they had delved together, she would consider him a potential mate...or maybe someone fun to have in her bed chambers. "She is becoming more of a problem since the demise of Michel."

He nodded in agreement. "That she has." Tomas lightly touched her cheek. "What do you wish for me to do?"

She smiled, playing coy. "Nothing, at least not by your hand."

He raised a brow. "What is it you are intending?"

Irina shrugged softly. "With your permission," *or not*, she thought, "I would like to experiment on her with a few ideas I have with the creature's blood."

Tomas continued to look into her eyes. He remained quiet for a moment, then spoke. "What is it you intend to gain from your experiments?"

"I hope to see where maybe this Alchemist, Amelia, left off. I hope to see if I can gain a helpful advantage in your war."

"My child," he started and slid his finger down her neck. Irina felt him trace the vein that thumped just slightly faster now and she swallowed. "This is not my war, nor did I start it. I am simply a pawn in the plan made by a damn mad man, Henry VIII, centuries ago. I fight to live in a war strategized by a coven of witches who no longer wished to see their blood-sucking creations kill for the sake of killing."

He held his finger to Irina's lips and shook his head. "Just as the shifters were created to be our destroyers, we were created to give eternal life. One cannot live without the other, or so often I have heard." He paused and turned away from Irina, placing his hands folded behind his back.

"Do tell me, Irina, what is it you plan to gain by playing this...game of yours?" He turned back to her and lifted a brow. "It seems quite obvious you are not here on your own accord, that you are fulfilling some position bestowed upon you. Am I right?"

Irina had not often been rendered speechless but in this moment, she could only stare at the man. She did not know whether to agree or shake her head in confusion. She opted for a different approach. "I have been asked to help in the securing of the cure. Nothing more."

"You realize said cure has been used and destroyed?"

She nodded. "And you saw what it did to James Maxwell."

"That I did." Tomas took a few strides to became almost flush with her. "Then tell me, Irina, what is it you seek to accomplish here?"

She held her breath for a moment and stared into his eyes. Irina tried to step back, but Tomas quickly grabbed her arms. She considered using her necromancy on him, but that would be along the lines of assaulting her elder.

I could easily end his life now and place the blame on Elena, she told herself. Instead, she smiled and tilted her head slightly. "I simply wish to acquire you the upper hand, Tomas."

Releasing her, he smirked and offered a short nod. "Good answer." He made his way toward the entrance of the house and paused. "I suggest you keep your plans secret," he glanced over his shoulder to her, "if you plan on interrogating René. I would not wish for her blood to be on your hands, figuratively or literally."

"Yes, of course."

As Tomas took his leave, she let out a sigh of relief and watched as he entered the house. Irina then glanced to where her guard would have escorted René and smiled. "You are now mine, bitch."

16

"Tell me, Miss Sarah," Marcus smiled at her as he set her hand in the crook of his arm, "how you found yourself alone on such a beautiful night?"

She smiled and lowered her gaze. The moon having risen, she felt fortunate the evening sky blended any blush that may have risen to her cheeks. "I suppose I needed time alone."

He nodded and walked her toward her horse. "I assure you, madam, I would not allow a creature such as yourself to be left alone. Your beauty is magnifying on many levels. I would be a fool to not admit as much."

"Oh, Marcus, that is quite forward of you." She laughed to herself and reached for the reins of the horse. "You also should be aware of something." She pulled the horse next to her. If she needed a quick escape or a distraction, she could spook the horse to kick him. *That is absurd*, she thought. *If I could only manage to climb on without help, then I could away easily enough.*

"What may that be, Miss Sarah?"

The moon shone in his eyes and for a moment, Sarah had been taken aback. This man was beautiful, vampire or not. She cleared her throat and forced herself to look to the horse. "I know what you are and you should know who I am."

He grinned and a chuckle sounded. "You know what I am?" He released her arm and took a step back from her.

She nodded. "I know you are one of the Undead."

"And I shall assume the speed I took earlier possibly gave that notion away?"

Her mouth opened in surprise. *Well, he does have a point*, she told herself. "Well then, as long as we are clear."

He chuckled again. "Miss Sarah, if I had intended to have you as my dinner tonight, I most certainly would not entertain the idea of playing with my food beforehand."

"Marcus, that is absurd!"

"Is it now?" he asked with a grin. "And here I am with a woman who seems to call on me being a creature of the night, whilst I stare at her beauty and wonder what I did to deserve such a slap in the face?"

She blinked. "Excuse me?" She shook her head and waved a finger at him. "No one is calling anyone anything."

"Oh, but you did, did you not?" He grinned again.

She stepped back and her hands rested on her hips. "You are enjoying yourself, right now, are you not?"

He smiled wide, then laughed. "I most certainly am but by all means, Miss Sarah, continue digging yourself further in the ground. Once the shoveling ceases, I shall help pull you free." He winked.

She groaned. "Marcus, please. Do not insult me."

His brows rose. "Oh, who is insulting whom?"

She turned her back to him and huffed. "I suggest you leave before I turn around and tell you exactly who I am. Who I *really* am."

"Oh, now I am intrigued and I do not plan on leaving until the sun begins to crest over the horizon. So please, Miss Sarah, continue with your threats."

Sarah closed her eyes and mentally yelled at herself for this banter she had been having. *This will not go over well when I return to the plantation.*

She sighed, then turned to Marcus, but found only emptiness. She looked to her left, then right. Satisfied he was gone, but also feeling almost sad, she patted her horse's neck.

As irritating as Marcus had become, he was also somewhat entertaining. She smiled and wanted to mentally slap herself for it. *Amelia will have my hide if I tell her of tonight.* Then a wind quickly blew around her backside, forcing her skirts to billow slightly. She glanced over her shoulder and almost screamed.

"Marcus! Where..." She shook her head and he chuckled. "Why did you leave just to startle me?"

"You were quite clear to not be here when you turned, so I moved."

She groaned. "You are awful! You know that?"

He chuckled. "So tell me, Miss Sarah," he stepped closer and reached for the reins. He placed them on the horse then reached for her hands. "Tell me who you are."

Sarah stared into his eyes and willed herself to step away. *Remember what Michel did to Amelia. Remember he killed her sister, tortured her with René, then attempted to change her for the sake of his own amusement.*

She summoned courage in herself and stood straighter. "You will not wish to have friendly relations with me, Marcus."

He smiled and leaned forward, almost as if being mischievous. "I am not positive as to why, however, I shall spend my nights changing your mind on this matter. What else should I know?"

She blinked. "Does it not bother you, my warning of friendly relations?"

"Why should it? Would we cause quite the scandal?" He grinned. "Assuming we were seen in town together."

I do not understand, she thought to herself. She pulled herself free of him, putting distance between them. She decided the truth was her best option. And most likely the most foolish.

"Please, do not pretend with me, Marcus. The company I keep...you must be well aware the Alchemist Amelia Rimos created, most recently, the cure for vampirism."

He nodded. "Yes, I am quite aware."

"You also may know her sister had been brutally murdered by the vampire who attempted to seduce her and kill her for this cure?"

He again nodded. "Yes, I am well versed of this fact."

She furrowed her brows. "Then please help me in understanding why you would want anything to do with me?"

"Simple," he began and took a few steps closer to her. "I am not Michel. You are not Amelia. You are not out to change me into a human. I am not out to kill you for this cure." He paused and his lips twitched into a bit of a smile.

Sarah raised her brow then crossed her arms over her bodice. "I agree on everything you have said, but you also need to know Amelia is like a sister to me. There is no way this could possibly happen. Even if it were on a friendly level."

He raised his brows and smiled. "Are you suggesting we court, Miss Sarah?" He placed a hand over his chest where his heart would beat if he were living. "I must say, I am flattered." He stepped closer to her and his grin softened.

"Marcus, please," she exasperated, "please understand why I could not possibly do this." She took a few more steps back as he slowly closed the distance. Bark scratched at her back and not able to move farther due to an oak tree behind her, she swallowed.

"Do what, exactly?" he asked as he approached.

She could see the hazel of his eyes as the moonlight shone into them. Her heartbeat picked up in rhythm and panic subtly built inside her.

"I do not plan to feed on you. I have already made that point clear." He stood a foot away from her and his eyes slowly trailed down her body, then back up.

Her undergarments, which had now dried, continued to cling to her body. The material grazed across her nipples and they responded as if asking for him to take them in his mouth and devour her. Her breathing quickened as she watched him.

"If you do not plan to feed, why corner me into the tree?"

"Oh, Miss Sarah, that was your own doing," he grinned as he placed a hand next to her head on the tree. He leaned in and inhaled, closing his eyes. "You have made my evening tonight," he whispered by her ear, "just by your beauty alone."

He leaned closer and his breath slipped across her neckline. "I assure you, I am not Michel, nor are you Amelia."

Sarah closed her eyes and her hands fisted in the material of her dress. She wanted to reach for him, to pull him close and wrap her body around his. She wanted to take him inside her and more than anything, she wanted to feel his naked body against hers. Her breath came in a rush and she swallowed.

At this, Marcus tentatively pulled away, but remained close enough to allow his nose to graze her cheek. As he looked into her eyes, Sarah felt herself holding her breath. If she simply moved her head at all, his lips would be on hers.

And how she wanted his lips.

Her tongue slipped over her upper lip and she began to move to him, as Marcus pulled away.

"I should escort you home, Miss Sarah. I would not want any harm, provoked or otherwise, to find itself on you tonight." He lowered his gaze as he took a few steps back.

Sarah immediately missed the absence of his body. *This is not right*, she told herself. *This cannot happen.* She removed herself from the confines of the tree and made her way toward her horse.

Shame, maybe humiliation, crept inside her as she reached for the reins. Her eyes burned slightly as tears threatened.

I wish to have someone to call my own, but not like this. I wish for someone to love me as I would love them, but again, not like this. She glanced over her shoulder to Marcus, who stood watching her, not moving. "What is it about me that entices you, Marcus?"

He lowered his gaze for a moment, as if considering his answer, then looked up to her. "I am simply curious about you, Miss Sarah. Nothing more."

She nodded, not quite content with his answer, but did not challenge it. "Help me into my saddle?"

In an instant, he stood next to her. Sarah flinched. "Oh." They stood close to one another, but not like at the oak tree. That had been quite intimate.

Marcus stooped and held his hands together. She placed her foot in it and as he lifted her, his hands gave way and Sarah fell toward him. Landing in his arms, their bodies pressed together, Sarah gasped and immediately looked into his eyes.

"Why, Miss Sarah, if you wished to be this close, you only need but ask."

She put distance between them and shook her head. "It was by your hand we were close to begin with. Now, if you do not mind, please help me into my saddle. And no playing, Marcus."

He smirked and stooped once more. He secured his hands as a step and he lifted her. She swung her leg over the saddle and settled in.

"When shall I see you again?" he asked her.

She lifted a brow. "I may be in town soon, or here at the lake. But if you really would like to see me, you know where I reside. It would not be in your best interest, however, if you were to come to the plantation."

"Ahh, thank you," he told her and reached for her hand. He kissed the top of it and smiled. "Until next time, my beautiful lady of this evening. Thank you for making it an experience I shall never forget."

She smiled. "Goodbye and goodnight, Marcus." Pulling the

reins to the side, Sarah lightly kicked with her heels and the horse left in a canter.

∼

Marcus watched as the silhouette of Sarah blended into the night. Satisfied in tonight's adventure, he made his way toward his coven.

Irina may not be pleased with the news her creature had been destroyed, but in the same breath, she would be pleased he found a way in.

And this way in was named Sarah.

17

*I*N A QUICKNESS that only a vampire could muster, he arrived to his coven. He entered the home and as he was about to call out for Irina, he paused upon hearing a scream. He grinned and lifted a brow.

"Seems someone has started without me." Marcus quickly made his way toward the basement where the deceased were-creature had been held. Guards stood by the door and upon his arrival, they stepped aside.

Seems I was expected. He opened the door and stepped through, and closing it behind him, he heard the scream again, followed by a voice.

He chuckled. "Oh, Irina," he began as he turned one of the corners and walked past the cells. Toward the end stood the torture chamber, or so she called it. Wooden doors separated the room from the cellars and on the inside laid tools of various degrees.

Bone saws, tooth extractors, hooks to hang one from the ceiling, amongst other devices. René had boasted about hoisting the woman, Eva, from one of the meat hooks as she had been killed to prove some sort of point to Amelia. This reason had become lost on him as he entered the room and found René hanging upside down with her legs bound, from one of the same meat hooks.

His brows rose in surprise as he entered the room. René's body hung lifeless as her body gently turned in a circle.

"Oh, Irina, where are you love?" he called out. To his words, René's eyes opened and when she saw Marcus, she sobbed.

"Please," she whispered, as her body continued to rotate from the hook, her hands bound behind her. A few knives had been shoved in her backside and Marcus stepped away.

"Oh, Irina, your work proceeds you."

"Marcus, please," René whispered. "Please..."

"Please what, exactly?" he asked. "Help you escape so you may seek revenge on Irina? No, I do not think so. You did this to yourself, René."

She closed her eyes and a tear slipped from her and landed on the floor, mixing with the blood she had lost.

A shadow fell across the floor and as Irina entered the room, she smiled to Marcus. "And he returns! What news do you bring?" She approached him and Marcus chuckled.

Irina had blood on her face and neck, her bodice, hands and arms. Her legs and feet were meticulously clean, however. She wore an apron over her outfit and Marcus thought she looked to be a doctor for a moment. "How is it, Irina, you manage to cover your entire body in blood, and miss your legs and feet?"

"What?" She glanced down and when she looked back up, she smiled. "I have no idea. So what news do you bring?"

"You will not get away with this," René announced, followed by a swift knife to her throat, decapitating the body. Irina pulled her hand away and wiped it on the apron covering her dress.

"Oh, dear, I already have." She smiled and her eyes lit in gleam as she stepped closer to Marcus. "Tell me!"

"Well, I have good and bad news. The good news is, I found a different way in to gain the favor of an Alchemist."

Irina lifted a brow. "I am not sure I follow."

"Then allow me to tell of the bad news from last night." Marcus went into detail of killing James Maxwell before he gave up the position they were in. He could see the disappointment in Irina and he continued. "Trust me, he would be a liability."

"As is–was–this one?" She motioned to René, sans head, on the hook.

He grinned. "Precisely."

"So, tell me of your adventures tonight and how you found a way in."

Relieved, Marcus smiled as he recounted meeting Sarah, her being an Alchemist and having close ties to Amelia and the wolf pack.

Irina smiled and touched Marcus's cheek, leaving a bloody streak. "You have done well. My elders will be very pleased."

"I had hoped as much. As for me," he said in a lowered voice and reached for Irina. He pulled her close and pressed his lips to hers. "I plan to claim what is owed to me."

Irina sighed against his lips and wrapped her blood soaked arms around his neck. "Shall we bring in a human for you?" She licked his lips and smiled. "I have no issue allowing you to have your way with me in their blood."

He growled and grabbed her body, pulling her hard against him. "Guard!" One of the men stepped inside and waited. "Bring me someone to feast upon," he said as he kept his gaze on Irina's. "Then lock the doors as you leave. We do not wish to be disturbed."

Marcus snarled and pulled his lips back as he made his way toward the woman. She screamed again to not hurt her and as Marcus grabbed her arms, he pulled her to her feet. He softened his features and watched the torment on her face.

She was beautiful in a way. Her hair was long and brown, it had been tangled and matted to her head. Her body was filthy from living in the dungeon and she smelled of death. Marcus grinned once more.

Her mouth opened to scream and he grabbed her hair, jerking her head to the side. He sank his fangs into her neck and her screams shifted and sounded as if she were drowning in her own blood.

He dropped her body and watched as her neck bled out onto the floor. Marcus removed his shoes, then his pants and undergarments. Sinking to his knees, blood covered his calves and he removed his shirt.

Hands grasped his shoulders and Irina circled him. She had removed her clothes and stood naked before him. Her breasts were full and blood settled between them. He reached for her and brought her to him. Marcus ran his blood soaked hands up her thighs and licked the lips covering her clit.

Irina gasped and watched him. She glanced at the woman on the floor as she lay dying. Glancing back to Marcus, she lowered to her knees and pressed him to the floor. As she straddled his body, Marcus reached under her and grabbed his dick and lined it up to her. As she lowered herself, he groaned and lay back in the blood of his victim.

He could feel the healing effects it had on his body. "You understand that bathing in the blood of our victims, we are able to keep our youthful appearance. Drinking blood gives sustenance, but the act of bathing keeps us alive.

His hips thrust against her and he grasped her breasts. Pulling her closer, he sucked on her nipple and bit lightly. Drawing blood to the surface, he licked it, tasting her.

She gasped and moved her body forward and back. Moving her legs up, she placed her feet down and readjusted herself. Lifting her body up and down, Irina continued to fuck Marcus on the floor. He snarled as she thrust herself harder against him.

I shall have Sarah and she will be on top of me, or under me. Either way, she will be mine.

Marcus leaned up and grabbed Irina around the waist, then thrust her on her back. He sat back on his heels and lifting her hips, he thrust hard against her at an unnatural speed. Moving faster and faster, Irina screamed as her body began to break.

"Marcus," she screamed, "STOP!"

He looked at her and immediately stopped. She panted and catching her gaze, he tilted his head. "You allowed me to fuck you this way, why did you not stop me yourself?"

She smiled. "Because, lover, you are mine."

He lifted a brow and leaned down to her. "I suggest you realize who is in charge right now." He thrust hard against her and Irina screamed out in pleasure. Then with each word, he thrust hard. "It. Is. Not. You!" With that, he fucked the necromancer until he saw fit.

Her hands reached for his forearms and she grasped him. A force like a fire suddenly raged through his body. He yelled out and released Irina, pushing her body away from his.

"What are you doing to me?" he screamed. "What is the meaning of burning me?" He glanced to his forearms and watched as the burnt skin began to heal.

"If I did not stop you, you would have broken my body in two." Irina scooted across the floor from him and rested her body against the wall. "It is one thing to torture your meals or your game. It is something different when it comes to me."

She panted a few more seconds, wiped her forehead and left a blood streak. "You will do good to remember that."

He snarled and stood. He knocked on the heavy wooden door. As the guard opened it, he shoved the tall man aside and in a flash, Marcus left the room, leaving a trail of blood behind.

18

Louis sobbed in his mother's arms as Amelia readied him for nursing. "Shh, it is all right, Louis, it is all right." She rocked in the chair as she smiled upon her son. In the den, the fireplace had been lit and provided a warmth to the room. Considering it was still summertime, she informed John he did not need to light a fire, but he thought otherwise.

"I do not wish for my son to catch a chill."

She smiled. "Then allow me to cover him in blankets. We do not need a fire."

The back door opened to the house and Amelia leaned over to catch a glimpse of who entered. White hair streaked by and she sighed. Sophie still had not said one word to her since the funeral. She had no idea how to get past this, except with time. Sophie spent most of her days and nights outside patrolling.

"It keeps me busy and away from her," she overheard Sophie say one night to Katherine.

Sighing, Amelia continued to nurse her son until he fell asleep. She placed him over her shoulder and carried him across the room to a bed made for him. She laid him down and pulled a sheet over his body.

"Sleep, my little prince." She lightly kissed his head.

The door opened again and this time, Sarah entered. Amelia smiled and as she made her way toward her friend, she flinched and took a step back.

"Sarah, what has happened? You look to have soiled your clothes!"

Offering a smile, Sarah nodded. "I took in a swim after visiting town this afternoon. That is all."

Amelia's eyes widened. "But it is late and the sun is down!"

"Yes, it is," Sarah confirmed. "I can handle myself, Amelia." She smiled and walked toward the staircase. John stepped into the room and stopped in front of her. He sniffed a few times, then furrowed his brows. Sarah's rose at him. When he did not say anything, she shook her head and headed upstairs. "I will be down later after I bathe."

"All right," Amelia called after her. She looked to her husband and gave him an expression as if asking, *what is it?*

"If I did not know any better, I would suspect she has been with an Undead."

"What?" Amelia asked in a raised tone.

John shook his head and stood next to her. "It could be the water she swam in, but I am telling you now, she smells of death. It, umm, reminds me of when you were friendly with Michel."

"Friendly?" she asked. "Friendly?"

"Well, I did not want to say intimate."

"Right." She rested her palms on his chest. "Are you well?"

He nodded. "Perfectly. Are you healing?"

"Yes. I should be good as new very soon." John smiled at this and hugged his wife. "Have you spoken with Sophie?"

John pulled back and sighed, then nodded. "Yes. She still wishes to remain alone."

Amelia nodded. "I wish there was something I could do." She sat on the couch and looked to her son sleeping across the room. His breathing deepened as his sleeping fell into slumber. The couch moved as John sat next to her. Soon, his lips gently touched her temple, then her cheek.

"I have missed you," he breathed by her neck. "When can I have you again?"

She turned to him and John immediately captured her lips. His hands cupped her face and he kissed her. A growl emitted from his chest and it vibrated against her lips.

Amelia grinned and pulled back. "That tickles, you know?"

He grinned and set into kissing her again. Leaning into her, Amelia lay back as John moved on top of her. He pushed a knee between her legs and pressed his pelvis against her.

She sighed into his lips and tightened the hold around his shoulders. "I need you," she whispered. "But I am scared it will hurt."

"I will make sure I am gentle," he mumbled against her lips.

"What if someone walks in? We are on the sofa."

"Mmm, I thought of that," he mumbled and continued to kiss her. "Unless they wish to die tonight, no one will interrupt." He palmed one of her breasts and squeezed. "Damn, I have missed you, woman."

She wrapped her leg around him and pulled him closer. "I have missed you inside me, John."

He growled and sank his face into her neck, kissing along her décolletage. Not giving her a chance to undress herself, John grasped the bodice of her gown and ripped the material. It tore down to her knees and Amelia gasped. He quickly discarded the shredded garment. John reached for his shirt, pulled it over his head and tossed it.

Amelia sighed at the warmth of her husband's body against hers. He reached between them and pressed a finger against her clit, massaging it.

"Oh," she gasped and pushed her legs apart farther.

"Is that good?" he asked in a gruff voice.

"Oh yes," she whispered. "Yes."

"Good." He pushed his finger inside her and made a 'come here' motion. She gasped under him and her nails dug into his biceps.

"Remove your pants," she ordered. John nodded and sat up on his knees.

He pulled his finger from her then brought it to his lips, licking it. "I have absolutely missed this and you." His eyes flashed golden as he made quick work to remove his pants and undergarments.

He kicked them off his legs, then pressing his naked body against hers, John growled into her neckline. He reached between them and grasping his dick, he pressed it to her entrance and pushed.

Amelia gasped and held tight onto John. "Hold on," she whispered. "It has been a while. Take it easy."

He breathed an exasperated breath as he kissed softly.

Their son had been approaching two months of age. Two months since Adam's disappearance. Two months since John's kidnapping.

Amelia pushed the thoughts to the back of her mind and focused on John. She moved her hips against him and kissed his neck. "I love you," she whispered.

John moved slowly against her and began to thrust gently. "I love you, my wife."

She sighed as his dick glided in and out of her with ease. Her pussy ready for him, she opened her legs wider, her body more open for him. "Oh my God, John, yes…"

He thrust harder into her and when Amelia did not wince, he did it again, and again. Soon, John picked up a steady rhythm as they made love on the sofa. She reached above her head and grasped the material of the sofa as he thrust harder against her.

"Yes, yes!"

"Shh," he whispered with a chuckle. "You do not want to wake our son."

"It would almost be worth the effort of containing myself." Her head tilted to the side as she arched her back. Her breasts pushed against his body and John growled, watching them.

"Your tits...my god, woman!" He moved faster against her and Amelia bit her lip to keep from yelling in pleasure.

"John, I feel it coming, I feel...John!" She struggled to keep her voice at a minimum.

John growled into her neck and his momentum became fast and hard. Amelia knew he would finish soon and this fact turned her on more than sex alone. She loved having this effect on him and suddenly, her body exploded in an orgasm that caused her body to buck hard against him.

"Amelia, shit!" He thrust one more and held himself as he groaned. He panted on top of her and slowly pulled himself free. He sat back on his heels and stared down at her body with a grin.

"We need to do more of that, soon," she said with a smile.

He chuckled. "Yes, we do. But first, let us get you upstairs to clean up before anyone comes in the room."

She grinned with a nod. Amelia grabbed her garments and quickly made her way up the stairs as John pulled his pants on. Upon reaching her bedroom, Amelia pushed the door open and stepped inside. Closing it behind her, she dropped the linens and made her way toward the bathroom. She sat on the edge of the basin and began to draw water into it. She hummed to herself as she waited while the edge of the water rose. Slowly, one foot at a time, she stepped inside, then lowered herself in.

The heat of the water enveloped her as it continued to rise. She closed her eyes, thinking of John and sex with her husband. She smiled to herself as her body relaxed. Already soreness began to set in between her legs, but the pain made her smile.

"Amelia?"

Sarah's voice interrupted her thoughts and she sat up. "Sarah? I am bathing. Are you all right?"

"Yes, I am fine. Once you are done, come find me if you would. We have some things we need to discuss."

"All right, please give me some time as I just sat." Amelia relaxed in the basin, intent on not worrying about anything for the next half hour, if possible. Whatever Sarah had to tell her could wait. She sighed and closed her eyes.

∽

SARAH STARED AT herself in the mirror, contemplation coursing through her. *How do I tell Amelia I had an evening with a vampire? I am pretty sure John smelled him on me. I cannot hide this for long, so rather than hiding, the truth may be more useful here, especially if I can gain Marcus's trust.*

She picked up her hair brush and ran it through her locks; the thick drop curls separated with each stroke.

Marcus seems harmless but then again, Amelia thought the same of Michel.

She recalled the moment Amelia told her ashes were all that was left of the self-proclaimed vampire king.

"John went down to check on him, but he had aged to dust," Amelia informed her.

"How fast does this cure of yours actually work?"

She shook her head. *"That is just it. I did not have enough time to test the long-term effects it would have on a cadaver. The one I saved, well, last I heard he was recovering in the hospital."* Amelia lightly shrugged. *"I would have to assume it would age the person to the rightful time of life they should be; in Michel's case, many centuries old."*

Sarah cringed as she thought of the aging process Michel had been through. "I wonder if it was painful for him? Nevertheless, he is gone and the world is a better place for it."

She set her brush down and made her way toward her bed. Removing her garments from the day's events, she pulled on her nightgown, the chilled material causing gooseflesh to rise on her skin. The gown teased at her nipples and the tautness pushed against the material.

"I need to tell John and Amelia about today," she told herself with a sigh.

"Tell us what?"

Sarah turned to find Amelia in the doorway. Her eyes wide in shock, she was curious how to tell her now that she had been questioned.

Amelia grinned. "Well, the look on your face indicates you are the cat who ate the canary. So tell me, Sarah." Amelia took a seat on her bed while she towel-dried her blond hair. "Who is the said bird in this equation?"

Sarah blinked and she felt her face become hot; not necessarily from blushing. She lowered her gaze and turned her back to her friend. "I have met someone, Amelia."

"Oh, do tell me!"

She shook her head. "I am not sure it is a good thing, or if maybe it could be." Sarah turned. "I went to town today."

"Yes," Amelia nodded. "I remember you leaving."

Sarah smiled softly. "Well, I went alone on horseback. It was nice to get fresh air, abandon some of what has transpired here."

Amelia nodded again with a smile, then patted the bed. "Please, sit. Tell me about your day. I think this will be an interesting story."

Taking a seat next to her friend, a sigh left Sarah. She glanced up to Amelia and studied her face for a moment.

She would have to understand, having been there herself with Michel. Although this is different...I hope anyway.

"I picked up the supplies I needed from Mister Quincy in town."

"Oh yes, he is very easy on the eyes." Amelia grinned.

Sarah nodded and her lips gave a small hint of a smile. "Well, after leaving his shop…"

"Wait," Amelia interrupted her. "Did Mister Quincy ask to court you?"

"What?" Sarah blinked at her, then shook her head. "In a way, yes."

"Oh, you should, Sarah! You most definitely should!"

"Amelia, please allow me to finish."

Amelia grinned and nodded. "Forgive me. Please continue."

Sarah sighed once more. "After I left his shop, I decided to go for a swim in the lake. You know, the one up the hill?" Amelia nodded and Sarah continued. "Well, dusk began to settle in and I knew I would need to leave soon." She began to wring her fingers in her lap. "I was swimming in my undergarments and when I began to come ashore, a man stood next to my horse watching me."

Amelia's grin immediately shifted to a frown. "Oh, Sarah, please tell me something did not happen."

Sarah quickly shook her head. "Oh no, nothing at all! I apologize for leading you to believe otherwise."

"Well, I am happy to hear that. Continue." Amelia set her towel across her lap.

"Well, he announced he did not mean to startle me and quickly left, allowing me to put my clothes on. A moment later, he was back." She swallowed as she continued telling her tale. "He is an Undead, Amelia. His name is Marcus."

She paused to allow Amelia time to understand, to allow her to ask questions. Instead, her friend remained silent as she stared into Sarah's eyes.

"Right," Sarah cleared her throat and continued. "He was kind and helped me gather myself…including my corset." Blush touched her cheeks and she felt her ears warm.

"Sarah," Amelia started with a soft voice. "He is no different than Michel. He is an Undead."

Sarah nodded. "I had a feeling you would say that." She lowered her gaze and fidgeted with her fingers once more. "I plan to see him again."

"What? Why?"

"I need you to hear me out, please?"

Amelia nodded. "I will listen, and I will speak my piece when you are done."

"Fair enough," Sarah agreed. She went into detail about their introduction, the kindness Marcus showed her, and the request to call on her again. "Amelia, I feel this would be a great opportunity for us."

"How so?"

"If I am able to gain his trust, I might receive information on Adam's whereabouts; maybe receive more information on where their coven hides."

Amelia's eyes widened. "No, absolutely not! I do not like this plan and I am sorry, Sarah, this is not a good idea. We already lost Adam, we cannot lose you as well."

"Amelia, you need to understand the purpose of this!"

"I understand plenty," Amelia told her as she stood, folding the towel over her arm. "I understand how these monsters work and I understand the deception, firsthand! The answer is no." She turned her back to her friend and walked toward the door.

"Amelia, I do not need your permission to do this."

She looked over her shoulder and raised a brow. "True, you do not, however, heed my warning, Sarah. Do not intermingle with the Undead. It will lead to heartache."

Sarah nodded and crossed the room to her friend. She rested a gentle hand on her shoulder. "Thank you for having my best interest. Trust me, I know what I am doing." She stared into her friend's eyes and Amelia nodded, then lowered her gaze.

"I do not like this, Sarah, but do what you feel you must."

Heavy footsteps sounded on the hardwood floor and Amelia turned, then smiled. "John, I was about to come find you." She turned to Sarah and took her hand. "Sarah has met someone and I feel you should know what she is getting herself into."

What the hell is she doing? Sarah stared daggers into Amelia's backside and when her friend turned, she lifted a brow. A smirk slowly replaced the chagrin she wore as she gathered her wits to explain her plan to John.

"Has something happened?" John leaned in and his nose wrinkled slightly. "Sarah, you smell like…I will be honest, you smell like an Undead."

She nodded, then explained her plan with Marcus. Amelia stood next to her husband who, in turn, crossed his arms over his chest. He listened intently to her plan of gaining Marcus's trust, finding Adam, and their coven.

"I see," he started, then rubbed his chin with his fingers. "I think this is a great idea."

"You do?" Both Amelia and Sarah asked together.

He nodded. "I do not like that it is you, Sarah, but regardless, if this is something you can work in your favor, then make it happen. Rest assured, someone will trail you at all times to guarantee your safety."

She nodded and smiled. Triumph built inside her and she exhaled a sigh of relief. "Thank you, John, I appreciate that." She turned to Amelia and took her hand. "I can do this. Have trust in me."

Amelia squeezed back. "It is not you I have trust issues with."

Sarah nodded, then turned back to her room to begin formulating details for her meet ups with Marcus. *This will work*, she told herself. *It has to.*

19

Three days later Sarah pressed her heels into the horse's sides and he picked up into a trot. The evening sun felt warm still and as she gave the command to canter, she enjoyed the breeze against her body.

She decided on a white long-sleeved shirt with a light tan corset, a small white hat set strategically in her pinned curls, and long white skirts. The front of the skirt had been hemmed just above her knees whereas the back almost touched the ground.

White lacy gloves on her hands, Sarah headed toward the same location she met Marcus prior. The bank of the lake appeared undisturbed as she approached a large oak tree. The shade from the tree provided a momentary reprieve from the setting sun. The horse bent his head and began to nibble on the grass and Sarah set the reins to step off the saddle.

"You are a sight to behold, my dear," came the familiar voice of Marcus.

Sarah grinned and glanced to her left to find her new friend next to her horse. He patted the horse's neck then glanced up to her.

"Marcus," she called casually.

"Miss Sarah. Allow me," he held his hands up as Sarah shifted in the saddle. He gripped her waist as she slid down into his waiting arms. "Perfect," he whispered.

She smiled and her cheeks heated with blush. "Thank you, Marcus." She cleared her throat and he took a step backward. "I took a chance to come out this way again. I hoped you would return to our meeting place."

"Of course, Miss Sarah. I would not have missed it for anything." He took her hand and lifted it to his lips, then placed a gentle kiss upon it. "What shall we do tonight?" He lowered her hand then released it.

She smiled to his politeness, then considered his question. "I do not feel up for a swim tonight."

"Obviously," he stated.

"Obviously?" she questioned.

He nodded. "Dressed as you have tonight, well, it gives the impression of importance, not swimming."

She laughed softly with a nod. "Right you are. So, as you were asking about tonight. There are a few places in town we could attend for a drink."

Marcus stepped closer to her, casually touching the side of her face. "Or we could stay here, allow me to understand who you are better. I would like to know what you enjoy, what you dislike, and what drives you, Miss Sarah."

She lowered her gaze with a smile. No one had paid this much attention to her in a while. *I need to focus*, she told herself. Glancing to her right just past her horse, in the woods, were sets of patrols who followed her. She knew they were there, and at the same time, she felt…awkward.

If she were to sit in the sand and talk with Marcus and they listened, it would be uncomfortable to say the least. Would Marcus know or smell the packs? There was no telling.

"Marcus?" She smiled and side-stepped him. "I would be fine if we went into town as well."

He nodded. "Would you prefer a crowd for your own protection?"

Her eyes widened. "What? No! Oh please, that is not what I insinuated. Please, trust me on that."

Marcus chuckled. "It would be understandable, Miss Sarah."

She blushed again. "Please, just Sarah."

He nodded. "All right, Sarah. Now, about this trip into town?"

She thought this over. They first met here on the beach while she swam, and he assisted in dressing her. The memory made her beam. "I think we are good to stay here."

"Perfect," he told her with a grin.

What a beautiful smile, she thought. Then she saw his fangs and the smile faltered slightly. Marcus wore dark gray trousers and suit jacket with a white button down top and matching gray bow tie. Atop his head sat a gray top hat. Small opticals rested upon his nose and they held a bluish-green hue to the lenses.

He removed the opticals and with his gaze to the sand below them, he took a step forward. "Miss…" he grinned and his eyes lifted to hers. "Sarah, if I may be so bold…" He lifted a hand and gently touched her cheek once more.

Sarah swallowed hard and gasped as he touched her. She held the eye contact as she stared into his hazel eyes and felt herself begin to drift. "Marcus," she whispered.

He leaned in slightly, his eyes darting from hers to her lips, then back up again. "I would be the happiest man on earth if you allowed me to kiss you, Sarah. Your beauty has become a welcome relief in my world. I wake in the evenings and the first thought is of you."

She inhaled sharply at the closeness of the proximity. "Marcus, we have only just met."

He nodded. "And when you have lived enough lifetimes to

know beauty when it is thrust upon you, you learn to take it." His finger glided from her cheek to her neck, just under her ear.

Sarah gasped and gritted her teeth in an effort to keep control of herself. "Marcus," she whispered, "tell me how you came about becoming an Undead."

Marcus stopped his movement on her neck and leaned backward, just enough to put a little space between them. "You wish to know how I became a vampire?"

She nodded. "Is this all right to discuss?"

"It is quite forward, I must say."

She grinned, then it turned to a giggle. Sarah lifted her fingers to her lips as she began to laugh.

"May I ask what is so funny?" Marcus lifted a brow as a smile threatened to claim his lips.

Sarah shook her head and a snort escaped. Her eyes widened, then Marcus chuckled. "Well? Honestly, Marcus, I feel the touching my body has received from you is quite forward as well. If we were to make love right now, I feel it would be the highlight of your evening. As we have only met a day or so ago," she paused as the blush crept up her neckline. "I hoped we could talk more, before things became…intimate."

He smiled, offered a nod and took a few steps back. "As you wish, Sarah." Marcus offered his arm to her and she placed her hand in the crook of his elbow. "It was a few centuries ago I was changed. I fought in a war I had no business being in. No one wanted to fight, but everyone wanted to win. I had been charging in on my horse, sword drawn and ready to fight. It was then I was struck with something sharp in my back.

"An arrow had plunged into my body and its head came through my gut. I fell from my horse and he galloped away out of fear, most likely from the screams and yells, the canons and whatnots.

"I gazed upward to the sky, awaiting my ascension…or

descension; whoever had the claim on me at the time. Instead," he paused for a moment and gazed to the ground.

Sarah felt her hand squeezing his arm as he told his tale. She may not have blinked the entire time.

He glanced to her and continued, "Someone peered into my vision of the skies. Someone with dark hair and blood on his face. That is all I could recall. The next moment, a pain erupted in my neck, however, it was a welcome reprieve to the pain in my back and stomach. I blacked out soon after, and when I awoke," he turned to face her and held his other arm up, as if gesturing 'here I am,' "I was a vampire."

"Marcus, that is quite a story." She meant every word, too. "You have lived a few lifetimes, you say?"

He nodded. "That I have."

"Have you had many lovers?"

Marcus stopped walking and faced her. "That is a bold question, Sarah."

She paused and glanced to him. "I did not mean harm. I simply ask as a woman who may be courted by a man if he has had many lovers in his past. I do not give my heart freely, Marcus. If the intent of our meeting is a conquest of sorts, we shall end this now and I will return home."

He grinned and nodded a few times. "I understand." Marcus stepped closer to her and smiled a little more as he looked into her eyes. "If I wished to have claimed you, I would have done so by now. I would have taken your body on the beach. Fucking is not something I enjoy…unless I am drunk, which is impossible in my current state."

Sarah laughed, then covered her lips with her fingers. "My apologies, I did not mean to laugh, but the thought of you drunk, it was funny."

Marcus shrugged with a grin. "I had intended it to be. Now," he touched her chin and lifted it slightly as his nose came a breath's distance from hers. "As I was saying. I do not fuck for the sake of fucking. I enjoy a woman's body."

His fingers gently glided down her throat, then up toward the back of her neck. He leaned in just slightly and Sarah tilted her head back further. "In time, I plan on enjoying yours. Not if, but when, you allow such delicacies."

Her breathing became rapid. She felt her stomach flip as what could be described as butterflies flitted about. *Oh my, what have I started?* she thought as she stared into his eyes. *This cannot happen, not this soon, not like this...* "Marcus," she swallowed and her heart pounded hard in her chest. She wondered if he could hear it. "Please..."

He grinned and his gaze lowered to her bosom, then back up to her eyes. "Please, what?"

She planted her foot firmly, then pressed her palm to his chest and pushed him from her space. Sarah stood and took a step back, then brushed her hands down her dress as if to straighten herself...and her senses. "Please, do not do that again unless it is welcomed."

Marcus chuckled and drew his hands behind his back. "Upon being asked if I have had many lovers, one would wonder if you were asking to be one of the selected few."

"Is that what you think? That I wish to be one of your mistresses?" Now it was Sarah's turn to laugh. "Well, rest assured, Marcus, my intention is to not give myself freely, if that is what you think."

"I would hope not." He offered his arm again as they continued their walk toward the woods that crested the beach. "Whores may be bought at a brothel or any of the bars in town. I do not wish for a whore, Sarah. I wish for a woman who understands what it means to be respected."

She smiled and lowered her gaze. "I am happy to hear this, Marcus."

A few moments of silence passed between them. A few owls

called in the darkness and the breeze whipped through the surrounding trees. Sarah shivered and pulled her arms around her body, then rubbed her arms.

"Sarah, are you well?"

She nodded, "Yes, just a chill is all."

Marcus ceased walking and unbuttoned his gray jacket. Pushing it off his shoulder, the jacket slipped down his arms. He turned to Sarah and opened it toward her. "Please, allow me to help keep you warm."

She smiled and lowered her gaze. "Marcus, you do not..."

"Nonsense. Put it on. I do not chill nor heat."

"Oh?" she asked looking up to him, then took a few steps toward the open jacket. Pausing for a moment, she smiled softly then turned. She felt the jacket touch her hands and Marcus worked the material as he guided it up her arms. She inhaled and could smell him, and it was sweet, like lavender and honey; maybe a hint of something spicy. She did not understand how the pack could consider this a smell of death.

Turning to face him, she smiled and bowed her head slightly to the right. "Thank you, Marcus, for the jacket and chivalrous action."

He shook his head. "It is nothing, Sarah. I would rather keep you warm, than chance you becoming ill. What would I do then? I could not simply head to your homestead."

Suddenly, her stomach plummeted. She swallowed and made a strong effort to keep her voice from breaking. "Well, maybe?"

"Good."

She visibly sighed and let a small laugh escape. "Yes, of course." She relaxed and smiled to him. "Maybe one day we can do that."

"I would like that." Marcus paused and looked up to the sky. The moon shone the brilliance of white toward the earth as a half moon. "It is a beautiful evening."

Sarah watched Marcus for a moment as he stared into the

sky. She smiled to his words and nodded. "It most certainly did become a beautiful evening tonight."

Marcus lowered his head and looked into her eyes, then smiled. "The evening had been beautiful, then became perfect merely with your presence."

"Oh," she gasped at his words.

Monsters.

Deception.

Amelia's words reminded her why Sarah was here with Marcus. She glanced to the coat on her body, the gray a dark contrast to the white of her garments. *This is almost the same contrast between Marcus and myself; his darkness to my light.*

She sighed and glanced up to him. Catching his gaze, a softness took his features, something maybe even deeper...something gentle. *I pray he is gentle with what I am about to announce.*

"Marcus, there is something about me I feel you should know now, before we continue this."

"All right, Sarah. I am listening." He folded his arms over his chest and in that moment, his muscles pulled against the constraints of the shirt. Marcus's body was indeed strong. His arms bulged and his chest, well, it pushed against the shirt as well and Sarah found herself staring at his neck, then his eyes, speechless. "Sarah?"

"Yes!" she announced quickly, then shook her head. "Umm, yes. Well? I am..." she paused and took a deep breath, exhaling as she lifted her gaze to his.

Marcus's brows rose and he offered a smile of encouragement. She could do this. Maybe it was something with Amelia that she could not tell Michel she was an Alchemist. "Marcus, I am an Alchemist."

He smiled again. "And?"

She blinked. "I thought...I understood that..." She casually rubbed her arm and shrugged. "I was under the impression the Undead would not willingly mingle with an Alchemist."

"Who told you this, Sarah? I shall right the wrong you have been unfortunately informed of."

She smiled and shook her head. "It does not matter who informed me. It seems they were maybe mistaken."

Marcus took a few steps toward her and smiled. "They were wrong on many levels. You are a stunning woman who glows with beauty and admiration. Any man would consider himself lucky to have you on his arm."

"Oh, Marcus," she smiled and lowered her gaze. Sarah held onto one of her arms and looked to the ground, watching as he moved closer to her.

He touched her chin and gently lifted her face to his. Staring into her eyes, Marcus smiled softly. "I would consider it a wonderful gift of life, this lifetime, to have you on my arm, Sarah. Your beauty knows no end."

Her lips parted and she glanced from his eyes to his lips, then back again. "Marcus, your words…no one has ever, I mean…" she trailed off as Marcus leaned in closer.

"May I kiss you, Sarah?"

He was so close, she could simply lift on her toes and their lips would meet. More than anything she wanted to feel his lips on hers. She longed to feel his arms around her. Letting go of her arm, she gently touched the arm that held her chin. She gripped it then brought her other hand to his chest. "Yes, kiss me."

Marcus did not waste time. He quickly captured her lips and held them for a moment, then pulled away.

Sarah kept her eyes closed for a moment, then slowly opened her lids to find him watching her. Neither moved in their hold of one another, at least until her hand tightened on the grip of his forearm. "I thought you said you would kiss me?"

He chuckled. "Then allow me to do so, properly this time."

Sarah held her breath a moment as their lips met once again. Marcus let go of her chin and his hand held the back of her head; his other arm moved around her waist, securing her to him. He leaned in and Sarah felt herself bend back just slightly.

His tongue swept across her lips and as Sarah opened her mouth for him, she exhaled and slipped an arm around his neck. Their bodies pressed together as the kiss grew deeper, and the heat between her thighs rose with the tingling sensation of need...longing for him.

Sarah kissed him back and her own grip tightened with his. Her tongue glided with his and when she scraped his fang, she whimpered softy. She could taste the iron of blood in her mouth and her senses immediately warned her to stop.

Breaking the kiss, she pulled away and covered her mouth with her hand. "I am sorry," she whispered.

"I understand, but Sarah..." Marcus reached for her and Sarah turned her back to him.

"I cannot, Marcus. My mouth...my tongue is bleeding."

"I know, I tasted you." His hands gently touched her shoulders and he turned her to face him. "I have had my fill tonight. I do not wish to feed on you, Sarah...my Sarah."

She considered this and felt grateful he had no thirst, then regretted this notion as someone out there had been his meal. Then reality forced her to see reason, and what stood in front of her.

"Marcus," she took a step back, "I do apologize, but I need to leave. Forgive me." She turned away and made a few steps toward the beginning point of their walk. She prayed her horse had not wandered off or she would be walking home...with the pack trailing her.

THE PACK! My plan!

Marcus reached her just as she turned to face him and they almost bumped into one another. "Marcus, please understand..."

"No, you need to understand, Sarah." He reached for her hands and took them in his. "I do not wish harm on you, nor would I ever consider harm. As we have just met a few nights prior, I have enjoyed my time with you and would like to continue seeing you, if you will allow me to court you."

Her plan had been coming along as she hoped, until he kissed her...and she kissed him back. She felt herself give in to him, give herself over to him. There was no way this would last. *Once he finds out I am helping the pack, he will either kill me and go after them, or capture me, make me into a vampire, then kill the lot.*

She sighed and shook her head. "I do not know if that is such a good idea, Marcus. We are different people who walk different paths."

"This is true, however, if I had a way to be with you in the daylight, would this change how you felt?"

She shook her head almost immediately. "No, it would not."

"Then why allow it to hinder us here?"

Sarah made her way to an old oak tree and leaned back against the bark. Marcus followed and stood in front of her, putting distance between them.

"I am an Alchemist. Does this not bother you?"

"Not in the least."

She smiled and glanced down. "You knew who Michel was, did you not?"

"Of course, he was one of our great rulers."

"You understand he attempted to lure my friend, and fellow Alchemist, Amelia, to her demise?"

"Yes," he stated firmly. "I am aware of the torture she endured alongside the insane René. It is unfortunate she experienced such the ordeal, however, I will tell you now, Sarah, we are not all the same.

"Whereas one enjoys the hunt, the torment and the kill of their victim, others appreciate the life itself. I have enjoyed myself with you, Sarah, and at no point had I considered conquering you for sport, or otherwise." He held his hand up and shook his head. "No, I apologize, that is a lie."

Sarah held her breath and her eyes widened to this confession. "What?" she whispered. Fear of death struck her and her heart raced frantically. The pack was there, watching, as they had her back, but it would be impossible to reach her in time if Marcus struck her.

He glanced to her with a double take. "Sarah, my word, what has frightened you so?" He stepped forward and Sarah shook her head quickly.

"No, just…keep back there. You said you would not conquer me for sport or otherwise, then changed your mind." She fisted her hands and pressed her body against the tree, willing it to absorb her body. A part of her longed for the ability of necromancy. She would force him away now…then not have to worry about him again.

"Sarah," he grinned with a chuckle, "you misunderstood, trust me. I wish you no harm in the least."

She stared at him, unwavering.

"Allow me to explain what I meant." He stepped closer and Sarah felt a lump catch in her throat. She wanted to scream, but the sound would not come from her lips. "I would love to conquer your body, just to touch you with my hands and my tongue, then make love to you. I would not wish harm on you, Sarah. I promise you this." He rested a hand over his heart, which struck her as funny. His heart did not beat, yet he held it.

The fear she assumed began to lessen and she exhaled the breath she had been holding. Sarah relaxed her hands and her body softened. "Marcus," she whispered and shook her head. "We must work on your delivery when you decide to tell me something of importance."

He chuckled again. "May I approach you again?"

She nodded and looked up to him. "Yes."

Marcus took a few steps forward and pressed a palm to the tree above her head. He brushed hair from her eyes and smiled once more, before he leaned in and kissed her.

20

The sun would be up soon. Marcus felt the oncoming change in the evening as the last bit of darkness began to fade into light. After assisting Sarah onto her horse, he waited as she cantered away, then he turned to face the trees.

"For what it is worth, I know you are watching her. For what reason, I do not know, however, if it is for her safety," Marcus shrugged, "heed my warning, mutts, I do not wish her harm."

With that, Marcus turned to leave as a growl erupted from the trees, followed by a sharp whine. Marcus grinned and sped into the night's remaining darkness.

He could smell the wolves in the trees before he arrived. He had a feeling they would have followed Sarah, and it surprised him she took the nobility of letting them in on their meeting.

She is stronger than I thought.

Grasping the handle of the door entrance, Marcus opened it and stepped inside as the sun began to crest the horizon. He closed the heavy door with a thud. Leaning against it, he closed his eyes and inhaled a deep breath; not that he needed it, of course.

"About time you return."

He opened his eyes to find Irina watching him. Wearing a dark green corset that barely covered her protruding breasts and a garter...and nothing else. "Well, are you not a sight to behold?"

"Where have you been?" She slowly made her way toward the vampire and ran her bare arms around his neck. She kissed him on the corner of his mouth, then pressed her body to his.

"Irina," Marcus groaned, "must we do this now? My evening has come to an end." He pulled her arms away and held her at bay. "Please, allow me to rest."

She raised a brow. "So you leave and frolic with who knows what whore in town, yet you do not have time to please me?"

"Trust me, I was not with a whore." He rubbed his face with his hands then took a few steps from her.

Irina could use a lesson or two in acting like a lady from Sarah. He grinned at his thought. *The Alchemist teaching the Necromancer.* He chuckled to himself.

"So how *was* your visit with the blond woman?"

Marcus stopped walking and froze. He glanced over his shoulder to Irina and raised a brow. "What makes you believe I was with a blond woman?"

"Well, for one, I smell her on you. She wears some perfume that does not bode well for you."

Marcus grinned and turned to face her. "Ahh, yes, well that was a mishap. Allow me to explain."

She shook her head. "Why should I?" She crossed her arms over her chest, forcing her bosom to ride a little higher.

Any higher, her breasts will fall from her corset. A brow rose as he pursed his lips together, contemplating on how to address this...politically.

"You asked me to watch the women at the plantation," Marcus stated.

She nodded. "Yes, I did."

"And you sent James..."

"The creature," she interrupted.

He shook his head. "James with me." He paused and shifted his weight, then smirked. "Given time, and an opportunity, you would have heard him speak."

"Oh, I did," she told him. "He growled and grunted like a child."

Marcus chuckled. "Not quite." He went into detail of their conversation and his demise as he went to attack Sarah. "I could not allow him to escape with blood lust. He would have killed them and honestly, was our purpose to lure one of them here?"

She nodded. "Yes, of course."

"Then allow me to do what you asked of me. James was in the way. I did, however, bring back some of his blood. It is in your laboratory below."

Irina raised her brows. "Is that so?" He nodded. "Well, that changes things."

"How so?"

She shrugged as she grinned. "You can come see now, or wait until later once the experiment is done." She smiled again. "Your choice."

Marcus sighed and rolled his eyes. "All right. Let us go."

She clapped her hands, excited like a child. She snatched a silken robe she had draped over the staircase and pulled it on. Tying it to her body, she made her way toward the basement door and descended the stairs. She lit a lantern, the golden glow lighting her features. She smiled at Marcus, then led the way into the dungeon.

Marcus followed, not thrilled with whatever plan Irina had concocted. *She is getting a little out of hand,* he thought to himself. *If she did not have the upper hand in most situations, I would end her. If she knew how to concoct this...cure...hell, I would have her do it and remove her head personally.*

She looked over her shoulder to him and Marcus grinned. Irina turned toward the entrance of the dungeon and the sounds of metal clanking filled the silence in the air. Marcus stepped forward and took the lantern from her, then entered. The dungeon smelled of mildew, blood, and death.

He held the lantern in front of him, extended outward, and approached one of the cells. The bars were laced with silver and he knew their captured could not escape. As Marcus drew closer, the clanking of the metal let up until it was completely quiet. He could hear the faintest heartbeat coming from Irina... and a stronger one inside the cell.

Marcus took another few steps toward the cell and as the lantern came close to touching the bars, a body jumped toward him and bounced off the bars in a loud clank. A growl from the creature erupted so fierce, it ripped through the room. Marcus fell on his backside and the lantern rolled to his side. Irina yelled in pain and held her ears.

"The sounds echo off the walls! Do not cause him any more distress! He will yell and scream more and it will kill me! If he causes my head to explode..."

"Oh shut it, woman!" Marcus yelled. "The mutt would be doing us all a favor if he killed you with his howl!"

Irina gasped. "How *dare* you!"

"How dare me?" Marcus chuckled as he got to his feet and picked up the lantern. He adjusted the wick and it burned brighter. He lifted it toward the cell and a wolf sat inside with a dark coat of fur. For a moment, Marcus wondered if his coat had been soaked in blood, or if his fur was a russet color.

Nevertheless, he turned to face Irina. "You need to remember why we are here, Irina. We are not playing games and we most definitely are not at war with one another. Now, what do you wish to show me?" Marcus straightened himself and picked up his hat off the floor, then set it on the counter.

Irina stalked toward him and drew her hand up to slap him.

Marcus raised a brow then grinned. "Lover, if you strike me, I will have no choice but to hurt you in return."

"I believe you would enjoy it too much." Irina lowered her hand to her side.

"Oh yes, I would. However, something tells me you would enjoy it more."

She smirked and leaned against the table. "I extracted some of the mutt's blood."

"All right," Marcus asked, curious. "And?"

She rubbed her hands together then reached for her goggles. She pulled them on, then went toward a box set on ice. She pulled out the dishes set inside it, then made her way back. "I found something you may want to see."

She sat the dishes down then adjusted the goggles. "Bring the lantern closer." Marcus did as she asked. Irina leaned in, and slowly a grin formed on her lips. "Ahh, as I suspected. Here, take a look." She removed her goggles and handed them to Marcus.

He took them, furrowed his brows, then looked to her. "And what am I supposed to do with these?"

"Carefully, look into the dishes, of course. I trust you with these."

"And I am looking for what, exactly?"

"Just...stop being difficult and look!" She reached for him and grabbed his arm, then pulled him to her side. "Look!"

Marcus pulled the goggles on and once they adjusted to his vision, he leaned forward and stared into the dish. "Tell me what I am looking at and looking for."

Irina placed her hand on his back and rubbed it up and down, an attempt at affection, he assumed. "I took the blood of the mutt and dropped a few droplets of...well, let us say a volunteer...into it."

Marcus sighed and stood up again, pulling the goggles onto his forehead. "All right, and what happened? It mutated into another monster creation?" He knew he had malice in his voice, but right now he did not care. The sun had risen and Marcus slowly felt himself growing more tired.

"Oh, Marcus!" She reached for a napkin on the table and thrust it toward him.

He reached up and touched his nose, then shook his head. "This is why I sleep in the day, Irina. Now, tell me," he patted his nose as blood continued to slowly seep. "What did you find?"

"Consider it for a moment. What if you fed your blood to a shifter?"

Marcus sighed and shook his head. "I would never create such a thing. Now, if we are done here?" He then felt blood trickle from his ear and he growled. "Irina, I am leaving."

"Marcus, he would become a vampire."

He stopped on his way to the door and looked back to her. "You are sure?"

She nodded. "Yes! I watched it myself take place! When the time comes to take what we need, he will be valuable leverage!"

Marcus nodded and held a hand up in an effort to wave goodnight, then let it drop, not caring. "Well done, Irina. Well done." With that, Marcus took his leave to his coffin.

21

Sarah closed the door to her room inside the plantation home. She leaned against it and considered leaving for the first time since Amelia joined the group and married John. She had been a welcome part of the pack for years and not until her plan with Marcus did she feel like a stranger.

She met Adam early on and considered him more than an acquaintance. He had been cordial toward her, at least until Amelia entered the picture.

Whenever the pack needed anything from medicine to compounds, they would call on Sarah. With Adam missing, the void in the pack continued to grow.

She sighed and pushed off the door, stripped her clothes off and pulled on her nightgown. She set her boots across the room and draped her skirts over the end of her bed. Pulling the covers back, she slipped inside and yawned. Not having been accustomed to sleeping during the day and being up all night, Sarah had a hard time adjusting.

Turning on her side, she stared at the wall across from her.

The kiss played repeatedly in her mind; the first initial one, then the next...the heated one she welcomed.

Why did I welcome it? Why did I allow myself to feel anything for an Undead?

She paused to her thoughts, then considered what Amelia had said. Are they monsters? Are they all callous? From my time with Marcus, I would beg to differ, especially at his proclamation to knowing what Michel did to her.

Why would he say that if he did have intentions to kill me? It does not make any sense. Only sense here is...he is an amazing kisser.

She sighed and lightly touched her lips. It had been a long time since any man had given her notice, at least notice she knew of. No one in the pack turned their heads in her direction, but then again, she knew exactly how Adam felt about that.

The giddiness soon left and sadness replaced it as she thought of Adam. He had been captured during the fight and lord knows what they would put him through.

Sarah closed her eyes, forcing them tight to will the image of him away from her mind. She recalled the torture Amelia said Michel and René put her through. She did not want to imagine what Adam could be facing.

"I should speak with Sophie," she whispered to herself as sleep won and took her under.

~

Irina made her way into town and came to the outskirts of where John's plantation resided. She smiled to the occasional passerby, and as she passed one of the stores, she caught her own reflection.

She wore a dark blue corset dress with a matching hat. Irina carried a parasol and she grinned to herself as the blue optical blocked her from seeing her eyes.

"Madam, may I assist you today?"

Irina glanced to her right and found a young man who stood outside a shop. She assumed he worked there, maybe owned it. Smiling, Irina took a few steps toward him. "Possibly. I am new to Savannah."

He nodded and held his hand out to her. "Then allow me to welcome you, officially. My name is Jeremy Quincy. This here is my store so if there is anything you may need, supplies or otherwise, I will be happy to fetch it for you."

She smiled. "Well, very nice to meet you, Mister Quincy. My name is Irina."

Jeremy opened the door to his shop and escorted her inside. "Miss Irina, is there a last name?"

"Irina is all you need to call me by, Mister Quincy." She smiled as she passed him, trailing her fingers lightly over his chest. "Tell me, Mister Quincy…"

"Jeremy, please, Miss Irina."

She nodded as she glanced to him, then back to the store shelves. "Jeremy, how long have you lived in this town?" She glanced at him and smiled sweetly.

"Oh," he rubbed the back of his neck then shrugged. "All my life."

Irina slipped her hand into her purse and her fingers found a small vial. She pulled it out and kept it secure in her palm, keeping it hidden. "So I may presume you know many people here?"

"Sure, many come and go through these parts, but eventually, they will find their way here to my store." He made his way behind his counter and took a sip from his cup.

Irina watched, then turned her back as she made interest in the wall next to her. "I may need some of this," she looked over her shoulder with a smile, "if you do not mind." Jars of different salts, jams and mustards sat in wait for purchase.

"Absolutely. Allow me to gather the supplies for you." Jeremy left the counter and disappeared from the other room.

Irina took the opportunity given to her. She quickly made her way to the counter and emptied the contents of the vial into his drink, then stirred it with her finger. Shoving the vial back into her purse, Jeremy came out with a ladder.

He placed it on the wall and climbed to the top. Pulling a few of the jars, he set them on the ladder then descended.

"All right, Miss Irina, here we go." He approached the counter and set the items down, then took his place behind it. Jeremy picked up his cup and took a drink, then set it down. He pushed a few buttons on the register and the drawer opened. "Six dollars and thirty-six cents, please."

She smiled and set her purse on the counter, then glanced up to him. "Jeremy, do you know of an Amelia Rimos?" He blinked and Irina noticed Jeremy stumble slightly. She grinned.

"Yes, I do…but as Hawthorne now."

"Ahh, yes, she married that mutt, did she not?"

"Come again?" he asked her, then held his head. "Whoa, what is happening?" Jeremy waved his hand in front of his face a few times. "Everything seems…distorted." He grinned then chuckled. "I feel as if I am floating."

"Oh, because you are my new friend." Irina reached over the counter and took a hold of his hand, then pulled him around to her. "Well, your mind is floating anyway."

"How? Wow, you are really beautiful." He leaned in and puckered his lips.

She laughed and pressed her fingers to his mouth. "Thank you, but I am not here for you." She glanced down his body with a smirk. "Although I should reconsider that sometime. You are quite beautiful yourself, Jeremy."

"Yeah, I am strong. Wanna see?" He flexed his arm and Irina shook her head.

"Sometimes I hate truth telling serum; it makes the mind believe the body is drunk." She pulled him toward the back room. Irina pressed Jeremy against the wall and held him there.

It seemed too easy; Jeremy appeared drunk and he wanted to be frisky with her. *This will take no time at all*, she thought.

"Tell me about Amelia, Jeremy."

He wavered on the wall. "She married that John Hawthorne. Lucky dog."

Irina snorted at the dog reference then spotted a chair. "Come here, love. Have a seat." She pushed him into the chair then continued her interrogation. "Who is the blond woman with Amelia?"

His face lit up and he smiled. "Oh, that would be Sarah. She is beautiful. I have requested to court her but alas, she always turns me down. She tells me it is never the right time, and–"

"Jeremy," she interrupted him, "I am not interested in what you think of her. I need you to tell me who she is and what she is to Amelia."

"Well?" Jeremy slouched in the chair and his eyes began to close. Irina smacked his cheek and his eyes flew open. "Oh, Sarah, right. From what I understand, she is some sort of chemist, or doctor, or something. I am not really sure."

She nodded. "Yes, yes. Now tell me, Jeremy, do you think you could let me know the next time she passes through your store?"

"Of course, Irina. Whatever you need."

"Good boy. Now," she shoved a piece of paper in his front pocket. "Next time you see her, make sure she receives this note. Understood?"

He nodded lazily. "Yes, understood. May I ask something?"

"Sure, you may." Irina stepped back as her plan had been set in motion. Now just to follow through.

"May I read the note?"

She smiled. "I couldn't care less if you did. Just make sure she receives it?"

"Yes, ma'am. Now," he stood from his chair, "how about that kiss?"

Irina took a few steps to Jeremy and rested her palms on his chest. "Jeremy," she tapped his chest lightly with a smirk. "You, love, would not live to tell the tale of our kiss. I would ruin you for anyone else. Trust me, you could not handle a woman of my caliber." She grinned and kissed his cheek, then pushed him back into the chair. "Go back and play shop owner. I will be in touch." She left the back room and the sunlight from the day filtered through the store windows, sending her shadow behind her.

She heard Jeremy rustle about, most likely having hit the floor. The effects would wear off soon enough and all he would remember would be to give the note to Sarah.

~

Sarah mounted her horse and pulled lightly on the reins. She headed into town with plans to pick up a few essentials for her date tonight, along with other things. As she rounded the corner toward town, the trees that camouflaged John's plantation began to fade in the background as the hustle of the dirt road and the town of Savannah came into view.

She dismounted her horse in front of Jeremy's shop then retrieved the list of items she intended to purchase. After tying her ride to the mounting post, she took the steps up to the patio then pulled the door open.

As the door closed behind her, she stepped in and made her way toward the counter. She glanced to her left and right, and found herself alone.

"Where is Jeremy?" she asked aloud.

"I will be right there," he called from somewhere in the back.

Sarah placed her parchment on the counter, then turned to locate the clothes Amelia asked her to buy for her child, a few

FATAL ALCHEMY

items for the kitchen, cheese, bottle of wine, and the beeswax Sarah wanted for healing purposes.

"Miss Sarah, as always it is a pleasure to see you." Jeremy's voice made her smile and as she turned, she took a few steps toward him. Wearing the familiar apron of the store, white button down top and black pants, Jeremy smiled.

"Thank you. I need a few supplies on the list there, if you do not mind."

"Not in the least. Oh, I do have something for you." He reached into his pocket and pulled a slip of paper out, then handed it toward Sarah.

She looked to it then back to Jeremy. "Who is it from?"

Jeremy blinked, then shrugged. He seemed to have an appearance of being lost, as if he arrived somewhere but was not quite sure how. "Honestly, I do not recall. I just know I need to give this to you." He smiled.

"All right," she whispered and reached for the paper. Holding it in between her fingers, she unfolded it and found ink inscribed on the parchment.

"Miss Sarah," Jeremy interrupted and she re-folded the paper. "May I call on you, say Saturday?"

She blushed and lowered her gaze, then tucked the parchment into her skirt pocket. "Jeremy, I am flattered, but I am afraid I will have to turn you down."

"Again?" he asked with a grin.

She nodded then pulled her money for the items. "I need to head back soon." Jeremy nodded and grabbed her list, then set out to find what she needed.

After paying and putting the purchases into the saddlebags, Jeremy assisted Sarah by giving her a hand up on her horse. She pulled him toward the way she came then smiled down to Jeremy.

"Thank you for your assistance. One day, maybe I will take you up on the call."

He smiled grandly.

"Until that time, I do suggest calling upon another lady friend. I will be happy to set something up, if you like."

He shook his head. "No, thank you. I appreciate the offer."

She nodded and lightly kicked her heels into the horse's sides. He quickly started into a canter and she directed them toward the plantation.

Oh, the note! she thought to herself. *I will read it as soon as I am back home. Night is falling and I do wish to see Marcus again.*

It thundered in the distance and as Sarah glanced up, gray clouds began to build into the skyline. A storm was approaching and Sarah did not fancy becoming wet in the rain.

However, if it were with a certain man, I may not mind, she smiled at her own inner thoughts.

As she arrived at the plantation, she led the horse to the stable hand, then made her way toward the house. She placed the items on the counter.

"Amelia, I am back."

The sound of boots from a distance in the house echoed. "Good, I need clean clothes for Louis and I also need to do the clothes washing. You would not believe how often he has to... well, poop!"

Sarah grinned as Amelia shook her head. "Right, well I need to freshen up."

"Another date with Marcus?"

Sarah noticed Amelia glancing at her from the corner of her eye. She nodded. "Yes, another date. I am getting closer to him trusting me, I believe. From his actions, anyway, I would assume so."

"What are his actions?" she asked.

Sarah felt her cheeks blush and she turned away. "Nothing to concern yourself with."

"Please, be safe." Sarah turned as Amelia took her shoulder. "I worry each time you head out."

Sarah nodded. "I know, and I appreciate that but trust me, he will not hurt me. If he wanted to, he would have by now, right?"

Amelia shrugged. "Maybe, but who knows really? Michel did not hurt me in the beginning, but it was when he realized he could not get what he wanted that he turned on me. Do you know what Marcus may be after with you?"

"Who is to say he is not after me for just being me? Why would he need an ulterior motive?"

"Oh," Amelia dropped her gaze. "I apologize, I did not mean…"

Sarah held her hand up in a stopping gesture and shook her head. "No, do not. It is all right. I will be leaving shortly." She turned toward the sound of Louis crying out.

"Your son needs you. I will be back by dawn." With that, Sarah turned and left the room, leaving her closest friend behind and in the dark. Who knew what Marcus's intentions really were? All Sarah knew at this moment was she wanted to see him, feel his lips on hers, and touch his body.

22

Sarah left her room and closed the door securely. She stood in the hallway and glanced down the short distance. *It is time I move out. My services are no longer needed, at least I do not think.*

She shrugged it off, pushing the thought to the back of her mind, and descended the stairs. The exit toward the back of the house was empty which, in a way, relieved her. She did not enjoy telling everyone she knew what she was doing with Marcus. No one seemed to trust she could handle herself.

"Well, that is just fine," she told herself. Sarah made her way toward the stable and took a few steps inside. The stable boy on duty tonight smiled to her.

"Hello there. Who may I saddle up for you tonight?" He was a young man, most likely no older than sixteen.

"I may ride bareback, so saddle pad and reins, if you please."

"Yes, ma'am."

When the stable boy left her, Sarah opened the bag and checked her contents. She packed glasses, wine, and some edibles. She closed it as she heard the clip clop of a horse approaching.

She set the bag to her feet and watched as a large draft horse named Dolly made her way down the stable walkway. Dark hair and black mane, Dolly stood tall. Sarah grinned and shook her head. "I may need a step stool for this one."

"I will be happy to tack one onto your saddle pad, if you need it?"

She shook her head. "Not necessary," she grinned. *Marcus will definitely help me up when I am ready.* "Help me, please?"

The stably boy hoisted Sarah onto the saddle pad and she adjusted herself until she felt comfortable. He laid the saddlebag over in front of her afterward. Riding bareback was no easy feat, but did wonders for the body in keeping in shape. She nodded and the stable boy let go of the reins. "Thank you for your help. I will be back around dawn."

The boy nodded and retreated into the stables as Sarah cantered toward the forest.

Laying a blanket in the sand, the sun had begun its descent behind the western hemisphere. Sarah took a seat and set out two glasses, a bottle of red wine, and some cheese she had packed.

I have no idea if Marcus will eat this or drink the wine. Maybe I am being foolish.

She shook her head with a grin and glanced toward the lake. This had become their meeting grounds since their first introduction. She enjoyed this lake, but enjoyed his company more.

Marcus had this way about him that made Sarah feel as if all the attention she could ever want, or ever need, was given to her solely by him. She smiled at the thought and felt her ears heat from blushing.

She sipped her wine then took a bite of cheese. *Am I being foolish thinking this could ever go somewhere? I am after Marcus for information, yet here I am excited to see him, excited for him to kiss me. What would it be like to make love with him?*

As the sun continued to settle, Sarah became lost in her thoughts. She laid back on the blanket and stared up to the darkening sky. The clouds continued to blow in and she knew soon there would be rain. Disappointment settled for a moment at the thought of closing their meeting too soon.

Then a shadow fell over her form. She jumped and sat up quickly, looking behind her to find a smiling Marcus.

"I did not mean to startle you so," he started then chuckled. "Although, you were quite fast."

"Not as fast as you, apparently," she told him with a smile. "Please, have a seat."

He did as she asked, then crossed his legs underneath him. "Oh love, you brought us cheese and wine." He glanced up with a humorous grin.

"I was not sure if…if you would eat or drink with me."

He chuckled again. "Normally no, I would not eat or drink human food. However, for you, for tonight, I will." He picked up a piece of cheese and placed it in his mouth, then chewed. Marcus raised a brow and his face contorted slightly as he swallowed. He cleared his throat and Sarah giggled.

"Tasty, I see?" she asked him playfully.

"Yes, something like that." Next, he picked up the red wine and sipped, then nodded. "Now this, this is not too bad. Thank you for thinking of me."

She grinned. "You are welcome, but Marcus?"

"Hmm?"

"You do not need to eat the cheese."

"Oh, thank goodness," he told her with a sigh.

She laughed. "What shall we do tonight before the rain starts?"

He sipped his wine again, then set the glass down. "I thought maybe we could head into town. There is a place there we could go for the evening and not worry about soiling our clothes."

She blinked, taken aback by the forward gesture of having a room with Marcus. "Are you suggesting…we…sleep together?"

"As much as sleeping would thrill me as I am a vampire, no," he smiled, then stood and offered his hand to her. She took it and he pulled her to her feet. "I am merely suggesting having somewhere to go so we do not become wet."

Sarah nodded and lowered her gaze. "Marcus," she whispered, "I am not…"

"Sarah, no," he interrupted her and touched her chin to lift her head. "Look at me, please."

She lifted her gaze slowly, then met his.

"I do not wish to do anything you are not ready for. I simply wish to keep your company. Nothing more."

She bit the corner of her lip for a moment, then slowly nodded. "All right."

"All right?"

She nodded again with a smile. "Yes, all right."

Marcus smiled, then leaned in and kissed her cheek. "You have made me a happy man," he whispered next to her cheek.

"I am happy to hear that." As Marcus began to pull back from her, he hesitated.

Sarah held her breath and turned her face slightly toward his. She could feel the chill of his body being so close to him. If he could breathe, she imagined his breath would fan on her cheek.

"Marcus," she whispered his name and in a second, he took her by the face and crushed his lips to hers. Sarah grabbed ahold of his jacket and pulled him close, thrusting her body against his. His tongue swept across her lips and as she opened her mouth, his tongue darted inside, seeking her own.

A light suddenly flashed in the sky as it lit up around them and thunder crashed, but their kiss did not end.

Sarah gasped against his lips and stood on her toes, willing herself to be that much closer to him. She whimpered and suddenly, Marcus growled against her lips.

He bent her legs and tilted her back as his arms supported her weight. Marcus held onto her body as if he coveted her eternally.

MINE, her mind screamed.

Marcus trailed his lips to her jawline and kissed down her throat. He pressed his lips over her vein, then licked it slowly. Sarah groaned as heat grew between her legs and lust built in her body. Slowly, Marcus kissed from her neck to her collarbone, then between her breasts.

He brought his free arm around and grabbed her waist, slowly bringing it up her body. As he crested her breast, she moaned again and tilted her head back. Marcus grabbed and squeezed her breast and her nipples became taut to his touch.

She wanted him to ravage her, rip her clothes from her body and make love to her right here on the blanket. Her breathing picked up in rhythm as he nibbled through the material of her dress on the nipple.

"You have too many clothes on, my love," he growled against her body.

She gasped once more and as Marcus pulled her to a standing position, he kissed her once more. Sarah's arms wrapped around his waist and thunder cracked once more.

One, two, five raindrops hit her shoulders as they continued their kissing. She softly moaned as he nipped her neck and his hands gripped her derriere. He pulled her hard against him and Sarah felt his erection as it pressed against her.

Releasing his waist, she felt bold tonight, and wanted to make a bold statement. She placed her hand on his hip and moved it around to his crotch. Sarah opened her hand and her fingers closed in around his shaft over his clothes. She squeezed him, then massaged the length and his balls.

Marcus groaned and the lust between them continued to develop. The few droplets of water produced into a steady sprinkle. "Sarah, it will rain on us soon enough," he whispered as he pressed his lips against her neck, kissing her underneath her ear.

She bit her lip and nodded. "I know, and I do not care in the least."

Marcus cupped her face and kissed her again on the lips. "I need you, please, I need to be with you," he begged. "Allow me to have a taste."

"What?" she whispered and pulled away. Her lips tingled from the kissing and she gazed into his eyes. "You wish to feed on me?"

He grinned and shook his head. "No, I wish to taste you." His hand pushed against her skirts as he pressed his fingers toward her pussy.

She gasped and her eyes widened. "Oh," she whispered. "Oh, well that...yes."

He chuckled and leaned in. "Allow me to have you," he whispered again. "It would be the greatest moment of my lifetime to be able to call you my own, Sarah."

Sarah touched his cheeks and ran her fingers through his hair. She stared into his eyes and saw nothing but patience, lust, and longing. She smiled and kissed Marcus again. Without words, she expressed to him through touching what she wanted...what she needed.

Marcus deepened the kiss once more and this time, he did it with a snarl. Sarah did not jump, nor was she struck with fear. Instead, the snarl sent a shock of lust through her body. Her clit twitched and her pussy became wet, longing for Marcus to be inside her.

She moaned softly as his hand massaged her breast again. The rain became stronger than a sprinkle as it began to pelt their bodies. It was obvious Marcus did not care, either.

Her fingers took to unbuttoning his shirt and the farther down she proceeded, the more she saw of his chest. He was chiseled and strong, from what she could already see. He had a tuft of dark hair in the center of his chest and she wanted to run her tongue across his nipples and lightly bite them.

She pushed his shirt off his arms and when she opened her eyes, she took in the man before her in only his black pants. Marcus was beautiful. The rain poured down his body and hair soaked around his head, barely touching his shoulders. His eyes remained on hers and his lips were parted.

Sarah fisted her hands and a smile crept over her lips. "I had no idea this was under your clothes, Marcus. You are beautiful."

He took a step toward her and gently ran a finger over her breasts. "Allow me to undress you."

She nodded and Marcus kissed her and held her face in his palms. He released her and turned her. She glanced to the ground as the rain continued to pour. The corset began to loosen and soon, Marcus tugged on it. She unfastened the busk and dropped it onto the blanket.

The rain poured down her naked upper body and she lifted her face to the sky, smiling. Strong arms slipped around her waist from behind and hands cupped her breasts. Marcus kissed her neck as he teased, pinched, and pulled on her nipples. Sarah moaned as she leaned her head back onto his shoulder.

Passion filled her, reminding her what it felt like to be wanted, needed, desired. She lifted her arm and ran her fingers into his hair, then tugged his face closer into her neck. Her body shivered, not from any chill the rain may have caused, but from the impact his body had been making on hers.

"I need to be inside you," he whispered against her ear.

She turned in his arms and her breasts pressed against his bare chest. "I have been dreaming of your naked body against my own." Sarah blinked the rain from her eyes as she stared into his.

Marcus's hair dripped onto his shoulders, chest, and his face, a few droplets touching his lips. She pulled him to her and captured him in a heated kiss as her tongue darted inside his mouth, careful to avoid his fangs.

Marcus made quick work of her skirts as they kissed. He broke away from her lips long enough to push her skirts down her slick legs. Sarah lifted each leg as he tossed her garments. She had been left in her garter and boots, nothing else. He gazed up her body with a grin that screamed 'I am consuming you.' And she welcomed it.

He made haste to remove his pants and tossed them to the side. He pressed his palms to her thighs and slowly stood, allowing his hands to move up her porcelain skin. Marcus made it as far as her bottom and his hands palmed her, lifting her into the air. Sarah naturally wrapped her legs around his body as she pulled herself to him, kissing his lips.

"I need you, Sarah, please." He held her weight in his arms and his erection pressed against his stomach. Sarah ground her body against his and he groaned aloud.

"Take me," she whispered. Sarah felt the wind suddenly against her body as Marcus took off in a speed unnatural for any human. Moments later, the rain ceased as he entered a cave. She glanced around but could not see much of anything; not that it mattered the least in this moment.

Marcus pressed her back to the cave wall and kissed her hard on the lips. He ground his body against hers, his erection teasing her clit with each ministration.

"Oh my god," she whispered. "I will not be able to hold on much longer before I fall apart. Marcus, please…"

He growled, mixed with a chuckle, a sound like an approval. "Say it again," he whispered as he moved from her lips to her neck. Thrusting his body upward, his dick pressed harder against her. "Fuck me, you are absolutely wet with pleasure, my love."

"What," she moaned louder as her fingers dug into his shoulders. "Marcus, please."

"That is it, my love, that is it." He reached between them and lined his head to her entrance, then pushed.

Sarah yelled out at the impact he made as he thrust upward. He paused for a moment and she opened her eyes, gazing into his. "Why did you stop?" she asked as she kissed him on the lips.

"Have I hurt you?"

She shook her head. "Not in the least." She moved her hips in a back and forth motion, then grinned. "Do not stop, please."

He lowered his face ever so slightly and a fierceness took over. A brief moment of fear claimed Sarah, then it disappeared when Marcus kissed her again, pulling her body from the wall and laying her on the ground. The floor of the cave felt softer than she had expected; possibly mud pressed against her body. Regardless, she was here with Marcus.

After adjusting himself against her, he gazed down and smiled, then pulled back and thrust into her. Sarah moaned and her neck arched. She reached for his arms and pulled him toward her. Their lips met in a heated kiss as he thrust against her again and again.

"Oh god," she moaned and her back arched, pressing her breasts against his chest.

Marcus took one of her wrists and pulled her arm up above her head, then followed suit with the other. He held her wrists in one of his hands while the other held his balance. "I have wanted you since the moment I saw you in the lake." He thrust again and Sarah moaned, the sound echoing throughout the cave. "The way your nipples were on display," he thrust again, "the way your clothes clung to your body," again, "I have wanted you. For. My own!" He thrust against her with each word and Sarah closed her eyes as Marcus took hold of her, claiming her.

Sarah's body fell under his spell as she gave herself to him. She did not fight the restraint on her wrists, nor did she struggle against his hold. Gazing up to him, she watched as he continued to move his body against hers.

He is so beautiful, she thought. Their eyes met and Marcus held her gaze as he moved against her.

"Mine," he whispered, then louder, "Mine!"

She nodded and closing her eyes, her head rolled back and her back arched. "Oh god, Marcus, harder, Marcus!" A warmth encased her as her orgasm pushed through her body, setting her blood aflame.

In that same moment, a sharpness jarred her side and as she glanced down, Marcus bit into her left upper breast. Oddly enough, it did not hurt. Instead, the pleasure, the orgasm she was having, everything in this moment suddenly exploded into a force she had not been prepared for.

Her clit throbbed and her walls clenched his shaft. Sarah's hands fisted as he continued to hold them above her head.

"You. Are. MINE!" he roared against her body. Marcus lifted his head, his lips crimson from her blood. He thrust a few more times, then as if experiencing his own orgasm, he growled and tossed his head back.

He stilled his body, then slowly lowered his head until their eyes met once again. Marcus released her wrists and brought them to his lips, kissing each individually.

"I did not hurt you?" he whispered.

She shook her head. "No, but the bite was unexpected."

"It did not hurt?"

"Not in the least. Actually," she felt herself blush, considering they just had sex, "it caused the pleasure to become much more intense."

"Ahh," he remarked with a smirk, then leaning forward, he licked over the wound, cleaning it. "I have the ability to drain, but to also heal."

"I have heard that," she told him. Sarah felt her body relax in the cave. Marcus lay next to her and opened his arm for her. She moved close to him and laid her head on his chest, draping her arm across his body. "Marcus?"

"Yes, Sarah?"

"Will you be able to return me home, or will I remain your captive here in this cave?"

He chuckled and the sound echoed. She enjoyed his laughter and smiled. "I promise to return you soon, just before dawn. I intend to spend this evening with you, if that is all right with you?" He turned his head and looked into her eyes.

She nodded with a smile. "Yes, of course, it is all right." She kissed him softly, then relaxed into his arms.

23

*T*HE STAIRS CREAKED, the sound that awoke Amelia.. She yawned and glanced toward the window. The sun had barely begun to crest the horizon. *Who would be coming in at this hour?* She turned toward John and nestled into his back. She felt herself begin to drift into sleep when the creak happened again.

She opened her eyes again and tapped John's back lightly. "John?"

He growled something then mumbled.

"John?" She kept her voice low as she tapped his arm. "John, are you awake?"

His large body stretched, taking up more than his half of the bed, forcing Amelia to move back. He turned over and faced the ceiling, then rubbed his hands on the scruff that covered his cheeks. "What is it?"

"Someone is running the stairs from the sound of it."

"I heard one or two sounds. That does not make someone running, Amelia. Go back to sleep."

She stared at him for a moment, surprised at his non-caring of the homestead. Amelia furrowed her brows and sat up. "SO

HELP ME JOHN HAWTHORNE IF YOU DO NOT GET UP AND SEE WHAT IS GOING ON OUTSIDE..."

John immediately sat up and faced his wife. "What happened? Who is there?"

She shook her head. "Go see who is in the hallway," she smiled, "please?"

"Woman," he threw the covers from his naked body and stood, displaying to his wife a full morning erection. "You will be the death of me!"

She grinned and raised a brow. "I will make this up to you, John, I promise." Laying back in the warmth her husband vacated, she pulled the blankets up her naked body. She watched John as he pulled on trousers, buttoned them and sighed.

He glanced to her and shook his head. "A lot of making up." John opened the door slowly and peered outside. No one appeared to be in the hallway. He took a step out the door then pulled it closed behind him. Taking a few steps down the corridor, he found mud prints on the staircase that led to Sarah's bedroom.

John's brows rose in surprise. "What is Sarah doing in the mud? Some Alchemist work of some sort?" He scratched his head and took a few steps toward her bedroom. His hand touched the doorknob, then he hesitated.

She might be naked in there, he thought and shook the thought away. He settled for a light tap. "Sarah? Are you awake?"

The floor creaked on the other side of the door. His home offered no silence to anyone who walked the floors or the upper hallways, especially at night. If anyone were to consider thievery from his homestead, their footsteps alone would give them away.

"Yes," came her voice, then the doorknob turned. As she opened her door, Sarah peeked out from behind it.

John blinked and took a step back. "Wow, are you, umm, are you all right?" He rubbed the back of his neck and glanced to the floor. She had been covered in dirt, dried mud and her hair was worse for wear.

"Yes, perfectly. Why?"

He glanced to her again and caught a slight smile on her lips. "Well? You are usually so...clean."

She smiled and nodded. "I decided a morning roll with the pigs was in order."

John smiled and shook his head. "I highly doubt that, considering I do not *have* pigs, but as long as you know what you are doing, I will leave you be."

She nodded. "I will need time with you and Amelia later today, if that is all right?"

He nodded. "I will let her know. You may want to..." he gestured around his face.

Sarah giggled and nodded again. "Yes, I know. I will wash up. Do not worry, I will be my normal clean self." She yawned behind the door, then sighed. "I need to rest as well. Maybe later, as the sun begins to set?"

John raised his brows. "You were out all night?"

"Yes. Why?"

He crossed his arms over his chest. "With this Marcus?"

She raised a single brow. "Yes?"

He stared at her for a moment and did his best to not pick a fight with this woman, the best friend of his wife. Her safety was a concern, but he could not dictate when she left or who she spent her time with.

However, if she planned to get information on Adam or the vampire coven, moonlighting as someone of interest could still get her killed.

"I have some information I would like to discuss. John, I really need to clean up. I will find you two later, all right?"

As John was about to answer, Sarah shut her bedroom door. John heard it lock and he sighed. He could easily knock it down if he wanted but not today, not right now.

Rather than heading back to his bedroom, John headed downstairs toward the kitchen. Mud had been tracked in from Sarah. He followed the path from the back door entrance, up to the stairs he just descended. He opened the cabinet that stored food and supplies and grabbed deer meat that one of the pack members prepared as jerky.

He gnawed on it and made his way toward the back door. One set of foot prints were in his home, and he wondered if he looked outside if he would see two.

Would she be foolish enough to bring Marcus to our home, knowing we are wolves? Hell, does he even know where she is staying?

He swallowed the jerky he gnawed and began to chew on another bite. John felt it was time for a hunt, and this hunt would be for the Undead courting Sarah.

∽

Amelia descended the stairs in a tan corset, brown and black striped trousers, matching striped jacket, and her hair set in curls, pinned to her head. Atop it, she wore a dark brown hat. She went through the home, looking for John, but only found Sophie. She cleared her throat and offered a nod to the violet-eyed woman.

"Good morning, Sophie."

The female shifter stared at her for a moment, then rolled her eyes. "Do not talk to me."

Amelia sighed. "It is not my fault."

"Yes, it is. If you never found your cure, if you never allowed yourself to be seduced by that vampire shit," she turned and her gaze burned into Amelia, "If John had never opted to rescue you, Adam would still be here…with me."

She raised her brows in surprise, her mouth agape. Amelia stepped closer to her as she closed her mouth and narrowed her eyes. "If that is how you truly feel, then you really should consider the facts."

"The only fact I need to know is he is missing, and I have no idea if he is alive or dead." She turned her back to Amelia and stared out the window. "Now, if you do not mind, leave me. I do not wish for you to be in my space."

Amelia rolled her eyes and shook her head. "Suit yourself. When we do find him, are you planning to join us, or will you stay here and sulk?"

"You honestly need to ask me that?"

Amelia shrugged, then smiled. "Just making sure I know where you stand in this hunt."

"I should be asking you the same when John was missing." She raised her brow. "Go to your son. I am sure he needs to feed."

Shaking her head, Amelia left Sophie's side and made her way toward the nursery. Sophie was right, Louis did need her, and she needed him. Her breasts were swollen this morning and she needed to relieve the pressure.

As she entered his nursery, she smiled at his bright eyes, soft dark curls of hair, and his baby grin. "My Louis! Did you sleep well?"

Her son made movements in excitement as she reached for him. Carrying him to her nursing chair, she adjusted him in her lap, opened her blouse and he quickly latched on. Relief began to settle in her breast and she relaxed her head against the wooden chair.

"Oh, Louis," she glanced to her son as he fed, "what will we do with you when we go to find Adam? I cannot take you with me and I certainly cannot allow your father to go alone in this quest."

"Miss Amelia?"

Amelia glanced up to a young woman who entered the room. She was young and beautiful with a dark head of curls and dark brown eyes. She smiled and stepped into the room. Macy, the younger sister of Tyler, one of the pack members, sat down on the floor.

"I could not help but overhear you, Miss Amelia. I will be happy to help if you need me. I love children, especially babies!"

Amelia smiled. "Is that so? Have you cared for children in the past?"

Macy nodded and explained caring for animals, playing with the other children in the pack growing up, and when other married pack members had children.

"I see," Amelia told her. "Well, allow me to discuss this with John and we will see where we stand. How does that sound?"

Macy smiled and nodded. "Lovely. May I hold him?"

"As soon as I am done feeding. Pardon me." Amelia pulled Louis up to burp him, then switched him to the other breast. The same relief settled in and the bursting sensation finally eased away. A few minutes later, Louis had his fill, Amelia burped him, then carefully lowered him into the waiting arms of Macy.

She was a natural. Macy laid him against her chest with his face just above her shoulder. She rubbed his back and smiled to him. "I will be happy to keep him this afternoon."

Amelia nodded. "Allow me to talk with John…"

"Macy?" John's voice filled the room and Amelia looked up then smiled.

"Well, speak of the devil and the devil shall appear." She winked at him.

He chuckled. "Macy, are you looking to keep Louis for yourself?"

"Oh NO, Mister John! I would never consider taking him!"

He grinned. "Of course not." He turned to Amelia. "Trust our son is in good hands."

Amelia stood from her chair. "If you trust her, then I will, too. Just," she glanced to Macy, "forgive me if I seem overprotective."

"I cannot imagine you would not be. It is all right." Macy smiled and cooed at Louis. He smiled at her and gurgled baby sounds.

"Amelia," John lowered his voice for just her to hear. "We need to talk about Sarah."

"Oh." She made her way toward the room's door, glanced to Macy and Louis, then back to John. "Did something happen?"

"Possibly, but I am not quite sure yet. She came home very early this morning. She is who you heard."

Amelia nodded, then took John's arm and led him out of the bedroom, just standing on the other side out of earshot. "What happened?"

"She came in covered in mud, dirty, and it looked as if she had been in the rain all night."

"Wow, all right, so I will venture to guess she had an evening with Marcus?"

"Seems that way," he crossed his arms over his chest. "I am not comfortable with her playing this game with him while staying in our home."

"I agree."

"Good, because she plans to speak with us about this later."

24

Sarah opened her eyes and stretched on her bed, then groaned from the soreness of her body. She lifted the sheets up and glanced down her body. Her nightgown rode up her legs, baring them to her. They appeared unbruised, which she felt happy about. Sarah then lifted her gown up and glanced to her chest.

She bit her lip at the bruise Marcus left over her breast when he bit her.

"I have the ability to drain, but to also heal." His words came back to her for a moment.

She gasped at the discomfort between her legs, then smiled as she remembered why the discomfort was there.

As she made her way toward the bathroom, her clothes from the night before lay on the floor, soiled and dirty. She kicked them to the side and quickly brushed her teeth. Sarah pulled her hair to the nape of her neck and fastened a black choker around it that hung a crescent moon. She dabbed on a bit of makeup then left the bathroom.

Deciding on a dark blue corset and matching trousers, she paired it with a gray jacket, small top hat, and black boots. She dressed and pulled the strings of the corset into place, then set everything.

As she made her way toward her door, she suddenly remembered the parchment she received from Jeremy. Sarah sought it out for a bit, then recalled where she had left it. Locating the parchment, she slowly opened it.

She did not recognize the handwriting at first, but when she saw Adam's name on the top line, she sat on her bed.

We have Adam. If you wish to see him alive, you will meet us at the island out to sea where the ships have become lost. Some call it Bermuda. Take caution as we will be watching, and waiting, for you to arrive. To receive him, we do need a trade of sorts. Bring us the Alchemist and you shall have your mutt.

Irina

Sarah felt her chest burning and realized she had not taken a breath. She quickly inhaled and stood, then ran from her door, took the stairs down, and headed toward the den. Voices of the pack, including Sophie, sounded. She glanced through the room and did not move.

John looked to her first and stood to his feet. Next stood Amelia, then Sophie, and Katherine.

"Sarah?" Amelia called to her, then crossed the room. "What is it? What happened?" She took her hand and squeezed it.

Sarah glanced down to their hands but could not move. She swallowed hard and felt a tear race down her cheek. Her gaze first went to Sophie.

Sophie's brows rose and fear touched her gaze.

Then Sarah looked to Amelia.

"You are as white as a ghost," she told Sarah. "What happened? Talk to me!"

Rather than say a word, she lifted her other hand. It shook and the parchment rattled like a stiff piece of paper. Amelia reached for it and tugged, but did not retrieve it.

"Sarah, let it go. It is all right, let it go." When her fingers finally released the parchment, Amelia squeezed her hand and remained by her side. She lifted it and read over the letter. "I will be right back, all right?"

Sarah nodded and lowered her gaze. Amelia released her hand and stood by her for a moment. Sarah nodded again, letting her know she was fine. Amelia nodded back, then rushed to John's side and handed him the note. She glanced to Sophie next, then sighed. "You need to see this."

Instantly, Sophie came to her side. "What? Is it Adam?"

Amelia nodded, then the other pack members stood to their feet.

"Where is he?"

"Is he alive?"

"When do we leave?"

"Who has him?"

Questions began to fly in the room and John turned to address all of them. Amelia patted his back then glanced to Sophie. She watched as the woman clenched the parchment to her chest, as if willing the paper to take her to Adam. Slowly, she approached her and touched her hand.

"Sophie?"

Violet eyes snapped to her own, filled with tears. "What if he is still alive? Have they tortured him?"

Amelia took a chance and pulled her into a hug. After a moment of hesitation, Sophie melted against her and sobbed. Rubbing her back, Amelia thought back to when Michel and René had tortured her, had sex in Eva's blood, when Michel tried to force his own blood down her throat...she quickly shook the memories away.

"We have a location to go to. We will find him," Amelia told her softly.

Sophie nodded against her, sniffed, then pulled from the hug. "I hope so." She palmed the tears away and wiped at her nose. "When do we leave?"

Then their moment of make up ended as Sophie approached her pack. Amelia glanced back to Sarah and found her covering her face with her hands.

"Oh hell," she mumbled and quickly made her way over. "Sarah, why are you crying?"

"I feel...I do not...what if..." She could not get her words out as she sobbed.

"Let us start from where you found this note."

Sarah nodded. "I went to the shop in town, the one Jeremy Quincy runs." Amelia nodded. "I went in there to fetch a few supplies, your baby clothes, and things for the evening I had planned with Marcus. Jeremy handed me this parchment, and honestly, he seemed a bit...strange. Maybe ill? I am not really sure."

"Did Jeremy say who gave him the parchment?"

She shook her head. "No, just that he knew he had to give it to me."

Amelia nodded. "Sounds like he may have been spelled."

Sarah slouched as if giving in to the feeling of defeat. "I was afraid it was that. I had been so overwhelmed with my own doings, going to see Marcus, going on with my own plans and selfish desires, that I completely forgot about this letter. Oh Amelia, I am so, so sorry!" She sobbed and covered her face with her hands again.

Amelia wrapped her arms around her, then whispered, "It is not your fault, Sarah. We will find him, all right?"

She nodded, then looked to Amelia. "It all happened within moments of each other though, Amelia. I cannot help but feel, and I really do not want to, but I feel Marcus has something to do with this."

"Really?"

Sarah nodded. "Yes. He is involved with the coven, he has told me as much. But he does not have the desires the others do. Or so he has told me."

Amelia slipped her arm around Sarah's waist and led her out of the room. "Come on, let us talk outside. No one needs to hear this, at least not yet."

The women made their way out of the house and stood in the yard. The sun had been drifting toward the western horizon and it would be setting soon. Sarah sighed and glanced to Amelia.

"We made love last night."

Amelia's brows rose in surprise. "Oh, I am not quite sure what to say to that."

Sarah blushed and lowered her gaze. "There is nothing to say. The pack has been following me but last night, Marcus held me in his arms and ran so fast...the wind surrounded me and moments later, we were in a cave." She shook her head. "I do not know if the pack even realized he had left with me."

"I will mention it to John later, all right?"

Sarah nodded. "I had a mission to accomplish and I allowed my own feelings to cloud my judgment. Amelia," she lowered her gaze and turned her back to her friend, "he treated me as if I truly mattered. He coveted my body and truly made love to me."

"I imagine he did, Sarah. I remember how Michel was–"

"No, Amelia," Sarah cut her off. "This is not like Michel. Please, do not compare Marcus to that blood sucking evil bastard."

Her brows rose and Amelia shook her head. "I understand he is not Michel, but Sarah, a vampire is a vampire. They are all the same."

"No!" she shouted, "No, he cannot be the same. He cannot! He has been so wonderful to me, just...amazing." She began to sob again and sank to her knees. "Oh, Amelia, am I a fool for thinking he actually cared for me?"

Amelia felt bad for her friend, so much so she wanted to hold onto her and tell her it would be all right. But it may not be, and that was what she needed to prepare for.

"Did he feed you his blood?"

Sarah looked up and sniffed. "What?"

"Did he feed you his blood?" Amelia lowered herself to her knees and set her hands on Sarah's shoulders. "Last night, did he…"

"Oh my god, Amelia, no, he did not feed me his blood!" She knocked her hands away and stood. "I would be a vampire by now, would I not?"

Amelia stood to her feet and followed her friend. "I…I honestly do not know. Maybe? Possibly? Did he feed on you?"

Sarah turned on her and if glares could be used as a weapon…she quickly pulled her top to the side and exposed the top of her breast.

"Oh…" Amelia touched her lips with her fingertips. "Are you…all right?"

"Physically, of course. Emotionally? No." She pulled her top into place and began to walk toward the stables.

"Where are you going?" Amelia called to her.

"Not that you can stop me, but I am fetching a horse to track down Marcus. I have an idea where he may be," she turned to look at Amelia, "and I plan on getting my answers, one way or the other."

"Sarah, wait for someone to go with you!"

"I will go," Sophie's voice called as she ran past Amelia. "I have been listening in and if she finds Adam, I want to be there."

Not liking this idea, Amelia backtracked toward the house. "Do you two know where you are going?"

"Yes, I know where to go," Sophie told her. "If we are not back by sunrise, we have left for the island. I have heard rumors of men with ships that travel to the island. We will meet you there."

Amelia shook her head and knew, without a doubt, John would be furious. Sarah and Sophie both left on a suicide mission. Sophie was hell bent on finding Adam and Sarah would definitely give in to Marcus.

"Well, hell," she told herself as she made her way back inside to find John, prepare for the Alpha to emerge, and pray they find and locate Adam, Sophie, and Sarah before it was too late.

25

CHAINS PULLED ON his arms and his head hung, slumped from exhaustion. His knees barely touching the ground, his shoulders burned from the pain of being held limp in the air. Adam's body had been mangled, bled, beaten, and close to the edge of being drained.

Just kill me, please, he begged with his inner thoughts. *End this hell.*

The bars serving as a window high upon his cell wall had the last remnants of sunlight pouring inside. Night would fall soon, and with it, the necromancer and Undead would venture inside for further torture sessions.

He swallowed the bile in his throat and coughed. The movement caused pain to radiate throughout his body and Adam cried out. His voice croaked and he coughed. A warmth slipped down his arm from his wrist. Glancing over, blood seeped from the wound inflicted by the one who called herself Irina.

Irina created a concoction to prevent him from shifting into his wolf after keeping him trapped in his animal form for weeks. Adam stared at the ceiling and willed it to reach down and unshackle him. If he could shift, he would, and he would be freed from the silver chains that bound him. Instead, he continued to fall limp to his capturers in a death sentence they seemed determined to draw out.

The light on the floor continued to thin as the sun fell behind the horizon. He closed his eyes as soon as the cell became pitch black. They would be here soon. The torture would begin again, the pain, the horrific, endless night of torture.

In the darkness, Adam could only hear the dripping of water from a nearby puddle.

Drip.

Drip.

Drip.

It was enough to drive him mad, but in the same instance, it was something he could hold onto that was still real.

As long as I continue to hold on, I know I am still alive. The moment I let go, everything will be lost. I will have failed my pack and my Sophie.

Then the door opened and heels struck the cement floor, followed by another set of steps. Adam listened hard, hoping to tell who would be coming for him. He did not have to listen for long as a match struck in the darkness.

The face of Irina lit in an orange glow as she set a small flame to the lantern in the room. She burned the light brighter then handed the matches to someone else.

She approached his cage and smiled. "Good evening, mutt. I trust you slept well?"

"Fuck you," he groaned.

"Oh, now that is no way to say good evening," she tsked. "Well, let us just say today will be your lucky day, your day to begin anew, mutt! How exciting is that?"

She bounced in her step and left his cage for the table behind her. One by one, the lanterns in the dungeon began to light. As the orange glow cast throughout the room, Adam found himself in company with other vampires; some he recognized from years of fighting, others were new.

"I think I am flattered," he grumbled.

"Oh?" Irina questioned as she prepared a syringe. "Why is that?"

"You brought all of these filthy vampires on my account? You must be scared of me to bring all this force just for me."

She laughed and turned her gaze to him. "You are a legend in your own mind, mutt. Now, if you will, I need one more sample."

Adam held his breath as she approached him, two Undead trailing her for protection. Protection from what, he was not sure. He could not move, even if he wanted to.

Irina was never gentle when she wanted something. She would take it, willingly or not; most of the time not. She grinned as she approached, then frowned. "My goodness, you smell like death!"

"That is because you are surrounded by it. Smell yourself, evil whore!"

A growl, maybe a snarl, erupted from her and she raised her hand then brought it down hard into his side with a scream.

Adam yelled out from the pain. He felt the warmth of blood trickle from the wound. Irina quickly yanked the syringe from his side and tapped it. She nodded and left the cage, leaving her Undead escorts behind.

"I am hungry and he is bleeding," said one.

"I hear he tastes like salt," said the other.

Adam eyed both and waited…nothing happened. He glanced toward Irina who, in turn, had her eyes on him, looking almost amused. He looked back to the vampires, then to Irina once more.

"What do you want from me?" he asked her.

"The Alchemist, Amelia. I need her."

"Why?"

"She has something I want," Irina stated plainly.

"If you are after the cure, she destroyed it and all directions on how to make it."

Irina's grin slowly shifted to a frown, then chagrin. "Well, that is not what I wanted to hear. You may have him." With that, she waved her hand and the vampires began to stalk forward.

"WAIT!" he yelled. "WAIT! Why kill me now? You could have told me this before! Did you not know she destroyed her evidence and used what she had actually created on Michel?"

"Yes, and now Michel is dead, our James Maxwell is also dead, thanks to Marcus, and we have nothing left to work with other than the blood left from James. Even that is now tainted."

Adam jerked in his chains, ignoring the pain in his body. The vampires drew closer and the first one took him by the hair, then jerked his head to the side.

Fuck, this is it, he told himself.

"However," she held her hand up and just as the fangs touched his neck, the vampires stopped. He felt the mouth shake against his throat, as if resisting what he needed, what he was naturally drawn to. The vampire slowly receded in a way that seemed unnatural.

Adam watched them and breathed a sigh of relief, then closed his eyes for a moment.

"I am in a giving mood," Irina announced. "We will have visitors soon and I would LOVE to have you as a dinner guest! What say you?"

He opened his eyes to her and watched as she flitted about the room. She danced around, humming a song unfamiliar to Adam.

The woman has gone mad, he thought.

She came to a stop in front of the table, picked up goggles, then looked into a dish on the table. She giggled and stood, removing the goggles. "Everything will be perfect tonight," she danced toward his cell and pointed to him, "just you wait and see!"

Irina giggled as she made her way toward the exit, carrying one of the lanterns with her. The vampires followed in what appeared to be a painful movement. Adam wondered for a moment if Irina had been pulling them along out of sheer enjoyment for herself. He almost felt sorry for them.

Almost.

She left him with a few lanterns in the room and with the light, he could see the surroundings, finally. The walls were obviously dark, or so he thought as the orange light glowed against them. Where the light burned, stains splattered in many directions across the floor and the walls, and he wanted to retch at the thought of whose blood it might be.

He held his breath, mentally preparing for the damage inflicted to his body. Adam closed his eyes and glanced toward his right arm, then slowly opened his eyes.

The forearm had skin slashed open, muscle tissue exposed and the wrist had swollen twice the normal size around the cuff.

"Well, could have been worse," he grumbled. He looked to his left and found similar wounds. Glancing down, his legs were bloody, but he could not tell if it was dripping from bite wounds or dozens of cuts. His entire body hurt and at this point, he could not tell what hurt where, other than his entire being.

Irina and the others left him in his underpants but at this point, they, too, barely clung to his body. Adam sagged again and welcomed the pain. It was a relief to the torment in his head of Sophie's screams. The last thing he heard before he was knocked unconscious was her voice, her screams, and her face. Now, it haunted him.

The necromancer said they were expecting company and he would be a dinner guest. "Well, either a guest or *the* dinner."

Closing his eyes once more, Adam tried to push the torture and mutilation from his mind and focus on the features of

Sophie. Her white hair, violet eyes, her succulent lips...damn, he missed her. "I am a damned fool for not telling her how I felt. If I get out of this and we find each other, I am making her my woman and marrying her." He groaned as pain shot through his back. "Fuck, if she will even have me after all this."

The doors sounded again and as Adam glanced up, he frowned at the sight of Irina. "Oh, I almost forgot! We are leaving on a small trip. So pack your bags, mutt!" She giggled and ascended the stairs again and in her place were the two vampires who threatened to feed on him just a few moments earlier.

"Oh, hell," he mumbled.

The two stalked toward him, one grabbed him by the throat, lifting him from the slumped position, the other yanking the chains from the walls. Adam hung in the grip of his assailant, short of breath from strangling. He coughed and felt darkness begin to take over. Just as he was approaching the darkness, pain erupted in his head and then, nothing.

26

Wind flying through her hair, Sarah rode her horse alongside a shifted Sophie as they made their way toward the coven of vampires.

"This may not be the most brilliant idea we have come up with," Sarah yelled to Sophie.

In a thick voice laced with a growl, she said, "I agree, yet here we are!"

The two continued to run; Sophie banking off trees and debris as Sarah's horse cleared fallen trees, shallow streams and a few bushes. Soon, a clearing came ahead and Sophie slowed to a precipitous halt. The pads of her feet gripped the earth as she left a thick trail in its place.

Sarah pulled her horse to a stop and turned him around. "What is it?"

"I cannot...it is so strong. The Undead. They are everywhere! I smell them!" Sophie's voice growled and her lip pulled in a snarl. Sharp teeth exposed, Sarah visibly shook at the sight of them.

"You have fought them, you have killed a few. Why stop now?" Sarah asked her. "Honestly, I do not smell anything."

Sophie's violet eyes shown in the moonlight as she gazed up to Sarah. "I will forget you said that and not remind you that every time you return from your courting with that Undead bastard, you reek!"

"Oh," Sarah whispered and lowered her gaze. "Well, this is not about me right now. It is about Adam." She sat up straighter and glared down at Sophie. "You can be brave and go in there fighting, or you can return home like the pussy you are acting to be."

This apparently angered Sophie…a lot. She suddenly jumped toward the horse, causing him to buck. The result threw Sarah off his backside and she landed hard on the ground, the breath knocked out of her.

She struggled to breathe as Sophie stalked closer. Lowering her snout to Sarah's face, she growled, baring her teeth. "Again, I will forget you said that. Never, ever, call me a pussy again, you vampire whore."

Sarah's lungs filled with air and as they did, she threw a fist at Sophie, landing it hard on her cheek. A shrill yelp erupted from the werewolf and she pulled back in a lunging position.

"I AM NOT YOUR ENEMY HERE!" She gasped as she continued to breathe normally. "Your enemy is behind those doors!" She pointed toward the home of the vampire coven. "Now, we can go in and find Adam, or we can continue to fight one another." Sarah reached behind her and yanked a long crescent moon-shaped dagger from her trousers. "What will it be, Sophie?"

The werewolf lowered her fighting stance and took a few steps back, then lowered her head. "Let us go," she growled. Her ears perked and Sophie quickly looked toward the forest, eyes wide. "HIDE!" she screamed to Sarah.

Not wasting time, she grabbed the reins of her horse and jogged into the forest, taking refuge behind a tree. Her horse trotted along and when she paused, he bent his head and chewed on grass.

Sarah peeked around her tree and watched Sophie and the grounds surrounding her when suddenly, a large mass threw Sophie onto her back. Snarls and growls erupted and Sarah held her breath. Whatever knocked her down was almost twice her size...and he had her pinned.

It was not like Sophie to put up a fight, but she resorted to remain still. The horse then neighed and trotted away.

"No!" Sarah whispered and reached for him. Another mass came from the forest and approached the horse who, in turn, acted as if nothing was out of sorts. Sarah scratched her head, then the moonlight caught the spheres of eyes staring at her.

She gasped and moved further behind the tree. The eyes appeared golden, or so she thought.

Wait, are the pack's eyes gold when they shift? Is that John holding Sophie?

A loud roar erupted and Sarah held her ears closed.

"SARAH! COME OUT!" came the deep, heavy voice of the Alpha wolf. She closed her eyes and knew, without a doubt, she was about to be scolded by a werewolf.

She inhaled deeply, then took the first step from behind the tree, then made herself visible. She held her hands up in surrender and approached the wolves. Looking to where the commotion had been, she found Sophie on her back and John on top. He then suddenly snapped at her neck. She yelped and he snarled, shaking his head.

Then he let her go and whined softly next to her head. "Never, ever, leave again the way you did," he growled. "I lost Adam, I cannot lose you as well."

"I apologize," Sophie told him in a soft growl. "I allowed the instinct of the fight to consume me."

John moved away from her and Sophie quickly jumped to

her feet again. Sounds of hooves in the distance became louder, and then Amelia appeared, breathing heavily.

"You wolves run too fast for me to keep up," she sighed.

Something of a chuckle sounded from John. "Are you all right, woman?"

She nodded. "Yes, I am good. Sore from the ride, but I am good."

Sarah came closer to the pack and lowered her arms. She glanced up to Amelia and nodded. "They know about the note?"

"Yes," Amelia started then climbed down from her horse, then brushed her hands down her trousers. "They know everything." She approached Sarah and took her arm. Then in a whisper, said "Really, Sarah, everything."

"Oh shit," she whispered back. "I will not be allowed back in, will I?"

Amelia shook her head. "Unfortunately it is too dangerous. But you may come to visit, only if you are alone. We will talk about that later. Right now, I need to relieve myself."

"What? You need to…pee?"

"Oh god…" she groaned and as Sarah rounded on her, her eyes widened to the sight before her. Amelia squeezed the milk from her breasts onto the ground as she lifted her face to the dark sky. "Give me just a moment. They hurt so goddamned much."

"Take your time." Sarah turned her back to her, then gasped at a dark form approaching from behind. Her breath held in her lungs for the briefest moment, just as she realized it was a werewolf. "SHIT!" she screamed.

"I am not going to hurt you," growled the voice of Katherine. "I am only here to make sure neither of you get into any trouble." Katherine stood on her hind legs and held the body of a wolf. This was something Sarah had never grown accustomed to, even living on the plantation as long as she had.

As Katherine's eyes roamed over Sarah's body, even in wolf form the disgust did not go unnoticed.

Great, Sarah thought. *Now they most likely will never trust me again. Then again, I cannot say I blame them.*

"All right," Amelia announced and closed her shirt. "I am ready. Sarah, get your horse. We need to ride to the edge of the waters. John said he has a contact there with a ship."

"A ship?" Sarah asked.

"Yes, a ship." John growled and ran back toward his pack, but not before he called out, "And this one not only floats on water!"

27

Sounds of the night teased Adam's hearing, the blackness continued to hover over his vision as his consciousness peaked. A sharp pain throbbed in his head and his neck felt stiff.

Adam attempted to move and open his eyes but could not. The crust dried over his lids pulled as he strained to see. Finally, faint light seeped in as his lids peeled apart. He groaned as the outside air burned his eyes. He squeezed them shut again and took a sharp inhale, then coughed as the salty air filled his lungs.

Where the hell am I? he questioned. *Am I bound? Goddammit, my body fucking hurts.*

Adam made an attempt to roll onto his side just as a boot came to rest on his hip. "Ahh, he lives," came a familiar female voice. Fingers touched his head gently at first, as if someone were inspecting wounds, then suddenly they pressed hard into what felt like a gash in his head.

"FUCK!" he screamed. "Where am I? What do you want with me?"

"Stop screaming, you little pussycat." The fingers that

invaded the wound on his head now pressed against his eyelids. The woman pried his eyes open and Adam yelled from the pain. It felt as if his lids were glued together and this woman, this bitch, ripped everything from him. "It is not you that I want, however, you have become an unfortunate pawn in my game."

Adam squinted his eyes as they adjusted to his surroundings. It was still evening, he could tell that much. How many days had passed since they took him from the dungeon? What were their plans for him? Would he survive this?

He sighed and looked up to the woman, Irina. "Will you at least untie me so I may stand?"

She smiled and bent over his body. Her eyes trailed from his to his chest, down to his legs, then back up. "I might," she smirked and stood, "but before I do..." she trailed off and reached for something behind her. Irina pulled a syringe she had hidden and held it in the air just before she plunged it into his body.

Adam screamed and he gritted his teeth, willing himself through the pain she injected. He recognized this immediately; Adam would not have the ability to shift, even if the moon were full.

As the pain began to subside, his hands and feet were then unbound. Pulling to his feet, Adam slumped against his capturers and felt as if death were knocking on his door of life, teasing him.

Come, take me, you fucking bitch. End this pain and just take me.

His capturers lurched forward and Adam slumped further into their grasp as his feet dragged behind him.

"It would help, ever so much, if you actually walked, mutt."

Adam smirked to himself and ignored the words of the vermin that held his body upright. Both men, the ones who thought he would be their next meal, now pulled him along the grounds.

When they stopped, Adam glanced up to what seemed to be something of a beach, surrounded by forest. He had no idea where he was, and when he sniffed, it smelled of salt.

When they came to a stop, Adam found himself in front of a wooden post, similar to a cross. He shook his head and allowed it to drop between his shoulders.

Maybe they will kill me now. Please, just get this over with.

His capturers deposited his body on the ground in a heap next to the post. He coughed and dirt flew from his face, as he glanced around his surroundings in hopes of spotting an escape.

Where are we?

"Now, we wait," Irina told the group.

"Wait for what?" Adam asked, not that he counted on an answer, but felt curious nonetheless.

Surprising him, Irina turned her attention to him. She took a few steps forward and squatted to his level. Irina touched his chin and lifted it ever so slightly. She grinned, "Your friends, of course. Bait brings the food." She winked and dropped his chin.

"They probably believe me dead. Why would they come?"

She looked to him over her shoulder and offered a slight shrug. "As I said, bait, lone wolf. Bait has been placed. I am positive we will be seeing your friends very soon."

"What is he doing here?"

Irina jumped to the sound of the new female voice. Adam glanced at a woman he had never seen, and the deepest part of himself hoped she would grant him mercy to end his life.

"He is the bait to bring the Alchemist, Amara. I told you…"

Suddenly, the woman backhanded Irina across the cheek. "You imbecile! Why would you bring him along? For your own delusional entertainment value? Get the change done and over with, woman!"

"Once they arrive, I wanted to do it then. I thought that it would…"

"No!" Amara screamed. "No! You do NOT think. You are

like a child." She made her way to one of the vampires who stood as guard to Adam. She lifted her hand in the air and suddenly, the vampire dropped to his knees, screaming in pain.

A part of Adam wanted to laugh, wanted to smile and point the blame to this Undead filthy monster. Then the woman looked to Adam.

"Oh shit," he whispered.

"You can make this easy on yourself, or you can make it hard." Amara bought out a dagger and sliced open the arm of the vampire. Blood seeped from the wound and it ran over her fingers, dribbling onto the ground.

Adam's eyes went wide with shock and fear. He vigorously shook his head no.

Amara stalked closer and pulled the vampire with her. "Open your mouth or I will force it upon you. Your choice, mutt."

Adam continued to shake his head no and kept his mouth closed.

"Suit yourself," Amara said with a grin. "You," she pointed to the other vampire. "Grab and hold his head, then pinch his nose. He will open his mouth one way or the other."

Doing as he was told, Adam's head was jerked backward and his nose held closed. He continued to press his lips together as he glanced at the blood, then Amara. He shook his head and quickly took a breath.

That was all the time Amara needed. She lunged forward and smashed the vampire's arm against Adam's mouth; the other vampire continued to pinch his nose. Blood smeared over his face as she pushed the arm harder against his lips.

Then he tasted it, the iron of the blood. It was in his mouth and too late. Adam closed his eyes and tears welled in them. His last thought tore through him with grief. *Sophie, please forgive me.*

Adam gave in and the blood pooled in his mouth just before the darkness settled in over him.

∼

Arriving near the docks, Amelia quickly pulled clothes for the wolves from her saddlebags and set them on the ground next to her. The wolf pack remained in the forest to shift back into human form. The echoes sounded through the forest and with each scream, she cringed. She shook her head and glanced toward the sound, staring into the darkness.

Sarah approached her side, hugging her arms around her waist. "Their bones break every time they shift?"

Amelia looked to her, then lowered her gaze with a nod. "Yes, every time they shift to and from wolf form."

"I could not begin to understand, or even imagine, how this would feel."

"Consider breaking your leg here," she pointed to her tibia. "Then here," she pointed to the femur.

Sarah shook her head, "I cannot…"

"Right," Amelia continued. "Now, imagine that all over your body." She motioned her hand around her body as she spoke. "John and his pack go through this every full moon, and times in between as needed…like today."

"What about Adam?" Sarah asked in a lowered voice. "The necromancers have the ability to cease the change, if they wanted."

"Fuck!" John yelled as he approached the sight where Amelia stood. Naked, he sighed and walked into the clearing with the others. Sarah gasped and quickly turned away.

John shook his head. "If the bitches did indeed give him something to stop his changing," John answered Sarah, "then it would make him very sick. There is a part of us that will *need* to change every full moon. It is not something we want to do; it is something we *have* to do. It is a part of who we are. If they stop him from changing, in time, Adam could die."

"Oh," Sarah whispered and kept her back to the wolves as they dressed. She glanced over to Amelia and motioned for her to join her. Taking her arm, she pulled her close. "What happens if Adam ingests their blood?"

"You know I can still hear you?" John voiced.

Sarah blushed and shook her head. "No, I did not think you could. I am sorry."

"What are you sorry about? It is a valid question," he told her.

"Not so valid, but something an idiot would ask," Sophie announced.

John growled and took a few steps toward her. "Know your place, woman."

"It *was* a stupid question, John. It would be as if asking, 'will a woman have a monthly cycle?' The answer is of course. Anyone would know that."

John stared at Sophie for a moment. "We will talk about this later. Right now," he turned his attention to his pack, "our mission is Adam. The ship's captain is just through the clearing. He will not be the only docked ship in port right now but trust me, he is hard to miss."

"What is different about his ship?" Sarah asked. Amelia nodded, thinking the same thing.

"He is paid to travel and no one else has a ship like he does." John grinned. "Just wait, you will see."

The pack, Sarah, and Amelia made their way through the forest and came to a clearing of beach property, docks, and ships. The air was salty and the view, in the darkness, well, it was hard to say.

Amelia glanced to Sarah and smiled. "Imagine this place in the morning when the sun is coming up. I bet it is stunning."

Sarah nodded. "The sun cresting over the horizon as it lights up the ocean." She smiled, then thought of Marcus. "I cannot imagine waking every day and not seeing the sun ever again."

Amelia squeezed her hand and smiled. "Let us not think about that right now. We can discuss this matter later. Right now..."

"Right now is Adam," Sarah finished for her. Amelia nodded and the women joined John's side.

He handed a rifle to Amelia and a handgun to Sarah. "Both weapons are loaded."

Amelia nodded to Sarah. "We had the bullets made with liquid sun and the shell is silver. No matter what species we encounter, vampire, werewolf or human, they will not make it out alive if we are attacked."

John grinned at his wife. "Well said. Let us go. Captain McGinnus's boat is different than what is out there. He has the typical ship standard housing, but no sails."

"No sails?" Amelia asked.

"Correct, no sails." John grinned. "Instead...hell, woman, let us go, you will see."

The group made their way down the wooden boardwalk of ships until they came to one without sails.

"So, this must be his?" Amelia asked.

"How may I help you tonight?" came a male's voice. The group turned to a man who stood alone, and definitely stood out. Amelia and Sarah both gasped and John chuckled.

"Albert McGinnus. Great to see you again."

The man grinned and as he stepped closer, he became more visible and more...inhuman in appearance.

Albert McGinnus had a mechanism atop his head that wrapped around to his right eye, but there was no eyeball. A mechanical sphere moved. His hair was long and dark, and appeared to be in dreadlocks.

Amelia took a step forward, as if to gain a closer look. Sarah grabbed and pulled her back.

"Ow!" Amelia whispered. "What did you do that for?"

"Did you see his arm?"

"No, did you see his face?"

Sarah nodded. "Now the arm, look!"

Amelia did and she gasped again. His entire left arm had been replaced with a mechanical one, and she recognized some of the features of her father's own work. Where his hand would be sat a hook. Inside the forearm sat a gun barrel, but not just any gun barrel. This barrel had at least eight shooters installed.

This man was ready to fight at the drop of a hat.

"Albert, this is my wife, Amelia, and her friend, Sarah. Ladies, this is Albert McGinnus. He is the captain of the ship we will be sailing out on shortly."

"Ladies," Albert greeted them with a smile. "Welcome aboard. Rest assured, you will get to wherever you need, however, I suggest you hold on and not look too far over the sides."

"Not look over the sides?" Sarah asked.

Albert chuckled. "Unless you care to fall to the earth."

Amelia blinked. "How would we fall to the earth?"

Albert grinned and John chuckled. "Let us go." John took Amelia's hand. "Trust me, you will see what Albert's ship can and will do. Besides, he owes me a favor and I am calling that in now."

The sailor chuckled again. "And now we are even, Hawthorne."

~

*A*FTER SECURING THE ship, loading everyone, and pushing out from the dock, Albert took to the wheel of the ship. He called to a few of the deck mates to do this and press that.

Amelia and Sarah took a seat near the back of the boat,

under where the wheel of the ship sat. A loud creak erupted in the air, causing the women to jump in their seats. The center most part of the deck opened and out came a grayish silver material that began to expand.

"What is this?" Amelia asked. "What is happening?"

"Welcome to my airship!" Albert McGinnus announced. "I am the only one in this area with an airship and if I can help it, I *will* remain the only one in my area!" He chuckled as the material continued to grow. It made its way across the floor toward their feet.

"Should we move?" Sarah asked.

"No, remain where you are," Albert told them. "Trust me, you will squeal in delight when you see what my airship can do!"

Albert lit a flame in the center of the ship and it began to grow. Then, the silver substance began to fill with air and expanded into a large balloon. It lifted into the air seemingly quick.

"Oh!" Amelia gasped as the ship suddenly tugged. "Oh my god, are we…flying?"

Albert laughed. "Yes! My ship flies! I told you, you have never be on a ship like mine!"

"Oh, he is not kidding," Sarah whispered as she gripped Amelia's hand. "How long until we are at this island?"

"Sailing upon water, a few days' travel," Albert told them. "By air, a few hours!"

"A few hours?" Amelia asked just as the ship shoved forward at a pace unnatural for any ship, air or water. Captain McGinnus grinned and as Amelia looked up to him, he pointed toward the very back of the ship with his thumb.

"Thrusters, love. Thrusters make for a speedy travel." He winked and Amelia, shocked, sat back in her seat.

She turned to Sarah.

"It is not often you are at a loss for words," Sarah told her jokingly.

Amelia nodded. "He has thrusters."

"What is a thruster?"

"Something that apparently makes a ship move very fast in the air."

Sarah laughed and shook her head. "Sooner the better. Once the sun is up, it will be difficult to track any Undead."

"Very true," John stated as he joined them.

"I am quite impressed with this airship, John," Amelia said with a smile. "I say we have our own."

He chuckled. "Any time we need a ride, Captain McGinnus will offer it."

She nodded. "What is our plan?"

"Hey, John," Albert called from atop. "Something you should be aware of."

"What is that?" John called up.

"The island you are venturing to. It has been taken over by the Undead, more or less."

"More or less?" John asked.

Albert shrugged. "Probably more."

"Ahh, well that knowledge helps."

Sarah gripped onto Amelia. "Do you think," she whispered, "Marcus would be part of this?"

"I have no idea," Amelia told her. "I would like to think not, just for your benefit, but honestly, you would know better than I."

Sarah nodded and lowered her gaze. "I feel as if we are charging into a suicide mission."

"Why is that?" Amelia asked.

"It is only the pack and me and you. We are not an army."

"No," Amelia started and she gripped Sarah's hand. "No, we are not an army, but if we can stop whatever they are doing before it starts, then we have succeeded."

"Even if we all perish?"

"I honestly had not considered that a possibility. I need to return home to my son so that is the only outcome for me and my family." She gripped Sarah's hand again. "That includes you, Sarah."

Sarah nodded and lowered her gaze.

28

Sarah grasped the side of the airship. Traveling for a few hours felt like days. Anticipation began to set in at what they were about to walk into.

The Undead have taken over this island. Are there any human survivors? Do the vampires want to be controlled by the necromancers? Sarah sighed and her grip tightened when the ship began to plunge.

"What is happening?" she screamed toward Albert.

In return, the man simply grinned. "We are descending to the ocean, beautiful lady. We will sail in from here, then take the smaller boats ashore."

She nodded and as she walked toward her seat, she gripped the railing even tighter. Amelia reached out and took her hand. Sarah knew she would not fall from the ship, but did not want to take any chances, either.

"Brace yourselves!" Albert called, then followed with a maniacal laugh.

"He is a madman!" Sarah announced.

Amelia smiled and giggled softly to herself.

"You find this funny?"

"Why? Do you not?" she asked Sarah.

"Not in the least!"

Amelia pressed her lips together and when she glanced to her husband, she smiled. John held onto the sides of the ship and smiled as the wind whipped against his body, his hair tossed in different directions.

Louis would have loved this adventure. Well, the ship ride that is.

The ship pulled up and as they slowed, the impact of the water splashed around them. The movement was quite abrasive, but nothing his ship could not handle, so it seemed. Cranks started up in the lower deck as the balloon expelled air. Slowly, it wound itself into the ship.

"Boats are at the ready, John. I wish you luck and I will be here waiting for your return."

"He is not coming?" Amelia asked John.

He shook his head. "This is not his fight."

Amelia glanced to Albert, then back to John. "He is…human?"

"Mostly," John answered with a grin.

"Mostly?"

"Well, he is with metal traits, as you see."

"Oh, shut it!" Amelia yelled and slapped his arm.

John chuckled. "Yes, he is human, wife."

"One day you will need to tell me the story of how you met Captain McGinnus and this favor he apparently owed you."

John nodded. "Upon our safe return, I will do just that."

Sophie approached and lugged a bag over her shoulder. "We have a few hours until day break. We need to get to shore as quickly as possible." She glanced to Amelia, then Sarah, then back to John. "Keep them out of my way." She turned her back to them and made her way toward the dinghy.

Amelia sighed. "Well, I am glad she is on our side, regardless."

John nodded. "Once we get Adam home, she will be back to her old self in no time."

"That is assuming–"

"Yes, now, let us go."

Albert anchored not too far from shore. The distance to the beach would take half an hour, at most. Pleased with the start, John rowed as quickly as he could with Amelia and Sarah in his boat; Tomas, Katherine, and Sophie in another. A few other boats held the flank with the rest of his pack.

As they approached the shore, John lifted a finger to his lips and the women nodded. He leapt into the shallows and pulled the boat ashore. He assisted Amelia, then Sarah, onto land. The wolves gathered and checked their ammo. Amelia pulled the strap of her rifle around her body and shoved a dagger in her boot.

Sarah shoved her gun into her belt, checked the position of her daggers in her boots, then stood at the ready.

"I am glad you two opted for trousers today," John began. "If we have to climb, skirts would not be your best asset."

Amelia grinned. "Right. Well? What is the plan?"

"I have an idea of where they are. Follow suit and do not split up." John looked to his pack as they all nodded, including Sophie. He then looked to Amelia and Sarah. "You two do not leave my side. My pack can defend themselves, but you two are humans with weapons. If you run out of ammo, you are dead. Understood?"

Both women nodded and they began their hike into the jungle of the island.

~

Adam groaned and the vampire continued to hold his head back. Amara shoved the volunteer blood donor to the side and stood over Adam's body. The vampire skulked away, cursing under his breath as he left the scene.

The vampire holding onto Adam tightened his grip. His body had begun to flail and a snarl erupted from his lungs.

"Release him," Amara ordered. The vampire did not need to be controlled for this task. He released Adam and stepped back.

Adam yelled in pain and squeezed his eyes closed. His teeth gritted and the remnants of the blood seeped from his lips. A sensation, as if he were on fire, consumed him from the inside out. He felt it in his heart, as it pumped the venom through his blood stream with each beat of the organ.

Pump.

Venom.

Pain.

Pump.

Venom.

Pain.

He clawed at his chest, his nails dragging across the flesh.

Must escape, I need to shed the skin, I must shift! It will heal me if I shift!

Adam focused on shifting but nothing happened, nothing except pain. Something inside his mouth, along his gum line, suddenly erupted and he howled a scream. Fangs pushed into his mouth, replacing the ones prior, and they fell to the ground, along with his now dead teeth.

He covered his mouth and felt blood fill his palm. Adam glanced down and blood, mixed with his saliva, streamed from his mouth.

"Help!" he screamed as loud as he could. "Help!" Adam sobbed upon the last cry, for he knew what had happened. The pain began to lessen, or maybe he was more in control of it; either way, his mind began to clear.

He scooted to his side and sat on his knees, his fingertips pushing into the ground. His head hung as his breathing slowly ceased. The pain in his mouth was replaced with a different kind of ache, something he had not known in his life as a werewolf.

His words came back to him, words he told Amelia during one of the gatherings.

"No one would willingly choose this life. No wolf in his right mind would ever want this for themselves. They would be declaring treason on their own kind."

Slowly, Adam opened his eyes to the new world he had been born into, a world he did not choose, a world that had chosen him. After a few moments of clarity, he looked to his left, then his right. He could see further, clearer, than he ever could as a wolf.

"Ahh, he lives!" yelled the vampire who held his head upon the assault.

"No, I died," Adam hissed. He slowly stood and glanced to the vampire who, in turn, smirked.

"Live. Die. Whatever. Welcome to the coven, brother."

Adam hissed, then charged the man. He struck him to the ground and held his hand around his neck. "I am not your brother!" He ripped the vampire's throat out and tossed it. Adam stood over the body as he watched it flail, then turn to ash.

He glanced across the grounds, licked his fingers, then grinned to the woman Irina.

Human blood.

"You. Are. Mine," he whispered as he quickly sped across the grounds to the unsuspecting necromancer.

Irina turned, shock claiming her for a split second before she screamed and threw her hand out toward him.

Adam immediately stopped. He tried to move forward, but could not. An invisible wall captured him. He felt himself turning in his step and he yelled out.

"What are you doing to me?"

"Saving my own life!" Irina yelled back. "You need to feed but it will *not* be on me!"

"Let me go!" he yelled. "Now or I will rip your head off!"

"Not likely," she stated firmly. "Bring me a human!"

Adam glanced over his shoulder and waited. He tried to move again, but nothing. He growled and let go of any force he had. When a woman's scream broke the silence, Adam whirled toward the sound.

"Ahh, your dinner has arrived," Irina told him in a pleasing voice. As the female was delivered to her side, Irina grabbed her hair and yanked her head back to the side. Exposing her neck to Adam, she traced a finger over the vein. "Now, you listen to me...what do you wish to be called?"

He did not look away from the woman when he answered. "Adam."

She rolled her eyes. "Fine, Adam. See this vein? You want to target this. Feel her blood, taste it, devour it. You also need to feel when her pulse begins to cease. Once she is dead, she cannot offer any more blood as it will have died. Do you understand?"

He shook his head.

Her vein, it pumped in her neck so gently, so softly. Her screams became muffled by the sound of the woman's pulse.

How am I able to hear her pulse?

He pushed the thought from his head and attempted a step forward, which he could make. Maybe Irina released whatever hold she had over him, or not, but Adam continued to take slow step after step toward the woman.

"Please, no!"

The woman screamed again, but Adam blocked the sound. He felt electric, in power, in control of himself. For so long, he had been under the watchful eye of John. Not anymore. Now, he obeyed no one.

He smirked and slowly, his hands moved around the

woman's body and pulled her close; Irina retained her grip on the woman's head.

"As I told you, over the vein."

Adam stared into the woman's eyes for a moment and studied them. They were dark brown, almost the color of chocolate. He tilted his head slightly, then looked at her neck. A burn erupted in his throat and his mouth pulled in a snarl.

"Take her!" at the same time, "No, please!" broke the silence around him, any sound other than the pulse the woman let off.

His free hand slipped over her head, as if he were petting her, then he grabbed a handful and yanked. She screamed just as Adam sank his fangs into her neck.

∾

Irina, pleased with herself, took a few steps back while Adam fed his thirst for the first time. She grinned and turned, almost bumping into Amara.

"Mistress?" Irina whispered.

The woman quickly looked her way and furrowed her brows. "What is it?"

"The change is made."

"Of course it is. I did it. Get out of my way." She pushed past Irina and found Adam on the other side of her. She sighed. "This woman was helping me." She looked back to Irina. "Watch yourself, woman, or you will be next."

Irina nodded. "Yes, ma'am."

Amara glanced toward Adam, who slowly pulled away from the lifeless woman. If anyone were to walk up right now, they would assume him to be dead with the blood over his body. Then again, being covered in blood does not exactly help the case. "Good. I am glad you had your fill. You will know soon enough what it means to be under *my* rule as a newborn." She grinned, then took leave and headed toward her dwelling.

Adam smeared his arm across his mouth and when he glanced to his arm, he stumbled back. "Why would you subject this madness upon me? Why?"

Irina grinned. "Welcome to the cause, newborn. You will see soon enough what that entails."

29

A SCREAM FILLED the silence of the air and Sophie gasped. "Did you hear that?" she squeaked as she lay on the ground and glanced over a hill she had been spying from.

"Keep your voice down!" John snarled at her. "You do not know who may be close or who is lurking!"

She stared at him for a moment and if they were mentally linked, she would scream at him right now. Instead, she huffed and turned back. She peeked over the hill again and an orange blaze caught her attention.

"John, there is a fire to the east."

"Possibly a trap?" he asked.

She shook her head. "I am not sure." Another scream filled the air and alarm set through her. She gasped and looked to John again. "I know you heard that! I know you did!"

He nodded. "I did, and the first one, also."

"It is Adam, it sounds like him."

"You have heard his scream to know for certain?" Amelia asked as she crawled toward John.

Sophie rolled her eyes and looked toward the fire at the campsite. "John, come on, let us take a closer look."

"No, not yet. It is too dangerous."

Sophie sighed in frustration. "The only thing dangerous is having these two."

"Excuse me," Sarah whispered, "I am tired of your jabs, Sophie. I did nothing to you, so please, drop it."

"No, I will not drop it," Sophie snarled. "You gave your body to a dead man, Sarah. You slept with a corpse, a vampire, an Undead piece of filth! So no, I will *not* drop it!"

Sarah gasped and her eyes widened, as well as her mouth.

"Sophie, stand down. That is enough. You are out of this fight. Go to the boat and wait," John told her.

"What? You cannot be serious!"

"I am very serious!" John ordered. "They are here to help, not to harm. You are causing more harm now than anything." He moved closer to Sophie and grabbed her arm. "I understand your distress, but you will stand down. You will remember who your enemy is and you will remember, she is my wife! Be careful with her." He pointed to Amelia as if to add effect.

Sophie stared at him, then her own shock was replaced with chagrin. "Fine. I will stand down, but you need to understand something yourself. Do you think we would be in this mess right now if it were not for Amelia? Honestly now, John."

"How does this even matter?" Amelia asked.

"Oh, it matters. If it were not for this damn cure of yours, we would still be home, hunting, and I would still have Adam. So yes, Amelia, it fucking matters."

John quickly held still and grabbed both women. "Enough," he whispered.

"What is it?" Amelia whispered.

"Enough!" he said again. He motioned to Tom with two fingers to head east. Tom nodded, then he and Katherine disappeared. The bushes a few yards away moved and his grip tightened on Amelia and Sophie. "Sophie, get behind me. Now!"

"Please, do not get upset upon my account," a man stated

calmly. He stepped out of the bushes and held his hands in the air. He grinned and motioned for the person with him to step out.

"Who the hell are you?" John asked as he moved from the clearing and stood. He sniffed the air and his eyes turned golden. "Undead? You have balls to come face to face with my pack!"

"Ahh, well see, that is just it," he started. "See, there is this group of necromancers with my coven. They have it in their heads they want to rule everyone and everything. Including your kind."

John blinked, not quite sure what to say to this. "Why are you telling me this?"

"Because I do not wish to be in her rule. Simple as that. Oh, where are my manners? Allow me to introduce myself. My name is Tomas Hector Santiago Mendez. Please, call me Tomas." He bowed slightly and swept his arm across his body.

John lifted a brow, at a loss for words. "I do not understand...why, again, are you doing this? And you have three seconds before I rip you apart."

Tomas lifted his hands in the air with a smile. "Please, do not threaten me. Understand I have my own army scattered in the forest. Trust in my word, we do not wish to live under her rule. I simply wish to end her, before she accomplishes what she is after."

"And what might that be?" John asked.

"Her, for one," he pointed to Amelia. "Irina wants to have this cure recreated in an effort to finish what Michel started."

The name Michel seemed to unsettle everyone in attendance. Amelia stepped forward and took hold of John's arm. She kept close to him for protection. "You do realize the cure no longer exists? It was destroyed."

Tomas nodded. "Yes, I do. And I also know the effects it will have on a man who was once a vampire, 'cured,'" he quoted, "then became a vampire again. This cure of yours had an alternate effect no one was prepared for, to say the least."

John nodded with a sigh. "I told you of this, Amelia, of the man who became that creature."

"Oh," she began, then tilted her head. "You said she wanted to complete what Michel had started?"

He nodded. "Yes. She plans to make as much of this cure as possible."

Amelia lifted a brow. "She knows this cure...cures, correct?"

He smiled. "Yes, of course."

"Then please, help me understand what her ulterior motive is here?"

Tomas stepped forward just as John blocked the path to his wife. "John, leader of your pack, trust me when I say I have no intentions of eating your wife, or anyone else here. At least not right now. Once this is over," he shrugged, "maybe."

John stared at him then sighed. "I think I am going to regret this decision later, but fill me in on your proposition."

"Amara is the leader, something like a prime goddess in her own eyes. Irina is one of her minions."

"Irina is who we saw that day, John," Amelia announced.

Tomas nodded. "She did that purposely for you to see her, so you would know of her association with our kind."

"Oh, well that makes sense, I suppose," Amelia said to Sarah who, in turn, shrugged.

"Her ulterior motive, as you put it, she plans to destroy everything magic or supernatural."

"What?" John asked as he readjusted his footing.

"You heard me correctly, John. She plans on targeting everything in the radius around her and destroying it all. She feels it is in her blood right to end what her ancestors so long ago started."

"But it was not her ancestors who started it," Amelia interjected, "It was mine. They created the first vampire."

Tomas nodded. "Yes, and it was her ancestors who created the first were-beast."

John took a step back. "What? How?"

"You are aware how–" Tomas started.

"No," John interrupted, "I know how my kind came into existence. I am asking how on her part? What is she doing?"

"Ahh," Tomas grinned and nodded. "Forgive me. Well, she had one of yours prisoner."

"What do you mean, had?" Sophie asked.

"Had as in he used to be, but is no longer," Tomas told her.

Shocked, Sophie sank to her knees. "No," she whispered.

"Oh, child, please stand. Not all is lost. She still has him."

Sophie looked up to him, confused. "But you just said he is no longer."

"That is correct. He is no longer a were-beast."

"Now I am confused," John interjected. "Tell me what the hell is going on."

Tomas nodded. "Let me try this again. My apologies." He smiled. "Irina had your were-beast captive. She wanted to lure you out." He waved the thought away as he continued. "Regardless of that fact, Amara took it upon herself to change him into an Undead."

"What?!" Sophie gasped.

John took a step back and shook his head.

Sarah and Amelia stared at one another, then looked to Sophie.

"No, please tell me it is not true!" Sophie cried, "Please!"

"I am afraid it is."

John dropped to his knees in front of Sophie. He stared in the distance for a moment, shock claiming his features momentarily. "No," he whispered and lowered his gaze. He exhaled a slow, long breath, then looked up to Sophie and took her hands. "When we find him..."

Sophie shook her head. "No...not you. I need to do this. He would want me to do it."

Amelia joined them and set her hand on John's shoulder. "What are you going to do?"

Sophie looked up, her eyes filled with tears. "I am going to end his life. He would not have wanted this for himself."

"Sophie, no! Allow me to..."

"NO!" she said as she got herself to her feet. "You have done enough." She turned her back to Amelia and turned to Tomas. "I am ready for this fight." She growled and her violet eyes lit up golden.

"You need to be prepared," Tomas warned. "She has ways of targeting those she intends to destroy, including vampires. She could turn us against each other."

"And that would be so different from...what?" John asked.

Tomas chuckled. "Well, there is that, yes." He grinned and continued. "She could force you to shift. She could force me to do things against my will."

"She had control over us, somehow, prior. We could not move from where we stood." Sarah stated.

"So I heard," Tomas told her.

Sarah pulled her gun out and checked the barrel. "I am ready to go in. How many vampires are with her?"

"Good question," Tomas said in a rushed breath. "We can ease in to count, but if we get too close..."

"Right," John offered with a nod. "Too close, we could be found."

"No, you could be targeted," Tomas told him. "Just...be safe."

"And I assume once this fight is over, this alliance between us will cease?"

Tomas grinned and shrugged. "We will see."

John grinned and nodded. He turned to Amelia, Sarah, and Sophie. "No one is to charge in. We need to figure out where the exits are, how to get Adam out, and get back to the boats."

The others nodded in agreement and readied their weapons. John glanced at Tomas. "Do you have weapons?"

The vampire nodded and hissed, displaying his fangs. "If needed, I will make a stake."

"Right." John turned back to his group. "This is it. Let us go."

30

As the fire pit came into view over the hill toward the targeted location, Sophie turned to John. "The fire I saw earlier."

He nodded and looked to her. "Keep yourself hidden until–"

She gasped and her eyes widened. Her lower lip trembled and John followed her gaze.

"Oh shit," he whispered, then looked to Sophie, tears streaming down her cheeks.

"Oh my God," she whispered. "I had hoped, deep inside, the vampire was lying about Adam, but there he is."

"Why on earth would I lie about something like that?" Tomas asked her.

"Because you are a vampire piece of shit!" She stood and John quickly yanked her back down.

"Do NOT move!" he snarled.

"You accuse me of something I am, something I did not wish to become? One could accuse you as well," Tomas threw back to Sophie. "You were born with your gene, were you not?"

"Yes, but it is not the same! Do not compare us!"

"Oh, love, it is the same. You and I are not that different. You had no choice in your shifting. I had no choice as it were thrust upon me, an unwilling victim. So consider yourself fortunate, child," Tomas hissed as he moved across the ground.

Sophie stared at him with a low growl emitting from her chest. "Please, let me have him."

"Remember who your enemy is," John told her.

Sophie pointed toward Tomas with a questioning gaze.

"How is he different than Adam now?" John asked her.

This sobered her quickly. She turned to see Adam standing near the fire. He lifted his hand close to the flames, then quickly jerked it away. A young female joined his side and Sophie watched as they talked.

"Who the fuck is that?" she prodded.

Amelia pulled her rifle out and set it along the ground, lining up the site on another vampire. "I do not know. I can shoot her now."

"No," Sophie started up, "if I go down there for Adam, I will be happy to take her out."

"Before or after you kill Adam?" John asked.

"No!" Sarah gasped and scrambled backward on the ground.

Amelia let go of her gun and quickly followed. "What is it? What happened? Sarah?"

"He is there, Amelia, Marcus, he is with them! He is there!"

"I told you he was a piece of shit," Sophie scolded.

"Sophie, please, shut up!" Sarah told her and ran toward the bank. John quickly grabbed her and pulled her to the ground.

"What the hell do you think you are doing?"

"I am going in now with my weapons. I will not be made a damn fool!" Sarah grabbed her pistols and pointed one at John. "Release me or I will shoot you, John." She pulled the hammer on the trigger back.

He stared at her for a moment, then slowly released her arm. John looked to Amelia, then back to Sarah.

Sarah nodded to him and lowered the gun. She turned toward the bank and took off in a sprint toward Marcus.

"This is not going to end well," Amelia sighed as she pulled her rifle to her side.

"I fear you might be correct, my love," John started, then squeezed his eyes closed. "Oh my God! Amelia, fuck!" He dropped to his knees and a loud crack sounded.

"John!" She took his face in her hands. "John! Oh God, John, no!"

"Go, Amelia," he screamed in pain as his body thrust forward and claws replaced his fingers. "GO!"

She shuffled back and looked toward Sophie, who had also fallen. Tom and Katherine were not too far behind as they closed the distance.

"What the bloody hell..." was as much as Tom got out before he and Katherine fell to the earth, writhing.

Amelia sobbed, looking for Tomas. "My husband and his pack can no longer be of help. Sarah took off on what will clearly be suicide. What the hell am I going to do?"

"It seems Irina has discovered your pack is here, and has targeted them. If I may," Tomas offered, "I will be happy to assist." He smiled and held his hand out to her.

She stared at the vampire for a moment and feelings of reluctance swept over her. "Why do I feel as if I am making a huge mistake?" Amelia swiped her tears as the growls and screams from the pack reminded her she needed help, no matter the source.

"Trust in me, please. What I would like to have done was present you as a captive, but since your Sarah has basically run in for that position, we shall go in fighting together."

"As a captive?" Amelia asked. John screamed in pain and Amelia bit her lip as she looked at him.

"Do not watch what is happening as it will only distract you.

And yes, I would have presented you to their lot, then as soon as their guard was down, we would have attacked."

Amelia nodded. "And now the plan has changed?"

"Right," he looked from her to where Sarah was fast approaching. "Now, we do like your friend here and charge in. Try to keep yourself hidden in the shadows, behind trees, whatever you can use."

She nodded once more and took his hand. Tomas led them down the hill, and a few at a time, vampires joined their walk. She looked to her left and right, not sure if she should be happy about this or terrified.

"Do not worry, they will not attack unless provoked by Irina or Amara."

"Oh, that does not exactly comfort me."

He grinned. "If my understanding is correct, the two mistresses before us, Irina and Amara, they are out to change the world." He chuckled and shook his head. "Your friend, Sarah. She was involved with one of the vampires?"

Amelia nodded. "Yes, someone named Marcus."

"Yes," he lowered his gaze and lifted a brow. "He spoke of her often."

"What? Why?"

"Marcus is like me, one of the leaders of the vampire kingdom. He wants power. He reminds me of Michel in many ways.

"Marcus divulged what he had planned for Sarah once he received what he was after."

Amelia swallowed. "What, exactly, was he after?"

"You, or the cure. Either way, he would get what he wanted. Now with Sarah down there, she has pretty much sealed that for him."

She nodded and glanced to the burning pit of fire. Amelia kept her eyes on where Sarah had run to, then to Marcus. Her heartbeat ran rapid in her chest to the anticipation of their fight. "I understand. Then I hope with lover's remorse, she is the first to step up to kill him. Oh!" Amelia repositioned her rifle on the other shoulder. "Before we charge forward, please tell me what Irina and Amara wish to change in our world?"

Tomas turned to her, chagrined. He shook his head. "Not now, Amelia. We shall discuss this topic later. Now, we move. Are you ready?"

She sighed and nodded. "Ready as I will ever be." John's cries caught her attention and Amelia opened the barrel of her rifle and double-checked her ammunition. She closed and cocked the gun. "Yes, I am ready."

~

"MARCUS!" SARAH SCREAMED and Marcus quickly turned to face her. "What are you doing here? Why are you doing this? Why?"

"Sarah?" Marcus jogged toward her and took her by the shoulders, then shook her slightly. "You should not be here. Why are you here?"

"Marcus, who is your pet?" Irina came into view and smiled toward them, then gasped. "You have brought us an Alchemist after all! Good for you!" She approached and grabbed Sarah by the arm.

"No, she is mine," Marcus told her with a hiss.

Irina lifted her hand and twirled it. Marcus suddenly dropped as a crunch came from his body.

"What did you do?" Sarah screamed at her.

"I broke his neck."

"What?!"

"Oh, do not worry. He will be fine in a little while. He will heal, and trust me, he will want to kill me for doing that." Irina laughed as she approached a tree.

"Do not worry your pretty little head about that. What I have in store for you will please him immensely." She grinned and thrust Sarah's body against the tree. "Did you know Marcus fucked me in a pool of human blood?"

"What?" Sarah whispered.

"Oh, yes. He is quite the animal when it comes to lovers." Irina slugged Sarah in her stomach, then yanked Sarah's head up and pushed her against the tree. Irina gripped the woman's neck and squeezed.

One of the vampires minions tied rope around Sarah's wrists. Irina took the bound arms of Sarah and the vampire hammered a nail into the tree. Irina lifted Sarah's arms above her head and slipped the knot over a nail.

She then let her hands slip down Sarah's arms, over her breasts. She squeezed them, then teased her nipples roughly. Irina met Sarah's gaze then smirked. "Lovely breasts. Too bad you are about to die or I would suggest having you for myself."

"I would never give myself to you!" Sarah screamed and kicked her legs about.

Irina quickly moved out of the way and smiled. "So feisty. We should begin here shortly, if Amara has not started already." She glanced toward a person approaching and smiled. "Speaking of, here she is now. Amara, may I introduce you to our new friend, an Alchemist."

Amara's eyes lit up in excitement. "The Alchemist?"

Irina shook her head. "No, but..."

Amara backhanded the woman again, knocking her from her feet. "Why do you do these things, child?" She rolled her eyes and glanced up to Sarah. "Tell me your name?"

"Why should I?" Sarah screamed.

"You can tell me your name or I shall force it out of you."

She swallowed hard and panted. "S-Sarah."

Amara smiled. "Did you have a death wish coming here, Sarah?"

Irina got to her feet and rubbed her cheek. "She is friends

with the Alchemist and I had Marcus seduce her for information."

Amara glanced to her then smiled. "Well, seems some of your ideas are worthwhile."

"You did what?" Sarah asked.

Irina smiled. "Yes, I had Marcus seduce you. I did not tell him to fuck you, though; that was all him. Funny, I thought I would be jealous. Maybe I am just a little." Irina pulled a dagger from a belt over her corset, and tossed it to Amara. She caught it and grinned. Irina looked to her side and gasped. "Oh look! Here he comes now!"

Marcus came into view as he massaged his neck. "That was uncalled for, Irina, even for you." He looked to the tree, then did a double take. "Sarah?" He charged Irina, snarling. "What have you done? What did you tell her?"

"Oh, lover," she grinned, "I told her everything."

"Why?" he snarled as he lunged toward her.

Irina grinned and held her hands up, using her force to keep Marcus at bay. "Do you wish to call her your own?" Irina glanced to Amara, who took a step next to Sarah.

"What?" Marcus asked as he looked toward Sarah, his eyes widened. "No, do not!"

"Save her then, since your priorities have obviously changed," Irina told him as Amara plunged a dagger deep into her chest. Sarah gasped and mouth agape, no sound emitted. Blood seeped from the wound and when Amara yanked it from her body, Sarah's body hung limp.

"NO!" Marcus cried. Irina released her hold on him and Marcus quickly shifted direction and ran toward Sarah. He tugged on the rope and Sarah's body fell into his arms. He held her close and her blood seeped onto his clothes, but Marcus did not care. "Sarah! Please no, Sarah!"

"M...Marcus..." Sarah closed her eyes as her head rolled limp to the side.

31

"No, Sarah," Marcus cried out, "not like this!" He quickly pulled the sleeve of his shirt upward, the material tearing. He tore into his arm and spit out a large area of skin. His arm bled rapidly as he slipped his other arm underneath Sarah's neck. Hefting her into his lap, he opened her mouth, his blood oozing onto her body, the ground, and himself. Quickly, he pressed his forearm against her open mouth.

"Drink, Sarah, please drink from me," he whispered and stared at her face. He willed her to live, to blink, to do something. "Please, Sarah, not like this."

Marcus felt her mouth twitch against his forearm and his eyes widened. She lifted an arm and slowly wrapped her hand around his. Sarah pressed him harder against her mouth, then she latched on.

"Sarah!" Marcus yelled, "You will survive this, love, you will survive."

"Well, is this not something?" Irina approached Marcus's side. "I did not know you had it in you to fall in love, Marcus.

Too bad you did not fall in love with me, but then again, I would have killed you anyway."

He looked up to her and watched as she grinned. Irina rested her hands on her hips and her eyes left his as she looked over Sarah's body. "Honestly, what is it you see in her? She is human. You are vampire. This does not make sense to me."

"Why does it need to make sense to you?" he asked her and continued to hold Sarah close. "And you just told me you wished it had been you. You may be a necromancer, but you are still human."

She shrugged. "This is true. Now, if you do not mind, we have something to complete." Irina turned her back to him and as soon as she was out of the shadows, he pulled his arm away from Sarah's lips.

"Oh my God!" A woman's voice shouted from the shadows.

Marcus hissed as he held Sarah's body close to him, protecting her. He stared at the darkened figure. "Show yourself unless you intend to die in two seconds."

"What did you do to Sarah?" Amelia stepped out next to Tomas. She dropped to her knees and took her face in her hands. "Why does she have blood on her...oh no. No, no! Marcus," she looked to him, "did you feed her your blood?"

The fear on Amelia's face caused him to flinch slightly. "I had no choice! Amara stabbed her in the chest."

"What?" Amelia cried and looked back to Sarah. "Why?"

"To hurt me? Who knows why these bitches do what they do." Marcus shifted his gaze to Tomas and raised a brow. "I will say, though, I am surprised to see you here."

Tomas grinned. "Why does my presence surprise you?"

Marcus looked to Amelia, then back to him. "Is it not obvious?"

Tomas waved him off. "You know as well as I do plans and intentions change. As soon as I realized what these two were after," he pointed toward the necromancers, "my plans changed. I dare not give my life to these bitches, Undead or not."

"I do not understand," Amelia started. "What do you mean, 'give your life'?"

Tomas turned to her and took her hands in his. "Listen to me, Amelia. I promise, after this I will fully explain. Until that moment, we need to avert what is happening. Your husband and pack are being tortured. Sarah will become a vampire soon."

She stared into his eyes and shook her head. "Oh, Sarah," she whispered.

He nodded. "Now please, they are about to begin the second part of their ritual. Take Sarah with you and hide in the shadows. Once she begins to come around, you will need to hide from her. She will not understand the blood lust she is feeling." Tomas turned to Marcus. "She will be your responsibility after this."

Marcus nodded. "I would not have it any other way. I want her to be mine. I...I am in love with her."

Amelia blinked and raised her brows. "It is not often I am speechless, but right now, I am." She shook her head. "My experience with vampires has not been pleasant...well, at least until now." She looked to Tomas and offered a slight grin. "And that we will talk about later, as well. Here," she pulled Sarah into her lap from Marcus. "I have her. Go."

Marcus nodded and stood, then turned to Tomas. Before the vampire began his plan, Marcus glanced to Amelia and watched the woman drag the love of his entire existence into the shadows. *Never have I ever felt this for anyone...human or not. If I survive this...*

"Marcus?"

Tomas brought him from his thoughts. He turned to him and nodded. "I am ready. What is the plan?"

"Amara needs to go down first. It will leave Irina vulnerable."

Marcus nodded. "I will take care of that bitch. She killed my

Sarah." He grinned and put himself into a stance to sprint. "It will be my pleasure to end her existence."

"Do not let her, or Irina, see you coming."

"Understood. And Tomas?"

"Yes, Marcus?"

"I pledge my fealty to you, as king of our Undead." Marcus bowed his head slightly, then turned to the necromancers.

Tomas grinned softly. "Thank you for that, but let us discuss our plans for moving forward once this is done and over with. I foresee many changes coming." He grinned a little wider as his gaze set on Irina. "Do not hesitate to rip her fucking head off."

A growl sounded from Marcus as he lowered himself a little more, and when Amara turned her back to him, Irina closed her eyes and tilted her head back. In a speed too fast for human eyes, he slipped through the air toward his target.

~

FIRE BURNED IN the pit, heating the surrounding area. Amara set a large stone basin in the center. "Blood of the wolf." She tossed in a glass vial of blood from Adam during his time in his cell. The vial exploded and the blood sizzled on the heat of the basin.

"Blood of the Undead." She tossed in another vial of blood taken from one of the guards of the coven. "Blood of the Alchemist." Next, she held the hilt of the dagger in her hand, the one she stabbed Sarah with. She tossed it onto the stone and it clanked as it landed. Amara grinned and pulled one final vial.

"And finally, blood of the creature." She tossed in the final vial and when it exploded, the blood in the basin combined, sending a bluish purple flame into the air.

Irina tilted her head back and held her hands in the air. Grinning, "Finally! Allow the world to be rid of all the supernatural created by our ancestors, and those who aided in their existence!"

Amara closed her eyes and held her hands up as well. She took a step back and began to chant. The sounds were soft at first, almost like a whisper. She grew louder with each beginning.

Irina joined her. She repeated the words until a loud crack sounded. Taking a quick step back and opening her eyes, she saw Amara had disappeared. She looked around, then swallowed the lump in her throat. Fear consumed her and adrenaline shot through her body.

"Marcus?" she called out to her former lover and took a few steps around the fire. "Did you take Amara?" She grinned. "You are no match for her!"

"Is that so?" Marcus called from the shadows. "How is it then that I was able to get the upper hand?"

Irina stepped toward the shadow, and when close enough to see him with a body in his arms, she lifted her arms toward him.

Arms suddenly surrounded her body and a dagger pressed against her neck. The other hand fisted their hand in her hair, yanking her head to the side.

"Go ahead, Irina," Tomas taunted her, "go ahead. Do your magic. It will be the last act you will ever do."

She sobbed in his embrace and struggled against his hold. *What happened to Amara? What did they do? This is not happening!* "Let me go, you filthy blood eater!"

"No, I do not think I will," Tomas whispered in her ear. "Come on out, Marcus."

Slowly, out of the shadows, Marcus took a step forward. Blood splattered the ground and as the bluish light of the fire brought his features into view, Irina gasped at the gruesome sight before her.

Marcus grinned and held his arm toward Irina. In his hand he held the head of Amara. Blood dripped to the ground as he took a step closer. "You ruined everything we had. Everything! You tried to kill my lover, you killed too many of my kind, and you forced a werewolf to become a vampire. Why? What gain and purpose did any of this have?"

"You are all abominations of this world!" she screamed.

Tomas chuckled. "And that makes you what, exactly? You bear magic as a necromancer. How are you so different?"

"I am human!" she screamed.

"And the wolf-beast was not? And Sarah, my Sarah, was not human?" Marcus asked.

Irina growled and attempted to lift her arm, until the dagger pressed harder against her throat.

"I would not do that, woman," Tomas informed her. "However, if you wish to die now, I shall grant that to you freely." He pressed harder against her throat.

"NO!" She panted in his hold and closed her eyes. "No, I do not wish to die."

Movement caught Tomas's attention and he glanced to his side. A figure stood on the edge of the bank where he found Amelia. "I see the magic has ceased, Irina."

Marcus turned to see John, Tom, and Katherine making their way toward the fire pit. Then a white-haired woman sprinted past them, screaming a name.

"What the hell is all this?" John asked as he stretched his arms. "Under normal circumstances I would have fought everyone here, aside from the human women."

Marcus nodded and grinned. "Well, yes, however, it seems times are changing." He quickly filled in the pack members on the necromancers' plans.

"And it seems to have failed, from what I see?" John asked and pointed to the head of Amara.

Marcus grinned and tossed the head into the open fire. Flames grew higher and the bluish blaze faded slowly into an orange, amber glow. "You would be correct." He wiped his hands on his pants and turned toward Tomas and Irina. "Why are you waiting? End her."

Tomas grinned and glanced down to the woman he held captive. "You will never hurt us again, the were-beasts or our human companions. I would heed this as a warning, but more of you will eventually come. Then again, with the death of one of your leaders, I may have sparked a war," he shrugged. "Time shall tell."

"All of you should be dead. DEAD!" Irina screamed. Then her screams turned into curdling as the dagger sliced her throat.

Tomas continued pressing the dagger into her body until her head severed. Like Amara's, he tossed it into the fire. He turned to Marcus and raised a brow. "You may want to check on your mate."

"Sarah!" Marcus yelled and left the scene.

"Where is he?" Sophie screamed. "Where is Adam? Where?"

Tomas turned to her, then John.

"Sophie, calm down," John ordered. "We will find him."

"Calm down? Did you see what they did–" Sophie stopped mid-sentence when a shadow moved before her. A figure stepped into view, eyes cast downward. She recognized him immediately. Sophie sobbed and sprinted toward Adam. She hugged him to her and sobbed harder into his shirt.

"Oh my God, I thought I lost you!"

Adam reached for her arms and pulled them off his neck. He then put space between them and continued staring at the ground. "Stop," he whispered. "Please, Sophie, just stop."

She wiped the tears from her eyes as she stood before the man she loved. "Talk to me, please. What did they do? We can get through this together, Adam. I love you, no matter what."

"No, you cannot love…this." Adam finally lifted his gaze from the ground and met her own. He took a step back and shook his head. "We cannot, Sophie…"

"Adam," she whispered, "oh no, God, no! No!" She dropped

to her knees. Sophie held her face in her hands as her shoulders shook with her sobs.

"You have to smell it on me, Sophie. Do not tell me you cannot. I am death. I am an Undead. I am no longer...a..." Adam paused and closed his eyes. "Holy hell, I am a fucking, goddamned vampire."

"What in the hell happened?" John roared and came to Sophie's side. "Adam?"

Adam met his gaze and took another step back. "I did not choose this; please trust in that."

John shook his head. "Of course you did not." He growled and his eyes glowed golden. "If those bitches were still alive, I would kill them again for this!"

"I could not do anything. They had me under some sort of... spell. I could not fight them, nor attack them!"

John shook his head. "If there was a way to go back, and unchanged this, you know I would."

"Adam," Sophie cried out his name. "Please..."

"Please what, Sophie? Please do not be a vampire?"

She shook her head. "No, not that. Well, yes, that, but no." She stood and wiped her eyes. Sophie took a few steps and held her hands out for him. "Please."

Adam shook his head. "No. We cannot, and you know this." He lowered his gaze and turned away from the people he once called family. "As long as I am alive...or whatever I am...no one will attack your plantation, John." He glanced over his shoulder to his former Alpha.

John offered a nod then lowered his gaze.

Adam nodded back, then ran in a speed so fast, only a soft breeze had been left in his place.

"Adam, no!" Sophie cried before she fell to her knees.

Katherine lowered to the ground and gently wrapped her arms around Sophie. "I have her. Go see to Amelia and Sarah."

"For what it is worth," Tomas began and looked to John, "it

was wrong what they did to Adam. No vampire would ever want to become a shifter."

"And no shifter would ever willingly become a vampire," John followed up.

Tomas stopped walking. "I meant what I said, John. Times will change with this. I hope to gain your support."

"Let us talk about it once we leave this island."

Tomas nodded and turned his gaze away.

32

Amelia smoothed Sarah's hair to the side as she continued to hold her close and rock gently. Memories of Rachel came back, of finding her bloody and beaten body in her basin. A tear slipped down her cheek and she sniffed softly.

"I miss you so much, every day, Rachel. I wish you were here to see your nephew, to know John, and to be with me." She closed her eyes and squeezed Sarah's body closer to hers. "You will be all right, Sarah. I love you, my beautiful friend, my new sister."

Sarah's body moved in her arms and Amelia gasped. "You…" Sarah whispered.

"Yes, Sarah, it is me, Amelia." She smiled down to her friend and brushed the side of her head. "I am here, Sarah."

Slowly, Sarah's hand moved, then she reached up toward Amelia. She gently touched her cheek, then opened her eyes.

Amelia grinned. "There you are! See? You will be just fine."

Sarah nodded and continued to touch her cheek. She trailed her fingers gently down her face toward Amelia's throat, then rested over her jugular. "I feel so…different." Sarah stared at her neck for a long moment and her lips parted.

Amelia's grin quickly shifted to fear when she saw something new in Sarah - fangs. She held her breath for a moment as a chill quickly crept up her spine.

Sarah sat up slightly and looked into Amelia's eyes. "Marcus saved me," she whispered. Amelia nodded and continued to hold her breath. Sarah lifted a brow as Amelia began to move beneath her. "Where are you going?"

Amelia shook her head slightly and made an attempt to smile. "Sarah," she whispered before she screamed. Her back hit the ground with force, knocking the breath out of her. She coughed as she tried to suck breath back into her lungs.

Sarah climbed on top of her body and grabbed Amelia's wrists. She pinned them above her head and held them with one hand. Amelia did not struggle as she wheezed uncontrollably. Sarah grinned and leaned in, hissing slightly. Her lips pressed to Amelia's neck and her fangs just grazed her skin…

"Oh no, no you do not!" Marcus quickly grabbed Sarah's body and lifted her into the air, off of Amelia. "You will regret feeding on her if I do not stop you!"

"LET ME GO!" Sarah screamed as she flailed in his arms.

Marcus shook his head. "I will find you, Tomas, to continue our discussion." Tomas nodded as he and John approached them.

"Amelia!" John yelled and he dropped to his knees beside his wife. "Did she bite you? Are you all right?" He pulled her up and moved her hair aside. Breathing a sigh of relief, he checked the other side then looked her in the eyes. "Are you all right?"

She slowly bobbed her head as the breath filled her lungs. "Yes," she coughed, "or I will be."

John sighed a breath of relief and pulled his wife close. "I thought I was about to lose you."

She smiled into his chest and rested her cheek against it. His heartbeat thumped and she wrapped her arms around him. "Sarah, will she be all right?" She looked up to John.

"I honestly do not know. I am positive we will hear from either Tomas or Marcus about her soon."

"We will? How?"

"I imagine they would come by the plantation, or send word to meet us somewhere." John stood and pulled Amelia to her feet. "Adam…" he sighed and shook his head.

"Oh no, is he…did he…is he dead?" she asked, horror ridden.

He stared at her for a moment, then shook his head. "Not exactly. They forced him to become a vampire."

"Oh no…I did not think…weres could become vampires."

"I do not know of anyone who has made the transition, at least willingly." He shrugged then rubbed the back of his neck. "I need to keep watch on Sophie."

"Where is she?"

"She is with Katherine." He paused, looking to his wife. "I am going to ask you keep your distance, at least for now."

She nodded. "I understand."

John wrapped an arm around her and pulled her close. He tilted her head up and softly kissed her. "Let us go home."

∼

"LET ME GO!" Sarah screamed. "Put me down this instant!"

Marcus reached the farthest part of the island in a dash. He sat Sarah onto her feet, then held onto her arms. "I need you to stop and listen to me, woman, please."

Sarah looked into his eyes and tilted her head. She blinked and took a small step closer. "You look…different."

He nodded. "That is because you are a vampire now and your senses have changed completely. Your sight, sound, taste…" Pain erupted in his cheek and Marcus growled. "Woman, you do not need to slap me. I saved your life!"

Sarah shook her head. "No! You deceived me! You lied to me!

I gave myself to you and you *lied* to me!" She slapped him again on the cheek.

Marcus closed his eyes and took what she was giving him. He deserved it, after all. "Sarah, if you would please stop and listen before the sun comes up. There are things I need to explain to you. Woman! Do not slap me again or I will be forced to pin you to the ground and trust me when I tell you, I will enjoy every moment of it!"

Sarah gasped and took a step back. "You are deceitful!" She turned her back to him and crossed her arms over her chest.

Marcus lowered his head and pinched the bridge of his nose. He took in her body; her clothes had become filthy in the fight, the stabbing, her transition…he knew she had to feel overwhelmed with all this. It had been centuries since his change happened.

"Sarah, please." He reached for her and gently placed a hand on her shoulder. He tugged gently until she turned. "Yes, I deceived you, at first. Then something happened, something changed."

"What changed?" she asked with malice.

"Me. You. Us. Everything. I could no longer do what I was tasked with. My charge was to bring in Amelia. When I realized you were with her, I thought I could get to her through you. But I could not, Sarah. I just…I could not."

"Why could you not, Marcus? You sure seemed to be helpful to Irina when I saw you with her." She lowered her head and closed her eyes.

If vampires could cry, Marcus imagined she would right now. "Sarah, I fell in love with you."

Her head quickly snapped up, eyes wide. "What?" she whispered.

"I fell in love with you. I could not do that, not anymore. I wanted to protect you. I wanted you so much, I came here intent on destroying everything and everyone involved. Please, I need you to believe this." He took her hands and squeezed them gently.

Sarah stared into his eyes, then took a small step forward. "Why did you do this to me? I did not wish to become a vampire."

"For that, I will beg for your forgiveness for all eternity. I could not lose you, not by murder. I acted on my heart's instinct and fed you my blood."

She nodded and continued staring in his eyes. "You really do look different." Her voice softened and she smiled softly.

"Is different...good?" he asked and took a step forward.

"It can be," she whispered to him.

Marcus released her hands and gently cupped her face. He leaned in and softly kissed her lips. "Please, forgive me, my love, my life, my reason for existing." His forehead touched hers. "Please, Sarah. I love you."

She touched his cheek and when Marcus pulled away, just a breath's distance, Sarah smiled. "I forgive you."

He smiled, although he still felt pained. "Sarah, I promise, I will work until infinity making this right by you."

"I believe I shall hold you to that promise."

Marcus smiled again, then gently tilted her head up. He took a step closer and leaned in, pressing his lips to hers. His tongue swept the crease of her lips and she opened them. He deepened it and Sarah slipped her arms around his body, gripping his shoulders.

The sun began to crest over the horizon of the island and Marcus reluctantly ended their kiss.

"I love you, too," Sarah whispered.

He tilted his head at this. "Why?"

"Why do I love you? You saved my life...well, so to speak. You changed for me. And I also fell in love with you." She smiled and leaned into his embrace. "Now, take me somewhere safe. I have this need for you I cannot explain. Please, I need you."

"Ask no further, my love. I shall have you fed upon our arrival." Marcus kissed her on the lips once more. "And the need you feel, that is my connection to you."

"Connection?" she asked as he took her hand in his.

"Yes. You have my blood inside you. We are linked, in a way."

"Oh, well I will need more on this later. Right now, I need to put this burning out in my throat."

Marcus grinned and the two quickly hurried to the vampire's hidden dwelling as the sun continued to rise in the distance.

EPILOGUE

A FEW MONTHS had passed since the events on the island. Louis would smile upon seeing his mother and father. John would lie on the floor and play with his son, rolling toys in front of him. Amelia smiled as she watched her family. *I love my life,* she thought. *I wish Rachel were here for this, and Sarah.*

She sighed and glanced out the window. The afternoon sun shone through the panes and appeared as spotlights on the floor. Amelia sat up as she saw Sophie walk across the porch.

"I will be right back," she told John, who nodded to her. She made her way outside and Sophie turned to look at her. She paused, not moving. Sophie lowered her gaze and looked out toward the plantation grounds.

Amelia closed the door behind her and slowly walked toward Sophie. "May I sit with you?"

"You will whether I wish it or not."

She sighed, gathered her skirts and lowered to the porch swing. The afternoon breeze felt nice. Autumn was fast approaching.

Amelia reached over and gently laid her hand on Sophie's. When Sophie did not pull away, Amelia closed her hand around her friend's. "Sophie…" she whispered and looked to her. "I am so sorry about Adam."

Sophie nodded and lowered her gaze. A tear escaped and she wiped it away quickly. "I know you are, Amelia, I know. I am sorry I blamed you for everything. I am sorry, but right now, I am not ready for this. I still need time."

Amelia sighed as a weight lifted from her shoulders. "Sophie, no matter how long it takes, I will be here. I love you. Please know that." She paused, then smiled softly. "Thank you for forgiving me."

Sophie turned to her. "Eventually, I will be my old self."

"I am not sure you ever will be, but we will do everything we can to get you back there." Amelia brushed her hair back, tucking it behind her ear. "When you are ready."

Sophie smiled, then leaned into Amelia's embrace. Amelia felt her body shake slightly and knew Sophie had begun to cry. She rubbed her arm and held her as the breeze gently brushed her hair across her body. The sun made its descent behind the horizon as twilight touched the skies.

Movement in the distance caught her attention and Amelia glance up toward it. "Sophie, look over there."

Sophie sat up and wiped her eyes, then looked toward the plantation grounds. "What am I looking for–"

"Sophie?" Amelia asked as she looked to her friend. "Who is it?"

"It is Adam." In an instant, Sophie left the porch and took off in a run toward her former lover.

Amelia quickly got to her feet. "John! Come quick! Adam is on the edge of the plantation!"

"You have Louis?" he called as he ran out the back door, not giving Amelia any other option but to say yes.

She smiled. "Yes," then she hurried inside.

∼

*E*XCITEMENT, NERVOUSNESS, FEAR, anxiety, and adrenaline hit Sophie at the same time. She reached Adam and as soon as she stopped, she felt she would retch. As much as she longed to see him, having him now pierced emotion inside her far beyond what she was prepared for.

"Adam?" She took a few steps toward him. She swallowed the bile threatening to expel and continued. "What are you doing here? Are you all right?" She paused and bit her lip. Sophie wanted to hug him, kiss him, just touch him to know he was really there, in front of her.

"Yes, I am all right. As all right as I could be, I suppose." He lowered his gaze and shifted in his step. "I was hoping to see you and talk."

"Oh, Adam," Sophie smiled and took another step closer. "I have missed you more than you know!"

He took a step back and shook his head. "That is why I am here. Sophie, we need to talk...about us. About all of this."

Fear spiked in her gut and she held her breath. *Please, no*, she begged internally. "All right?"

"Listen, I think it would be best if..."

"ADAM!" John yelled as he approached in a run.

Sophie growled and turned to her Alpha. "Please, John, give us a few minutes."

"This will not take long, Sophie, all right?"

She shook her head. John looked to Adam and stared at him for a moment.

Adam raised his brows. "John?"

John shook his head, then attempted a smile. "It is good to see you, Adam." He held a hand out.

Adam stared at his hand for a moment, then slowly took it and shook it firmly.

"I am glad you came. Please know you are welcome to our plantation, but the others..."

"What about the others?" Adam asked.

"I do not know them like I know you," John told him.

"You no longer know me as the man you knew, John. I have changed, due to my circumstances."

He nodded. "I understand–"

"No, you do not, and please do not pretend to." He held his hands up and shook his head. "I meant no disrespect, but please understand, there is no possible way anyone in my situation could understand any of this." He glanced to Sophie and continued talking to John. "I need a few minutes, please."

A strong hand gripped Adam's shoulder and when he looked to John, he held his gaze for a moment. John nodded and Adam returned it. John let him go, looked to Sophie, then left, making his way toward his home.

As soon as John was out of earshot, he reached for Sophie and took her hand. She turned quickly to him and took a step forward.

"I have a feeling I know what you will tell me," she began and closed her eyes as she lowered her head. "Just please, before you do, hold me. One last time." She looked up with conviction, vulnerability, and offered her heart to him.

Adam hesitated for a moment as he stared at the woman before him. Her white hair barely touched her shoulders. Her violet eyes were darker with her emotions. He took a step closer and pulled her into him, hugging her close.

Sophie melted into his arms. She sobbed softly into his chest. "I have missed you so much."

"I miss you, too," he whispered. A few minutes passed between them and Adam kissed the top of her head, then slowly released her. Sophie wiped the tears from her eyes then held her hands in front of her. Her gaze remained on the ground.

"Sophie, please, look at me."

She raised her gaze and locked onto his. Her brows worried as she waited for the news she prayed to never hear.

"We cannot be together. I am now a vampire and you are a shifter. There is no logical way to make this work. Things have changed drastically between us."

She nodded and held herself together, although her insides were screaming in pain. She wanted to beg him to stay, to tell him they could find a way to work this out, but a part deep inside her knew he was right. She pressed her lips to keep from crying.

"Our kind..." he paused and closed his eyes. "Your kind was created to destroy my kind. We are mortal enemies, Sophie."

"We do not have to be," her voice broke at the end and she cleared her throat. "John and Tomas have worked out a truce."

Adam nodded. "I am aware of the truce." He paced for a moment, then turned to her. "I do not wish to be with you, Sophie. The part of me that held onto the hope we could be together disappeared. I crave blood, flesh, so much of what you are against. It is my nature to kill, where it is in your nature to destroy everything I am. There is no possible outcome for us."

Sophie closed her eyes and lowered her head with a nod.

"I am sorry," Adam whispered.

A soft breeze touched her and when she opened her eyes, Adam had disappeared. Her lips trembled, her fingers covered her face, and Sophie cried out. Her knees hit the grass as she collapsed in tears.

A moment later, a warm hand touched her back. She flinched and looked up, falling to her side. Tyler, one of the pack members, squatted beside her. His dark hair fell slightly over his forehead and his tanned skin appeared darker in the evening sun. His sleeves were rolled up to his forearms and the black button down shirt had been paired with a crimson vest. His dark brown eyes poured into hers.

"Sophie, come back to the house. We can get drunk, raise hell, and get naked in the rain." He grinned.

She blinked, looking at him. His words sank in and she

offered a small smile that grew into a giggle, then Sophie began to laugh out loud. It was not her typical laugh of humor, as it sounded of madness.

Tyler sat next to her and wrapped an arm around her. Her laughter slowly faded into sobs. She leaned into him and Tyler held her. "We will stay out here as long as it takes. Then once we are inside, I will pull out the whiskey and we will get drunk enough to pass out wherever we are."

She nodded against his chest and sniffed. "I would like that… a lot."

"Good. When you are ready, we will go into the barn so as not to disturb John and his offspring."

Sophie nodded and moved to stand. Tyler quickly made his way to his feet and reached for her hands. He helped her up, then brushed hair from her eyes. "In case I have failed to tell you in the past, you are one of the most beautiful women I have ever seen in my life. It would be my pleasure tonight to get drunk with you." He bowed slightly with a grin.

Sophie smiled and this time, it reached her eyes.

～

Marcus held Sarah in his arms. He kissed her softly and lightly licked her lips as he teased her. "I brought you something, my love. Or well, someone."

Her brows rose. "Is that so?" The burning spiked in her throat and she touched her fingers to her neck.

He smiled, then looked toward the entrance of the room and waved whomever was standing there forward. "Someone had been found beating a woman in an alley. I thought he deserved what he put out." He looked to the man and grinned. The man, dirty with greasy black hair and smudged skin, shook his head.

"I agree," Sarah offered and took a step forward.

"Now, love, I have taught you about being gentle, correct?"

She nodded, not moving her gaze from the man.

"Do as you please with this one."

Sarah looked at him and raised her brows, then she smiled. "Will you feed with me?"

Marcus took to her side in an instant. "Bathing in blood shall keep the youthful appearance, my love."

She licked her upper lip, then looked to the man. The guards held the man by his arms as he struggled. He yelled profanities but Sarah did not listen, nor did she care.

Any man who beats a woman deserves what he gets, she thought. Her fingers gently glided over his neck as his jugular thumped under her touch. She forced his head to the side and with a snarl, she bit into the man's neck. He screamed from the impact and Sarah bit harder.

Marcus pushed his head back and quickly sank his fangs into the man's opposite shoulder. The guards continued their hold on him until he no longer provided a fight.

Sarah released her bite and gasped as she pulled her head back. Her lips and teeth were covered in crimson. She glanced to Marcus and realized he was watching her. She grinned as blood trickled down her lip, over her chin to her neck.

"My God…" Marcus quickly took her in his embrace and forcefully kissed her; the man's body dropped to the floor, dead.

The guards made work of his body while Marcus held Sarah close to his.

"I want you," he growled, then gripped the front of her corset and ripped it apart. Her breasts fully exposed, her nipples grew erect with need.

She licked her lower lip, tasting the man's blood. Marcus pulled at her skirts until she stood naked before him. He kissed her neck, his arms holding her her close to him. He bent her back, holding her weight in his arms. Marcus licked against her neck, slowly moving his tongue down her collarbone, then between her breasts.

At the sound of a door locking in place, Marcus glanced up while keeping his lips on Sarah's body. Alone in the room, he glanced to the floor at the pool of blood left for them, minus the body.

Grasping Sarah's body, he lifted her and she wrapped her legs around his waist.

"Why are you still clothed?" she asked him.

"That will change very shortly." Marcus lowered her to the floor, into the blood pool.

She lifted her back, pushing her breasts into the air. Marcus leaned over and sucked on one, then massaged the other. He stood and quickly removed his shirt and pants, discarding them across the room.

Sarah moved her legs apart and Marcus settled between them. He kissed her and moved his body against hers, his erection brushing her. "Marcus," she mumbled against his lips. "Stop teasing."

He chuckled against her lips, then reaching between them, he lined up his head and pushed. Sarah gasped and arched her back as Marcus thrust. She closed her eyes and moaned softly, the blood smearing across her skin. Immediately, she felt the effects of it in her body. Sex as a human had no bearing on what she felt with Marcus in this moment.

Marcus thrust against her again and kissed along her neckline, then nipped where her jugular once beat. Crimson beaded upon her neck and he licked the substance. "I love you," he whispered.

"I love you," she told him in return.

THE END
Continue the series with Wicked Alchemy!
Here's Chapter One!

NOW AVAILABLE!

Now Available!

The Concubine and Her Vampires, book two, a reverse harem novel

When destiny becomes reality...

Born a blood demon, Olivia Martin's sole purpose is to become a blood slave to a vampire. She is nothing more than a blood bag.

With a vampire as her master, she would want for nothing, her every need and whim catered to, but becoming a prisoner was not the life Olivia would have chosen for herself.

At least, until she met Jared and his four brothers-at-arms. Giving yourself to one person was easy. Having fun with two, exciting. But a harem of lovers? It was more than Olivia ever considered possible.

Need, lust, and blood drive Olivia to find a strength inside herself to not only accept her five sexy-as-sin vampires, but to also protect herself from an evil hell bent on claiming her for its own.

Now Available!

The Human and Her Vampires, book two, a reverse harem novel

Can dreams become reality...

Tawne O'Brien loves adventure and dreams of living in a world where paranormal creatures exist. Orphaned at a young age, and with a string of failed relationships only adding to her misery, her books are the only salvation from a mundane existence in a universe where she feels completely alone. When her best friend asks her to come visit, her dreams of a new life suddenly become a possibility.

Tawne is introduced to four sexy-as-sin vampires and given the opportunity of a lifetime with no strings attached...or so they say. When she discovers she may only be a guinea pig to the vampires, disappointment regains the upper hand, reminding her of her place in this world.

Can Tawne find the strength inside herself to fight for what she deserves? If she doesn't, she'll lose everything...including any memory of her life with her vampires.

Now Available!

The Demon and Her Vampires, book three, a reverse harem novel

A world unknown, a destiny discovered, and a blood oath that will change her life forever.

Sadie McKenzie has no experience with love, giving or receiving. She's never had a family of her own and lives her days alone with a dream to become a published author.

The day of her first ever book signing, she takes a short cut down a dark alley that leads her on an unexpected path, altering her life forever. Sadie is about to discover her life up until now has been a lie, nothing is as it seems, and her new world has creatures she's only ever read and fantasized about.

In her new life, she'll never want or need for anything. What does she have to lose?

ALSO BY JULIE MORGAN

The Covenant of New Orleans series (Available Now)

The Concubine and Her Vampires (book one)

The Human and Her Vampires (book two)

The Demon and Her Vampires (book three)

RISE OF THE ALPHA SERIES

Alpha Rising (book one)

Alpha Risen (book two)

Alpha Redeemed (book three)

CHRONICLES OF THE VEIL (Magic and Mayhem Universe)

The Sassy Goddess (book one)

The Sassy Queen (book two)

DEADLY ALCHEMY SERIES (Available Now)

DEADLY ALCHEMY (book one)

Deadly Alchemy (on audio)

FATAL ALCHEMY (book two)

WICKED ALCHEMY (book three)

FAIRYTALE CHRONICLES

THE BEAST UNDERNEATH

THE HUNTRESS

ELLA'S PRINCE

STAND ALONE STORY (Available Now)

DRAGON MASTER
THE SASSY GODDESS
DICK
STONE OBSESSION

ABOUT THE AUTHOR

USA TODAY and Award-winning Bestselling Author, Julie Morgan, holds a degree in Computer Science and loves science fiction shows and movies. Encouraged by her family, she began writing. Originally from Texas, Julie now resides in Central Florida with her husband and daughter where she is an advocate for Special Needs children and can be found playing games with her daughter when she isn't lost in another world.

For more information please visit her at www.juliemorganbooks.com
To receive a free ebook, join Julie's newsletter!
www.juliemorganbooks.com/newsletter.html
Facebook: https://www.facebook.com/juliemorganbook
Twitter: @juliemorganbook
Web site and blog: www.juliemorganbooks.com

Made in the USA
Middletown, DE
04 April 2024